GHOST
HUNTER'S
GUIDE TO
SOLVING A
MURDER

F. H. Petford ran his own creative agency and was involved in writing projects for corporate clients and the London theatre world.

A Ghost Hunter's Guide to Solving a Murder, the first of the Alma Timperley mysteries, was written following the success of three crime novels set in the Oxfordshire village of Great Tew at the end of the Great War. The supernatural elements in his work are inspired by his own experiences of the paranormal. He was signed to Hodder and Stoughton in 2025 and lives a quietly pagan life in Somerset.

A GHOST HUNTER'S GUIDE TO SOLVING A MURDER

F.H. PETFORD

HODDER &
STOUGHTON

First published in Great Britain in 2025 by Hodder & Stoughton Limited
An Hachette UK company

The authorised representative in the EEA is Hachette Ireland, 8 Castlecourt Centre,
Dublin 15, D15 XTP3, Ireland (email: info@hbgi.ie)

1

A CIP catalogue record for this title is available from the British Library

Paperback ISBN 9781399749831
ebook ISBN 9781399749855

Typeset in Sabon MT by Manipal Technologies Limited

Printed and bound in Great Britain by Clays Ltd, Elcograf S.p.A.

Hodder & Stoughton policy is to use papers that are natural, renewable
and recyclable products and made from wood grown in sustainable forests.
The logging and manufacturing processes are expected to conform
to the environmental regulations of the country of origin.

Hodder & Stoughton Limited
Carmelite House
50 Victoria Embankment
London EC4Y 0DZ

www.hodder.co.uk

For Marguerita, Milly and Imogen.
The three graces in my life.

Chapter One

Alma Timperley was no admirer of the subterranean world, much preferring the heady delights of the top deck of an electric tram. But on Christmas Eve 1914, there were two compelling reasons for her to bend her rules. Firstly, a biting wind that had originated somewhere near the North Pole was turning London's streets into conduits of sleet and misery. Secondly, her destination was close to Charing Cross Embankment, a new underground station that had been completed just a few months earlier.

As the work appeared to have been done solely to meet her requirements that morning, she forsook the civilised world, walked the short distance from Whitton Road, and descended one hundred and ninety feet into the labyrinthine horrors of underground London via the Hampstead station lift.

During the journey, to her quiet astonishment, she appeared to be the only passenger battling a compelling need to jump to their feet and scream, *'The tunnel is going to collapse, and we'll all die an appalling death!'* Not that anyone would have known it, as she exchanged pleasant smiles with a middle-aged couple sitting opposite.

They're happy. They've had good news. She automatically registered the thought.

When they got off at Tottenham Court Road she considered her reflection in the window behind their vacated seats. There, hovering like a ghostly twin outside the carriage, travelled neat and tidy Alma, her short dark hair tucked into a bright red beret. Aged twenty-two, five feet one in her stockinged feet, and the owner of a cosy terraced house courtesy of her deceased mother. She was walking out with Jack Waring, currently somewhere in France, and she wondered where he was sometimes, but had recently come to the view that she didn't do that often enough and was glad that she'd refused to marry him before his embarkation.

Alma had obtained permission from her employer to make the journey, having received an unexpected letter from one James Nascent, Solicitor, of Carlisle House, Embankment, proposing a meeting on a matter that concerned her. There had been no further information, so it was a curious Miss Timperley who rattled nervously southwards deep below the bitterly cold streets.

Carlisle House was a narrow, three-storey brick building that faced the River Thames. It was fully exposed to the sleet and wind, so Alma was in some disarray as she arrived in the deserted entrance hall. A door on her left bore the instruction:

James Nascent, Solicitor.

Please knock and enter.

There was a mirror on the wall and, pausing only to make some essential adjustments to her beret, she complied. Inside, she was welcomed by a bird-like woman with bright eyes who introduced herself as Mrs Neal and directed her to a seat, then went next door. Moments later, Mrs Neal re-emerged and said, 'Five minutes. Would you like some tea, Miss Timperley?'

Shortly afterwards a gentle hail sounded from the inner sanctum. With a nod and a smile, she rose and led the way into the office, bearing the tea tray before her like a high priestess delivering an offering to the altar.

James Nascent was a striking-looking man, magnificently bald and with a skin colour that suggested his parents had been Spanish or Italian. His eyes were deep brown, heavy-lidded and sensitive, and he was clean-shaven. Alma realised to her surprise that, whilst his eyebrows were notably present, they were hairless and had been drawn on with considerable skill, or perhaps even tattooed. They rather gave him the look of a repertory actor waiting in the wings for his cue.

As his secretary placed the tray on his desk, Alma caught a glance between them and knew instantly that their relationship was more than employer and employee. He was in his mid-fifties and Mrs Neal certainly wouldn't see forty again, so not of an age to get carried away with passion, she mused, with the unwitting naivety of youth. And the woman wore a wedding ring, but Alma had a clear sense that the solicitor was not her husband. She wondered whether the relationship was an illicit *affaire de cœur*, or publicly acknowledged, at least in company they trusted.

'Tea, Miss Timperley?' His enquiry was a relief. Alma's intuition had plagued her for all of her relatively short life, and as a child she was regularly chastised by her mother for saying what she was thinking. She was normally right and therefore often in trouble. She was also occasionally wrong, which was invariably worse.

'Or perhaps something stronger?' he added with a gentle gesture towards a small group of bottles on a side table.

Well that is intriguing. Is he expecting to shock me? She shook her head. 'Tea will be most welcome, Mr Nascent.'

As Mrs Neal silently played mother, Alma eyed the buff-coloured file on his blotter and imagined a trapped bird emerging and flying away as he opened it.

3

Am I the bird? she wondered.

When tea had been served and the secretary had left, he cleared his throat and addressed her. 'Miss Timperley, thank you for coming to see me. I am glad we were able to find you.'

'Might I ask how you did?'

'Your address is contained in a letter that is attached to the last will and testament of a women called Gladys Timperley. I am acting as her executor. She was your mother's sister and, therefore, your aunt.'

Alma stared at him. All her life it had just been her mother and herself. As a child she'd asked about her father but had simply been told he had died young and, despite Alma's cunning attempts to elicit more information, her mother had refused to expand on this verbal cul-de-sac. So the news that she had a secret sister was astonishing.

'Golly,' she said. 'I had no idea.'

His eyes crinkled. 'So I surmise.'

'Did my mother know about her?' she asked.

'She was aware she had a sister, yes,' he observed carefully.

'Did you know her?'

'I did. I drew up her will . . .' he tapped the file '. . . and handled the conveyancing when she acquired a property in Falmouth.'

Alma frowned and pictured a map. Falmouth was a seaside town in Cornwall she recalled. 'A property?'

'Indeed. A hotel in fact. A hotel in which you now have an interest, Miss Timperley.'

He paused and permitted himself a gentle smile as a look of astonishment appeared on Alma's face, then continued, 'Shall I outline the contents of your aunt's will and we can then discuss what happens next?' He received a silent nod of acquiescence, then opened the file, leaned forward and began to read, as a fleeting moment of sunshine penetrated the window and gleamed charmingly on his nut-brown pate.

'The property in question is the Timperley Spiritualist Hotel, of Swanpool Road, Falmouth. It has eight bedrooms and as far as I am aware it is a successful enterprise, that area being popular with holidaymakers. Although of course, the war will have had an impact.'

Alma nodded silently, struggling to take in the implications this news would have on her quiet existence in a backwater of Hampstead. 'Sorry, tell me the name again would you please?' she asked.

'The Timperley Spiritualist Hotel.'

'Yes, I thought that's what you said.' Her mind whirled but when he failed to offer any further intelligence she continued, 'So I have an interest in this hotel, Mr Nascent?'

'More than that, Miss Timperley. You own it – lock, stock, and barrel. The building, the grounds, the bank accounts, and the guest list. It is yours in its entirety.'

* * *

She took a sherry from him in the end, just for the shock, and then lunch. The sleet had eased and in weak sunlight they hurried down the pavement for a hundred yards to a busy Lyons Tea Room on the corner and managed to get a table for two.

The combination of the crowd and a roaring coal-fired stove meant the place was mercifully warm. 'This is nice,' Alma observed as they took their seats and inspected the menu. And it was. Mr Lyons went to great lengths to create nice interiors for his premises. A polished floor of black and white tiles, starched tablecloths, neat uniforms for the waitresses, who everyone knew as 'nippies', and even an aspidistra perched in the corner lifted the place well above the standard of common cafés.

'I am a regular, although my favourite waitress no longer works here. She was of German extraction and quite charming, but Mr Lyons fired all such people when war broke out, I'm afraid.'

Alma nodded. Even for children born and raised in Britain, the taint of German or Austrian parents was enough to mark them. She supposed Mr Lyons wanted to protect his business from allegations of a lack of patriotism, and he had a point in her opinion.

A thought struck her, and she said, 'Was my aunt's death unexpected?'

'That is a very perceptive question.' As though gaining time, the solicitor's eyes drifted towards another table and when he looked back there was a rather complicated expression on his face.

'Two months ago, I received a letter from her in which she told me that she feared she would not make old bones and reaffirmed that she wanted me to act as her executor. Perhaps she had a premonition, because on the 10th of December she fell from a balcony on the upper part of the hotel and died. It was a most tragic accident, but when you say unexpected . . . ?' He gave an eloquent shrug before continuing, 'In her letter she specifically asked me to render you every assistance in your new role as the owner and custodian of the hotel.'

Alma looked at him. In the short time she had been aware of her inheritance, the idea of selling it had been in the back of her mind. His assumption that she would remove herself to the Cornish coast and assume command of the place brought the implications of her aunt's bequest into sharp focus.

'It was her intention that I retain the hotel, then? Rather than selling it?'

He nodded gravely. 'There is no doubt about that whatsoever, Miss Timperley.'

She exhaled slowly and watched a pair of office girls bustle in through the door and shake the sleet off their shared umbrella. Mr Nascent, in turn, watched her through his heavy-lidded eyes, a slight smile on his face. But there was tension there too, and a clear sense that there was some further, unrevealed, provision in the will swept over Alma.

'What happens if I say no?' she asked.

'Then regrettably our delightful but brief association will be over, and I am charged with pursuing another option.'

'It's all or nothing, then?'

'That is the sum total of it, yes.'

'Do I have to decide now?'

He shook his head. 'No, not at all. I was going to suggest that once the festivities have concluded we travel down together and have a look at your inheritance.'

She hesitated. 'Would there be a cost? Only I fear a daily rate for a man of your standing would be beyond me.'

His eyes creased again in what was becoming a familiar expression. 'Your aunt left provision for my fees to be covered. In any event I would classify it as a pleasant trip to the seaside and off the clock.'

'Would Mrs Neal want to come?' It was out before she could stop it. She blushed bright scarlet as the words hung in the air between them and embarrassment showed on his face as well. It was an awful moment. She'd let herself down by blurting her thoughts, and not for the first time.

Will you never learn, Alma Timperley?

Eventually, with a wry smile, he said, 'I see there is more to you than meets the eye. I wonder if you have inherited your aunt's gift as well as her hotel?'

In the confusion of the moment, she missed this oblique reference and babbled, 'I'm terribly sorry, Mr Nascent. My remark was unforgivably rude.'

'Certainly, its implications were. Tell me, what brought the question to your mind?'

Alma stared at him in an agony of shame. 'I saw the look you gave her.'

'Ah.' He nodded slowly, then said, 'Mrs Neal is a widow, and I am not married, but nevertheless your discretion would be appreciated.'

'You have it.' The words tumbled out in relief. 'You can be assured I will go to the grave with your secret.'

'Then I will ask her, and I would imagine she will say yes. More tea, Miss Timperley?'

Chapter Two

Two weeks after New Year's Day the three of them caught the train from Paddington to Falmouth. So far, January 1915 had been still and cold, and a hard frost lit the woods and rolling downs of Berkshire with a seasonal glitter.

The first-class carriage was a new experience for Alma, and she stared out of the window reflecting on her Christmas Day with Jack's parents. They had been kind to ask her but his absence at the front had thrown a pall over the celebrations, especially as – three doors up from their house in Tottenham – their neighbours had been horrified to receive a letter from the War Office bearing news of the death of their only son. There had been rumours of an informal truce between the British and the Germans on Christmas morning, and even a game of football in no man's land. The papers had been full of speculation about this but, in truth, in London and beyond, there was a dawning recognition that the war would not be over quickly, and more beloved fathers, husbands and sons would die.

Across the empire the festive season had been more sober than usual.

The time off work had given Alma an opportunity to reflect on the remarkable news she'd received and the stark choice that now lay before her. Her life in Hampstead was quiet, predictable and, she had to admit it, boring. The Timperley Spiritualist Hotel had lit a fuse that smouldered and crackled in the background all the way through the muted seasonal celebrations. It almost felt as though the place was reaching out to her, which was a strange thing, but nevertheless quite discernible. Alone in her little house its presence was increasingly hard to ignore and, ultimately, became irresistible.

Barring an unpleasant surprise, Alma knew she was travelling to see her new life and, in so doing, to answer the questions that were rattling round her head about her mysterious aunt. What had she been like and how had she come to own a hotel in Falmouth?

Her travelling companions were the only other occupants of the carriage and in the reflection in the window she saw Mrs Neal take Mr Nascent's hand and lean against him. He gave her a gentle smile. It was sweet and Alma felt envious of their affection for each other. Jack Waring was a nice man, and she admired the fact he'd volunteered to join the fight against the Germans, but she couldn't imagine him summoning the same feeling in his own eyes as he looked at her.

Maybe it's time for a complete change.

* * *

They arrived at Falmouth Town station at half past five and disembarked from the train onto a crowded platform. As they shuffled forward Alma wondered at the delay, but her curiosity was soon satisfied. As well as a ticket officer, the exit from the station was manned by two privates carrying slung rifles and a sergeant who was eyeing the crowd under the station lights.

'What's all this I wonder?' she remarked to Mr Nascent.

'Falmouth has defended-port status because of the naval dockyard and so on. I imagine security is pretty tight,' he replied.

'Do you live in Falmouth, sir?' the sergeant asked as they came to the barrier.

'No, I am a solicitor from London. Down to assist a client with a legal matter.'

'Your name?'

'James Nascent.'

The soldier looked at Alma and Hilda. 'Party of three is it, sir?'

'That's right.'

There was a pause as the sergeant inspected them and Alma had a feeling he'd recognise them again if he needed to. *They're serious. I'm closer to the war down here.*

'Where are you staying in Falmouth?'

'The Timperley Spiritualist Hotel.'

'Do you have the booking confirmation?'

The solicitor produced a letter from his inner pocket and passed it over. The sergeant read it carefully, then handed it back with a smile. 'Very well, sir. Welcome to Falmouth – enjoy your stay.' He nodded to the privates who eased out of the way.

They emerged from the building and took a horse-drawn cab to the hotel where Mr Nascent had booked rooms. 'Perhaps it would be best to sample the hospitality as an anonymous guest before declaring your interest,' he had observed. And she could see the sense in that.

It was a ten-minute journey before they passed through a pair of open gates. In the darkness Alma had a brief impression of a drive lined with large bushes, before the cab swung round a corner and the outline of a statuesque building appeared to the right. Mr Nascent grunted in surprise and murmured, 'Well, well,' and, peering upwards, she was rather taken aback too. In her mind's eye she'd pictured a slightly down-at-heel seaside hotel sandwiched into a terrace of houses, but as they climbed

11

out of the cab she realised any preconceptions she had about her inheritance were likely to be wrong.

The solicitor led the way up the steps and they entered a reception area containing a large counter upon which a bell reposed. There was no one in sight, so he pressed down, and a single bright ping floated off into the nether regions of the premises. Alma barely heard it, because as she crossed the threshold of the hotel she felt a sudden reconnection to something she had walked away from five years ago. A distant bell had chimed once more and a familiar tingle of goose bumps crept up her arms.

What is this place?

The murmur of conversation drifted into the entrance hall from a half-open door on the left. Glancing that way Alma saw the beginnings of a room filled with warmth and light. Seconds later a door behind the counter opened and a woman in her late thirties with a pleasant, open countenance and pinned-back brown hair emerged.

'Good evening, may I be of service?' she enquired with a smile.

'Mr and Mrs James Nascent and Miss Alma Nascent. Two rooms, reserved by letter,' the solicitor replied.

Well that settles any doubts about the nature of their relationship. And I am to be their temporary daughter.

'Of course, welcome to you all. If you'd just sign the register, Mr Nascent.'

Much later, as she lay in bed, Alma's thoughts returned to her first meeting with the solicitor before Christmas. When she had asked him if her aunt's death was unexpected, his face had displayed a combination of sadness and acceptance. But as she listened to the wind in the trees outside, she realised that the one emotion she had missed at the time had been anger. Something about her aunt's death had left him very angry.

Ostensibly Mr Nascent was here to provide her with every assistance, as dictated by the terms of the will. But as sleep drifted over her, she wondered if he had his own reasons for visiting the hotel. And if so, what they were.

* * *

Excitement and curiosity vied for the upper hand when Alma opened her eyes in the luxurious bedroom the following morning. She was still struggling to understand how Alma Timperley, who earned 13/6 shillings a week in Hampstead town hall could possibly merit such luck, and she lay daydreaming under the eiderdown until a gentle knock sounded on the door.

'Come in,' she called, sitting up.

A freckled face topped with mop of curly blonde hair peeped round the door. It was a girl in a smart maid's uniform. 'Good morning, miss. It's eight o'clock and I've brought you a cup of tea. Breakfast is served at half past.'

'Right,' she said. She'd never stayed in a hotel before, or been served tea in bed, and could think of nothing further to say. As the tray arrived next to her, she added, 'What's your name?'

The girl produced a warm grin. 'It's Polly, miss.'

'And who else works here?'

Her wide-eyed look suggested this enquiry was unexpected, but she rose to the occasion. 'There's Kate, she's a chambermaid like me, and we work for Mrs Banks, the housekeeper. Then there's Mrs Wilson who comes in and cooks, and her daughter Maisie who serves, and Alf the odd-job man.' She paused then added, 'And the dailies who come in to help with the cleaning.'

Suddenly curious, Alma asked, 'Who is in overall charge?'

Polly looked at her in some distress. 'Oh, miss, if you're not happy with the arrangements you'd better tell me, and I'll tell Mrs Banks, and we'll see what can be done about it.'

Alma hastened to put her mind at rest. 'No, Polly, I am very happy. I'm just wondering about the ownership of the hotel, that's all.'

Her face clouded. 'It used to be Mrs Timperley of course, but since the accident we've been muddling along as best we can. Mrs Banks has been in charge I suppose. There are bookings you see, and Mr Weaver and Mr Wragge to be kept satisfied.'

'Are they guests?'

'Bless, no, miss. They are, were I should say, sort of partners of Mrs Timperley. In the work, I mean.' She hesitated and glanced towards the door. 'Begging your pardon, but I've more tea to deliver before it gets cold.'

'Of course, on you go, Polly.' She sent her on her way with a positively regal wave and sipped her tea thoughtfully.

The work? What is that?

Breakfast was taken in the pleasantly appointed dining room where they had eaten the previous evening. When they'd ordered, Mr Nascent said, 'I had a word with the housekeeper, who we met last night. She appears to have assumed command after the accident. I explained that I am Mrs Timperley's executor and that matters regarding the will are in hand.' He smiled across the table. 'I hope I didn't speak out of turn.'

For Alma it was more than a question. It was her future. She took a long, slow breath and looked about the room. A girl who she took to be Maisie Wilson was serving two well-dressed women who were sharing a table. She heard her say, 'Here we are, your ladyships, fresh from the farm.'

She looked back at the solicitor as he continued, 'A meeting with the staff where you are presented as the new owner would be most desirable, but that pre-supposes that you are going to accept your aunt's bequest and become the principal of this hotel. Is that your decision?'

An electrifying pulse of pins and needles infused Alma's body, and for a moment it felt as though time had stopped. Then, with a silent scream that combined joy and terror in equal measure, she replied calmly, 'Yes, Mr Nascent, it is.'

Half an hour later they were standing in the office with the housekeeper, where Alma was introduced as the niece of Mrs Gladys Timperley and henceforth the new owner of the hotel.

'I'm Gracie Banks. You arrived incognito then,' she observed as they shook hands. Alma squirmed inside at the implication that she had been underhand, but it was said without rancour, and she was further reassured when the older woman smiled and added, 'That was very sensible, Miss Timperley, I'm sure I would have done the same.'

'I am inexperienced and took advice, Mrs Banks,' she replied. 'Would you be kind enough to tell me about the hotel?'

The housekeeper inclined her head. 'Your aunt set up the place twelve years ago having bought the house from the estate of the gentleman who had lived here prior to that. By then Mrs Timperley was well established and had a following amongst the upper classes.'

Alma nodded. 'In the dining room I noticed that the clientele seemed well heeled.'

'That's right. Reputation is everything and people are prepared to pay very well in order to enjoy the unique service that we provide here.'

'And what is that? What are they buying, exactly?'

'Didn't you realise?' She looked at Alma with a surprised smile. 'Guests staying here are offered the chance to contact the dead, Miss Timperley. And since the start of the war, we've never been busier.'

Chapter Three

Later, and much occupied with her thoughts, Alma went outside
to inspect the grounds. They had arranged that the staff would
be assembled at eleven o'clock so she and Mr Nascent could
address them, and she didn't want to invite questions by wander-
ing about the place in the meantime. Besides, she needed some
fresh air to assuage her nerves and to absorb the news regarding
the hotel's true purpose.

'Mrs Timperley was a well-known medium who had a genuine ability to connect with the other side,' the housekeeper had
told them. 'Nearly everyone who stays here wants to contact a
dead relative or friend. This dreadful war means that these days
we are almost exclusively working for families who have lost sons
in France. You are unusual guests in that respect and are lucky
we had room.'

Standing on the gravel she looked up at the hotel's façade, which
rose for three storeys. On the ground floor tall sash windows
reflected the turning circle, and these were mirrored by smaller
windows on the first floor. Above these, dormer windows pro-
jected outwards on either side of an ornate tower, which ended in
a stumpy spire clad in grey slates. Delicate iron railings ran round
its base and, with a shock, Alma realised that it must have been
from up there that her aunt had plummeted to her death.

Standing there, rather stunned that her move from the safe
familiarity of Hampstead was now permanent, she found her

thoughts turning to Jack Waring again. Even though they had only been apart for four months, the incredible changes she was going through made their time together in London before the war seem very distant. Jack had been part of her old life, but she wasn't sure there was room for him in the new one.

Mind busy, she wandered round to the back where a large lawn was edged with deep borders, much of it evergreen. To her left, beyond the garden, open ground ran downhill towards the sea. Three fine cedar trees stood in a clump at the far end and Alma noticed a gate leading through a stone wall that marked the end of the property. As she watched, it opened and a tall man appeared. He was wearing a long dark overcoat and trilby hat and appeared to be making a beeline for the back door of the hotel.

When he was six feet away, as though making a spur-of-the-moment decision, he stopped and removed his hat. His skin looked as though it was stretched a little too tightly across his face and, with his hair sweeping from right to left across his forehead and intense blue eyes, his gaze bordered on being alarming. Indeed, Alma had to brace herself to avoid taking a step backwards under his unrelenting examination.

A striking-looking man, though. No mistake about that.

He offered her his hand and said, 'George Weaver, spiritualist.'

She recognised the name from her conversation with Polly. One of her aunt's partners in 'the work' and about thirty-five years old.

'Alma Timperley, hotel owner,' she replied. He clearly registered the surname, but it took a moment for the penny to drop.

'Owner?' he queried faintly.

Alma nodded gravely. 'That is so, Mr Weaver. My aunt has left the hotel to me, and I am here to take possession.'

There was a silence, and she sensed a great deal of speedy thinking going on behind those striking eyes. She chose to wait him out. As her old headmistress Miss Bede had drummed into her at school: 'Men are different, but we should not assume they are better. Nor should we let them assume it.' It was a fine theory, although difficult to put into practice in the male-dominated hierarchy of Hampstead Town Hall. But down here, with her aunt's reputation and the hotel behind her, who knew how things might play out.

'What are your plans, may I ask?' he said eventually.

'For the moment I plan to carry on as normal, notwithstanding my dear aunt's demise.' Then some instinct prompted her to add, 'The work must go on, Mr Weaver, as I'm sure you agree.'

He nodded and she saw relief in his eyes. 'Yes, I do. That is good news, Miss Timperley.' He glanced towards the hotel and added, 'If you'll excuse me, I have a client waiting, but I hope that we can have a longer conversation over the next day or two.'

'I will enjoy that, Mr Weaver. Adieu for now, then.' She gave him a smile of dismissal and he nodded his head in a militaristic fashion before heading for the entrance. She watched him go and felt a quiet surge of elation. It was not Miss Timperley, council filing clerk, who Mr Weaver had just met, but Miss Timperley, hotel proprietress.

And Alma rather liked her.

At eleven o'clock the staff assembled, and a rather uncomfortable silence reigned until everyone was there and Mrs Banks shut the door, at which point Mr Nascent stood up and commenced speaking.

'Good morning, ladies and gentlemen, my name is James Nascent. I am a solicitor and executor for Mrs Gladys Timperley. To my right may I introduce Miss Alma Timperley, who was Mrs Timperley's niece, and is the sole beneficiary of her will. To be absolutely clear, she is the new owner of the Timperley Spiritualist Hotel and, as such, your mistress from this point onwards.'

Alma watched as he let the staff assimilate this news. Mrs Banks was unsurprised of course, but in the little arc of chairs spread in front of her she saw a mixed reaction. Polly gaped, wide-eyed, and nudged the dark-haired girl next to her, who she took to be Kate, her fellow chambermaid. Mrs Wilson, the cook, nodded slowly. Her daughter looked surprised but not unduly concerned and Alf the odd-job man introduced an element of humour into the loaded moment by nudging her and saying in what he clearly considered to be a sotto voce, 'Eh, who is she?'

'The new mistress, Alf. Mrs Timperley's niece. She's inherited,' the girl bellowed back at him. She saw Mr Nascent trying to smother a smile as she stood up.

Here we go then. Try to get it right, Alma Timperley.

'Good morning, ladies and gentlemen. I will make a point of speaking to you all personally when I get a chance but for now, the salient facts are these. Prior to what is an unexpected bequest I was employed by Hampstead Council in London, so I know what it is like to work for a living. I have no experience in the hotel trade, but I am a quick learner and will rely on you all to show me the ropes. To set your minds at rest, I have no plans other than to continue to operate the hotel to the same high standard that you clearly maintain . . .'

At this moment her carefully planned speech was interrupted by the door opening and a large man in his mid-fifties, with a shock of tousled and suspiciously black hair, appeared.

'What's going on?' he asked shortly. 'Lady Winterson requires a cup of tea and the whole bally place is deserted. Who are you, might I ask?' he finished, catching sight of Alma.

'Mr Wragge, I presume?' she said with a smile.

'Indeed.'

'My name is Alma Timperley, and I am the new owner of the hotel. I have inherited it from my aunt.'

Mrs Banks craned her head round to see him. 'I couldn't find you, Mr Wragge. You must have been out when arrangements were made this morning.'

He stared at her and then back to Alma before asking, 'Where's Weaver?'

'With a client – I will speak to him later,' she replied. 'Perhaps you could join us then, Mr Wragge? If you're busy at present.' He hesitated, obviously torn between staying and going, so she continued, 'Maisie, would you make a cup of tea for Lady Winterson,' and the girl rose and departed silently. Mr Wragge followed her.

First crisis averted. Heart almost beating out of her chest, Alma took a deep breath and carried on. 'As I was saying, there will be no immediate changes. My aunt clearly knew what she was doing and had the benefit of an excellent staff. You have all done splendidly in her absence and I hope that you will support me in the same way that you have supported her. I will be moving into her rooms today. Any questions?'

'She's moving in today, Alf,' shouted Polly, in response to a further enquiry from the odd-job man.

And with that her troops dispersed.

She looked at Mr Nascent and he nodded back. 'Well done. That was an excellent beginning. You must call me James from now on, and Mrs Neal is Hilda. I think we will have a long and happy association, and I look forward to it with great pleasure.'

Hilda gave him a look that Alma didn't understand as he reached into his jacket and removed an envelope. 'This is the final element in your aunt's bequest. My instructions were to give it to you when you were fully confirmed as the new owner of the hotel. I think that moment is now, Alma.'

She took it and said, 'Do you know what it contains?'

'I'd prefer not to speculate.' But his eyes were alight, and she felt a shiver pass through her body. It was a familiar sensation. Something was about to happen.

'Perhaps now is the time to inspect my aunt's private rooms,' she observed and five minutes later followed Mrs Banks up the stairs to the first floor, and then up again to the rooms with the dormer windows at the top of the house.

'Gladys had a bedroom, bathroom and sitting room up here, Miss Timperley,' the housekeeper said as they paused in the corridor outside a door. She unlocked it and handed Alma the key, then hesitated and produced an apologetic shrug.

'It's just as it was when she died. I did wonder, but it wasn't my place to clean it out. I hope you understand.'

Alma nodded. 'Yes, I do.'

The housekeeper seemed relieved. 'It's very nice to have you here and I hope we can make a good go of things. I'll let you have a look round on your own.'

Alma watched her retreat to the head of the stairs, then turned the handle and walked into her new home. She had a brief impression of a small but comfortable room before sitting down in an armchair and ripping open the envelope. There were two sheets of paper inside and, utterly absorbed, she unfolded them, noted the hotel letterhead, and began to read.

18th May 1910

Dear Alma,

I'm writing this on your eighteenth birthday in my sitting room at the Timperley Spiritualist Hotel in Falmouth. I own the hotel and if, at some time in the future, you read this letter I will be dead, and you will have decided to accept my bequest and take up the reins.

22

What a surprise it must be! I suspect that you will have had no idea that your mother Harriet had a sister. If that is the case, then she will have upheld her side of an arrangement we came to many years ago. In 1892 in fact. I was sixteen years old that year and had got myself into trouble. A silly mistake by an inexperienced girl and an older man who let their passion get the better of them one night on Hampstead Heath.

There was no hiding it, as there never is. When I told my father he threatened to horsewhip me, but after a few days a quiet and bitter rage settled over both Mum and Dad. They held strong religious beliefs and were terrified of the news getting out among their friends in the congregation. As it happened Harriet had just married John Timperley and a deal was struck.

I would have the baby and give it up into my sister's care, where it would be passed off as the first of her children. I would then leave the house never to return and never to be mentioned again. It was only much later that Harriet told me John had walked out early in their marriage and, once our parents had died, she had raised you alone. My parting gift was your name, dear Alma, and at the time I believed that leaving you in Harriet's care was the best and safest thing I could do for you. I had no home, no trade, and no money. Your birth father was a decent fellow but I'm afraid in my rage and grief I pushed him away.

But, although I walked down Whitton Road in tears, I felt some relief too. My eyes are watering as I write those words because it is a terrible admission, but it is the truth. A new baby is a burden for a free-spirited girl, and I sensed I had another role to play in the world.

When I finally settled here in Falmouth and established the hotel, I wrote to Harriet begging her for news. Since then, I have received a brief letter every Christmas. It's been thin gruel to a starving woman, but at least I know you are growing into a fine and capable girl, and that fills my heart with joy. It is also me who provides the funds for you to attend St Joseph's school. Nevertheless, the awful truth is that I am your mother, and I left you. In my guilt and despair, I even adopted the surname Timperley, knowing that would be your name.

You might wonder why I haven't contacted you now you are grown up, but my isolation is the penance I deserve. I left you when you needed me most and I have no right to you now. Oh, the bitter irony! I can contact the dead but not, in your case, the living. Sometimes I dream of you and sense that you are powerful in the same way as me, and I am sure that you will make a success of the hotel for that reason. There is another life awaiting me and, at some point in the future, I will be not far from you on earth. We may come to know each other, but until then I will be far away, so do not seek me in the Hall of the Dead.

Do not forget me, my darling Alma, but concentrate on your life here and now. That is what matters.

With all my love, your affectionate and regretful mother,
Gladys Timperley
P.S. James Nascent is a good man. You may rely on him.
P.P.S. I will leave notes in the file in the bedside table.

Alma was sobbing by the time she was halfway through the letter, and as she read the neat signature, she leaned back with it clutched in her hand and bawled her eyes out for a full five minutes.

Then she settled down and reread it carefully three times. It explained many things, especially the sense she'd had when growing up that she was in some way a cuckoo in that little North London nest. And her mother, who she henceforth resolved to refer to mentally as Harriet, had been unable to have children of her own, which no doubt added a telling piquancy to what had happened. With only one parent, who worked long hours in a haberdashery and was often tired, Alma's upbringing had been functional but not affectionate and she had occasionally wondered why she wasn't hugged by Harriet the way her friends were by their mothers.

Now she knew. Not only had Harriet been deserted by John Timperley, the man who was supposed to be her father, she was keeping a huge secret of her own. No wonder she had been distant with Alma at times.

And it also explained how, aged eleven, she had been suddenly and inexplicably uprooted from her rough-and-ready local school and inserted, complete with new uniform, satchel, and boater, into the exalted academic halls of St Joseph's School for Girls on Hampstead Heath, where she'd flourished under the brilliant guidance of Miss Bede and her able team of teachers. The school was also where she had first got involved in the spiritualist world. The headmistress had been a talented clairvoyant and Alma had been part of a little group of her 'special girls' who had conducted séances. Her own raw but powerful ability had emerged in those teenage years, although the jealousy of the other girls had ultimately led her to withdraw from the group, to the frustration of Miss Bede.

When James Nascent had first mentioned the Timperley Spiritualist Hotel, it hadn't just been her surname that had chimed in her head. Yesterday, Gracie Banks's announcement regarding the true purpose of the hotel might have astonished James and Hilda, but it hadn't shocked Alma.

She knew what the word 'spiritualist' meant.

There was a magazine sitting on the bedside table and she picked it up. It was a copy of *The Spiritualist* dated June 1910 and as she studied the colourful front cover she drew in her breath in surprise.

The headline read, *Gladys Timperley, Medium to the Nobility*, and below the words there was a photograph of the woman who was her mother. She stared at it hungrily, immediately seeing the family resemblance to Harriet. But there was more depth to her somehow. Much more. She was looking boldly at the camera as a small smile played on her lips, but her eyes were soft. The overall effect made her seem both strong and vulnerable. Her hair was swept back off her face and an artfully placed mirror showed a long French plait on her back. Alma guessed she was in her mid-thirties and as she stared emotion welled up in her again and she wiped her eyes.

If only I'd known. I would have come. I could have been here with you.

She read the article avidly, but it was a lightweight and rather fawning piece that contained no specific details about how she had risen to such prominence in the world of mediumship.

Frustrated, Alma put the magazine down and stared sightlessly out of the dormer window. Neither the letter nor the article had answered the questions that burned in her mind. Where had her mother gone when she left Whitton Road? How had she ended up as the owner of the hotel, and what had become of her birth father?

* * *

Half an hour later, as Alma reached the bottom of the stairs that led to the entrance hall, she was almost overwhelmed by an explosion of pins and needles that suddenly coursed through her body. Shocked by the intensity of the moment, she was instantly transported back to St Joseph's school and her early clairvoyant experiences with Miss Bede. She put a hand on the reception counter and struggled to maintain her composure as a well-dressed, middle-aged woman entered the foyer through the glass front door. Beyond her, Alma could see her maid struggling with the baggage and a horse-drawn cab turning back towards the drive.

To her surprise, a young man in army uniform was standing just inside the door, but the woman walked past him without even a glance. An affectionate smile played over his face as he watched her approach the reception counter.

There is something wrong about him.

Light-headed with the swirling energy that filled the hall, Alma almost faltered as the woman came to a halt. She was dressed entirely in black and even through her veil the hollow emptiness in her eyes was compelling. As though a blazing bonfire had been reduced to smoking ash.

'Good afternoon, madam. May I be of assistance?'

'My name is Lady Watson. I am booked in for the week to see Mr Wragge.' She had a low voice, flat and unemotional, and it was a simple enough statement.

'Are you travelling alone, madam?' she asked.

'Yes. My maid is with me of course.'

'Of course.' The maid came through the door, a suitcase in each hand, and placed them where the soldier was standing. He moved to one side. Alma realised she had not seen him.

Neither of them had.

'Well?' Lady Watson was looking at her. Alma pulled herself together and consulted the register. To her relief she saw that Mrs Banks had allocated a room and she indicated where the new arrival should sign.

'Welcome to the Timperley Spiritualist Hotel. I hope that your stay here provides you with some solace for the loss of your son, Alexander.'

27

Lady Watson drew in a sharp breath. 'How do you know his name?'

Because he's here. Ten feet from you.

Alma looked back at her. 'I don't know. It just came to me.' To her horror she felt tears welling up. 'I am so sorry for your loss.' Out of the corner of her eye she could see the maid staring at her. Alexander Watson was still there too. He looked faintly amused.

The woman's gloved hand reached onto the counter and enclosed hers and they looked at each other. 'It seems I have come to the right place,' she remarked quietly. 'Miss . . . ?'

'Timperley. Alma Timperley.'

'Ah.' She nodded, as if things had become clearer. 'Any relation to Gladys Timperley?'

'She was my aunt. I have inherited the hotel and only arrived recently.'

She nodded again. 'I saw your aunt conduct a séance at a private party some years ago. She was a remarkably talented woman, and her death was a tragedy.'

At that moment the housekeeper appeared. She took in the scene with a practised eye and introduced herself.

'Good afternoon, my lady. I'm Mrs Banks. I will show you to your room and see you settled in.' Turning to the maid who had picked up the bags again, she added, 'You come with your mistress now and I'll have Alf bring your bags up. He'll show you your room upstairs as well.'

As the little group ascended the stairs, Alma looked towards the door, but the soldier had disappeared. She stood, slack-faced and unmoving, as the implications of what had just occurred sank in. Because the Timperley Spiritualist Hotel had reawoken something deep within her.

* * *

Nine hundred miles east of Falmouth, in his office just off Unter den Linden in Berlin, Felix Muller the deputy head of the German overseas intelligence service, leaned back in his chair and considered the telegram he had just received from the embassy in Lisbon.

The message had originated in Falmouth and was signed *Excalibur*, like the ones he'd received previously. It included details of ship movements in and out of the port, the regimental shoulder badges of soldiers in the town and information about the increase in bread prices and other food items, all of which was useful intelligence that he could feed into the bigger picture of how the British were fighting the war on the home front.

The information arrived in letters via the *Lisbon Rose*, a neutral Portuguese-flagged ship, which plied a regular route between Falmouth and Lisbon and, as the embassy informed him that a sailor delivered the packages to them, he assumed that Excalibur had an arrangement with one of the crew to smuggle the letters on board in Cornwall.

The messenger had also been willing to accept any replies going in the other direction and Muller had sent the agent a book called *Der Antichrist* by Friedrich Nietzsche to use as a code key.

Excalibur was clearly well connected as he often included information about senior officers in the military and the government, which gave Muller a precious insight into what was happening behind the scenes in the highest echelons of British society. Given the woeful state of German espionage operations in Britain, he was glad to have at least one agent who had managed to avoid being scooped up by the British. And as it happened, this particular cable included something very interesting.

Pendennis Castle is armed with two six-inch guns sited at Half-Moon Battery facing the sea. There are two more

*in St Anthony's Battery on the other side of the estuary.
The entrance channel is covered by two quick-firing
twelve-pounder guns on the ramparts of the castle.*

This was the first time Excalibur had produced such information
and he would pass it along. In the meantime, he wrote a brief
note and walked through to his secretary who stood up as he
approached. 'This is for Excalibur. Encode it and send it to the
embassy in Lisbon with a covering note requesting onward despatch via the *Lisbon Rose*.'

As he reached for his copy of *Der Antichrist* the young man
read it.

*Starts Excalibur excellent information in your last message
stop Great interest in any vulnerabilities you can identify
stop Also gossip from senior figures stop Muller ends.*

Chapter Four

September 1909, Hampstead Heath, London

Few lights burned in the Gothic bulk of St Joseph's School for Girls as it crouched high in the darkness surrounded by trees and an intimidating wall. But in the crenelated clock tower above the foliage, a single uncurtained window glowed in the night sky, like a lighthouse guiding Londoners to their beds in the streets below.

Inside the simply furnished room Miss Alicia Bede, the eccentric and wildly gesticulating headmistress of the school, was sitting at a circular table. She was not alone. With her were four girls called Rose, Alma, Greta, and Letitia, although the latter, a redhead, was universally known as Lettuce by both staff and pupils.

The meeting was a regular one, although Alma was a new arrival. The headmistress had sensed something special in the girl the moment she'd arrived in the school four years earlier, but the little gathering was only open to fifth-formers and above, so she had waited until her birthday the previous week before quietly issuing an invitation.

What happened in the room required a certain degree of maturity.

Miss Bede rose, walked to the door, and turned off the gaslight. In the sudden darkness a single candle in the centre of the table lit the girls' faces with a warm glow.

'Hold hands,' the headmistress said quietly, resuming her seat. When she was settled, she closed her eyes and raised her head slightly. 'Concentrate now, girls. Open your minds to the other side and welcome the presence of those that visit us.'

A studious silence fell in the candlelit gloom as the five of them let their minds drift and reach out to the spirit world.

Or rather four of them did. Alma had her eyes closed but she wasn't reaching out to anything. In fact she wasn't sure she wanted to be there at all, but Miss Bede's glittering personality had overridden any doubts. At St Joseph's, when the headmistress asked, one obeyed. Joyfully.

Despite the girl's reluctance, the older woman – who was a gifted medium – felt the impact of her presence immediately. Many teenage girls had a raw ability to connect with the world beyond, but Alma was different. It felt as though the power around the table had been doubled in a moment.

The girl is a beacon.

Alma gave a low moan. Miss Bede opened her eyes and looked through the candlelight. 'Don't worry, my dear,' she said quietly, 'it's completely natural and there is no threat. Let it happen. Open the door.'

Across the table Alma was squeezing her partners' hands to the point of pain as fascination and terror vied for the upper hand. Inside her head she was drifting without purpose through a widely spread crowd. A man watched her as she passed but gave no sign of recognition, but then her heart thumped. A young woman aged about twenty was standing slightly apart from the rest and looking directly at Alma. They made eye contact and the woman smiled and nodded, her gaze intense.

As Alma stared back, in the far distance she heard Miss Bede's voice. 'Welcome to you.'

Reassured she smiled back at the woman and said, 'Hello. I'm Alma.'

'Anne-Marie.' The reply was in her head. A Scottish accent.

'Can we help you, Anne-Marie?' asked Miss Bede. This time her voice was much stronger and with a shock Alma realised she was standing next to her.

'You can tell my ma and pa that I'm all right. I miss them and I know they miss me, but I'm all right.'

Alma looked at Miss Bede. She was glowing with a graceful radiance that gave her face an extraordinary, almost angelic, quality. 'We'll do that, Anne-Marie. Is there any other message?'

'No. I've got to go now.'

'Very well. We wish you Godspeed on your journey.'

Afterwards, Alma wasn't sure what happened next. The woman turned and walked off, and then Miss Bede was gently calling her, and she came to the surface as though waking from a sleep and was surprised to see the room and the table.

Confused and disorientated, she stared at the headmistress. 'What was that place?' she asked.

'Clairvoyants call it the Hall of the Dead. People who have died pass through it on their journeys, but some will stay there for a while. It is the easiest place for us to reach.'

'I recognised the girl.'

'It was Anne-Marie Harton, wasn't it? One of the maids from the juniors' house. She died from typhoid last month.'

Alma nodded. It was true. 'Do you know where her parents live?'

'Yes. I'll go to see them and pass on the message.'

Alma looked at the other girls and asked, 'Did you all see her? And hear what she said?'

They all nodded. 'We weren't there with you, but we could see,' Greta clarified.

33

'And that's normally what happens,' Miss Bede said, her eyes fixed on Alma. 'But for you to not just come with me, but to lead the way . . .' She smiled, her eyes alight with warmth and excitement. 'You have a remarkable talent.'

Alma was silent, uncomfortable with the intense looks she was getting from the other girls. They were jealous; she could feel it. A new girl in the group. And doing better than them in the competitive world of approval from Miss Bede.

'We will have to explore your abilities a little more, I think,' the headmistress continued. 'If you are amenable.'

'I'm not sure,' she replied. 'I'm really not sure.'

'Oh but we must – you cannot ignore a gift like yours.'

* * *

With a sigh Alma suddenly stirred, opened her eyes, and stared in momentary confusion at the unfamiliar room. It was the middle of the night, and she was in bed in her aunt's quarters in Falmouth. The dream had been intense and unwelcome, brought on by the incident with Lady Watson some hours earlier. The sight of her dead son standing, a silent but interested observer as his mother had arrived at the hotel, was an unwelcome return to a world upon which she had turned her back when she had walked out of the gates of St Joseph's for the final time.

She reached out for the bedside lamp and sat up in its comforting glow. There was more. In the middle of the evening Valentine Wragge had sought her out, clearly displeased about something.

'I have arranged my first consultation with Lady Watson for tomorrow evening. She has requested that you are also present.'

Alma looked at him in surprise. 'I'd really rather not.'

'My thoughts exactly, Miss Timperley. What has brought this on, might I ask?'

34

'We met when she arrived at the hotel. Beyond that I have no idea.'

He was looking at her intently. 'She tells me you conjured up her dead son's name and that she felt some connection with you.' He raised his eyebrows. 'Can you explain that?'

'No.' Her refusal to offer any further comment momentarily threw the man standing over her. He sat down and continued in a more reasonable tone.

'I have explained to Lady Watson that a consulting session is an intimate affair between the pair of us and the spirit world, and the presence of a third party would not be constructive. She, however, will not be moved. I am at the start of what I hope will be a fruitful week with my new client, Miss Timperley. I would not wish her to be distracted.'

Alma's mind cleared. Wragge's concerns were financial, not spiritual. 'Believe me, I have no desire to impinge on your relationship with Lady Watson and wish you every success in your work with her. I am not at all keen to sit in on the consultation, but if that is what she wants then I will accede.'

'But say nothing. Not interfere . . . ?'

'I will be a shadow at the table, nothing more.'

But as she stared at the faint outline of the window, Alma felt uneasy. That undertaking had been easy to make and was genuinely meant, but her experiences under the tutorship of Miss Bede suggested otherwise. *'You are an open door, my dear,'* she had observed. *'Spirits are tempted towards you like cats to catnip.'*

* * *

That evening Alma found herself sitting in a room everyone called the nook. It was used as a rest and dining area for the staff and was also where the guests' servants ate. She was alone and waiting for Lady Watson's consultation to start. Restless and uneasy at what lay ahead, she walked over to a large dresser and started randomly opening the drawers. The contents were a predictable mix of cutlery and other table-ware and with a mental shrug she moved on to the cupboard below. Both shelves were crammed with old kitchen equipment and pots and pans.

Driven by an instinct she would wonder about later, she craned her head. A single cooking pot stood at the back and even in the gloom Alma could see the traces of finger marks on it while the others were dusty and unmarked. Curious as to why it had been used recently, she pulled it towards her and took off the lid. A brown leather-bound book lay inside, its title, *Der Antichrist*, embossed in gold lettering on the cover. She picked it up and flicked through the pages, noting that some paragraphs were underlined in pencil and the wear on the spine suggested it had been well read.

Odd. It feels as though the book is concealed here.

She replaced it and then returned to her seat. Shortly afterwards her reflections were interrupted by Wragge who put his head round the door and said, 'Shall we go through, Miss Timperley?'

Five minutes later they were sitting with Lady Watson at a small table in Wragge's consulting room. The lights were low, a single small candle lay in the centre of the table, and heavy velvet curtains added to the sense of being cocooned in the semi-darkness.

'As I explained earlier, Lady Watson, we will now hold hands and I will reach out to the spirit world to see if we can make contact with Alexander.' He spoke in a low and intimate tone, and Alma saw the older woman lean towards him slightly. She'd removed her veil and the flat blankness in her eyes had been replaced by a yearning that Alma found heartbreaking.

He raised his hands above the table and the two women took them, linking their own to form a circle. 'And now we begin,' he said and, with that, closed his eyes, drew a long slow intake of breath, and began to speak.

An hour later Alma took a cup of tea up to her room and sat down in the chair to gather her thoughts. There was no doubt that Lady Watson had been delighted with the consultation. It appeared that Wragge had indeed made contact with Alexander Watson and the ensuing exchange with his mother, during which the spiritualist had acted as a go-between, had moved her deeply. Twice she had sobbed as her dead son had made some remark about their home life before his departure for the front. And his confirmation that he was 'doing all right and with friends from his regiment who had also fallen', had reduced her to visible tears.

But despite this success, Alma was more interested in the two notable pieces of information that emerged from the evening.

Someone in the hotel spoke fluent German and was apparently keen to conceal it.

And Valentine Wragge was a fraud.

Unable to sleep, she ran through the hotel rooms in her head, starting with the high-ceilinged entrance hall. The main staircase rose to the left of the reception desk, which lay below the half landing. Behind the desk a door marked 'Staff only' led to the office, storerooms and other areas devoted to the running of the hotel.

A door in the right-hand wall of the hall gave access to the dining room and its partner on the left led into a well-appointed lounge with a fine fireplace and settees and chairs arranged in little groups.

From the back of the hall, a corridor led to the rear of the hotel where double glass doors gave onto a veranda overlooking the garden. Two short wings were built out of the main block. On the right, the ground floor housed the kitchen and the nook. The left-hand wing comprised three consulting rooms where the main business of the hotel was conducted.

Upstairs a corridor gave access to the eight principal bedrooms, four along the front and two in each wing. A further and less grand stair led to the top floor where Alma was now ensconced. The staff accommodation was also up there, along with rooms for the guests' servants.

As she lay there, she realised that George Weaver was in bed less than twenty feet from her. It was an oddly distracting thought and she wondered if he was asleep or awake, and if he had a significant woman in his life.

The questions lingered in her mind for a long time, before she drifted off to sleep.

Chapter Five

After breakfast, before departing for an appointment at the bank, Alma and James sat down with Mrs Banks and went through the bookings for the next few months.

'I expect we will miss the income from my aunt's work,' Alma observed.

The housekeeper looked at her. 'Yes and no, Miss Timperley. Your aunt charged her clients directly for her consulting work, so the hotel won't miss that. I wrote to the people who were booked in to see Gladys, advising them of her death, and received some very moving letters in response, but very few of them have cancelled. They've all asked to see Mr Weaver or Mr Wragge instead.'

'How does it work?'

'Your aunt always suggested people stay here for a week and have three sessions. She was clever like that. It meant a week's worth of money rather than a couple of days. All three of them worked in the afternoons and evenings, depending on who was staying. Mr Weaver and Mr Wragge will be able to take up the slack if we book further in advance.'

'And is it still all right for people to travel to Falmouth? We were checked by some soldiers coming out of the station.'

'Yes. When war broke out the government fortified the town and tried to restrict visitors, but there was a right to-do and the council and the local MP made representations saying that tourism was essential for local jobs. In the end they said if you could prove you'd booked a hotel you could still come.'

'Mr Nascent had to show the letter at the station.'

'That's right.' The housekeeper tapped the reservations ledger and added, 'We're nearly fully booked for three months, and new clients are writing all the time for reservations.' She gave Alma a sad look. 'The war is a dreadful thing, but it is very good for business.'

* * *

Alma and James returned from the bank in time for lunch and as they took their seats in the dining room, her escort remarked with a smile, 'Well, it seems you are now a woman of substance.'

It was true. The manager at Lloyds Bank had given them a summary of the accounts, which showed the position to be very healthy. 'Even with suppliers' prices rising by ten per cent because of the war, the hotel remains a profitable concern,' he had concluded. 'But that is not all, Miss Timperley. Your aunt also had her personal accounts with us here and she has just shy of four thousand pounds on deposit. If you are in agreement, we will open new current and deposit accounts for you and transfer the balances over, before closing your aunt's.'

Astonished by such riches, Alma could only nod. A silence followed and, seeing she was rather overwhelmed by the news, the solicitor cleared his throat. 'May I ask how things have been managed since Gladys Timperley died? The payment of salaries and supplier invoices and so on?'

The bank manager replied. 'Mrs Banks, who I believe is the hotel's housekeeper, came to see me and explained the situation. I undertook to keep things ticking over until matters were settled.' He looked at Alma. 'She strikes me as being a reliable and sensible employee.'

'Yes, I think so too,' she replied. 'In fact I was wondering about promoting her to assistant manager at the hotel.'

He nodded thoughtfully. 'She has been with Mrs Timperley from the beginning and is known in the town. It's your choice of course, but you could do worse.'

Deciding to act on this advice, after lunch Alma again sought out Mrs Banks and with James Nascent sitting next to her, offered the housekeeper a new role as assistant hotel manager, with a matching uplift in wages and status.

'Apart from anything else, I suspect the correspondence regarding guest enquiries must be time-consuming,' Alma added.

'It is that, Miss Timperley, and I'll be delighted to accept your offer. Thank you.'

'Very well. From now on, in private, we shall be on first-name terms, Gracie.'

'Yes, Alma. That will be lovely.'

* * *

Later the same afternoon, Alma sat down with Mr Weaver and Mr Wragge. James Nascent joined them. He was, for the moment, utterly essential to her confidence.

'Would you tell me about the work, gentlemen,' she asked, 'and perhaps something of your personal histories? How did you meet my aunt, for example?'

The men glanced at each other and then Wragge said, 'I was working as an actor, quite successfully, as it happens, when I first came across Gladys. She did a private séance for some people in the theatre world, and I was present. I quickly realised that I had some ability as a medium, which was a surprise, I'll admit.'

'When was this?'

He pursed his lips in thought then said, 'Fifteen years ago, I'd say. Anyway, the whole business interested me, and I persevered and built up my skills whilst keeping in occasional touch with your aunt. She was further down the path than me and often featured in spiritual magazines, but her big break was getting the endorsement of Arthur Conan Doyle. He is a great advocate for spiritualism and wrote very favourably of her work with the bereaved. That was picked up by the national newspapers. I even think he might have been a silent partner in the hotel in the early years.'

Arthur Conan Doyle! A bona-fide celebrity. This is fascinating.

Alma leaned forward, completely absorbed by his tale. 'So when did you arrive at the hotel, Mr Wragge?'

'In the summer of 1908. She wrote to me saying she'd set up in Falmouth and the signs were that the thing would be a success, and did I fancy buying in. As it turned out the timing suited me. I was in funds and tiring of my rather peripatetic life.' He looked at the man next to him and added, 'Weaver joined us a year later on the same terms.'

Alma looked at him and was treated to a penetrating stare, accompanied by a slight smile. She swallowed, momentarily losing concentration. 'Er, the same terms . . . ? What would those be, might I ask?'

Weaver answered. 'We both paid your aunt a one-off fee to operate as mediums in the hotel with our own clientele and consulting rooms. As Wragge says, we think Conan Doyle was a partner and our contributions enabled her to buy him out and gain sole ownership.'

Nascent stirred and spoke. 'But neither of you have a share in the property, per se.'

Weaver shook his head. 'Correct. We have the advantage of working under the umbrella of the hotel, which has a unique reputation in our field, and charging clients direct for our medium work, as did Gladys. She also received the fees for board and lodging from all the guests. As part of the arrangement, we both stay here all found for a reasonable monthly charge.'

So that was it, thought Alma. Her aunt had bought the hotel with a partner and then, when the concern was going well, found a way to raise the capital to buy him out, while at the same time increasing the potential for the business. The bank manager was right: she was astute.

'The arrangements seem very sensible to me, and I can see no value in stirring things up. Is it clear to you, James?' she enquired.

He nodded. 'I'll draw up a new set of documents with Miss Timperley's name on them, but there will be no other amendments. Is that acceptable, gentlemen?'

Alma thought Wragge seemed relieved and Weaver looked inscrutable but gave a little nod. His eyes really were deep blue, she noticed.

'Then perhaps I should tell you a little of myself,' she said. And for ten minutes she regaled them with a brief life story to which she noticed the solicitor also listened intently, although she didn't mention Gladys had been her mother. Shortly afterwards they departed.

Grateful at last to have some time to herself, Alma climbed to the top floor and began a thorough examination of her quarters. Sudden death leaves loose ends, and she was fascinated and moved in equal measure as she looked though the dresses and private bits and pieces that shone a bright light onto the life of the mother she'd never known.

She discovered a file of papers in the bottom drawer of a bedside table and, as promised, it appeared to contain various notes on the running of the hotel. But it was the sealed envelope on the top that had caught her eye. It was titled, 'Read this first'.

Sitting in the armchair she tore it open and did just that.

Dear Alma,

I promised to leave you notes and you should read this first as it explains what happened to me after I left Whitton Road and how I came to establish the hotel.

For the first year I drifted around doing pick-up work in hotel kitchens and general skivvying. I felt so raw and guilty at leaving you and teetered on the edge of doing something foolish many times. I saw less and less of your father as time passed, although we've always had an invisible silver thread that has bound us together, even if we are far apart. That is you of course, my darling.

Finally, I left London and simply walked out into the country-side. And I kept walking for weeks. Summer was coming and there was work to be had on farms and places to sleep in barns. The journey seemed to put me back together again, and I began to see some kind of future for myself. And un-beknown to me someone else thought so too, because one afternoon as I walked through some thick woods near a town called Dorchester, I came upon a little group of caravans.

The people in the camp saw no threat in a single seventeen-year-old girl and gave me food and drink. Then I was taken into a vardo where an old woman sat alone. She looked at me and said, 'So you've come. I thought you were close.' And the odd thing is, I knew what she meant. In some way I had been coming there ever since I'd left London three months earlier. As I looked into her eyes, I understood I was in the right place.

The woman's name was Marran. She was the leader of their group and had what they called 'the sight'. She took me under her wing, became my teacher and, in the end, my

Romany mother. I stayed with her for ten years and travelled all over southern England. During that time she taught me how to talk to the dead and I became very good at it. Better than Marran in fact. The whole thing came naturally to me – an unsuspected latent ability, which my time with the travellers turned from a dry seed to a full bloom.

In the winter we'd find a good site and wait out the bad weather, but in the spring, normally in April, we'd set off. The routine was always the same. If it was the weekend we'd call in at big estates and offer to read the fortunes of the residents and house guests, who were always keen to have us in for a bit of entertainment. At other times we'd set up on the outskirts of towns and send the men into the pubs. Word soon filtered back to their women and they'd come to see us.

And my own reputation grew, especially among the landed classes. They talk to each other, you see, and we began to get invitations to visit big houses when it became known that we were in the area. People wanted to know my name and that was when I began calling myself Mrs Gladys Timperley. Marran and I worked as a team. She would tell fortunes and I would do séances. We were successful and made money, so much so that after five years I had a tidy sum tucked away in a bank. The manager used to joke that I turned up every November with a bag full of money. And the bag got heavier every year.

One Friday in June 1898 we pulled up at a place called Woolsey Hall and were enthusiastically received when word was passed to the hostess that Gladys Timperley and Marran Gray were at the door. We did our stuff and I remember getting a clear connection to the father of one of the guests who had something important to say. The woman was astonished and then tearful, but the man sitting next to her in the circle just stared at me. Even when my eyes were closed, I could feel his gaze running over me like the sun's rays on a hot day.

As we were leaving, having been well rewarded for our work, he approached me. He had a fine moustache, which was waxed to a point on either side, and I remember the intelligence and humanity in his eyes. Speaking in a Scottish accent he said his name was Arthur Conan Doyle, professed his admiration for my work, and asked for a private meeting the following day. There was something about him, and I invited him to the camp, which was rarely done, but I could see Marran approved of him too.

And that was the start of our friendship. He had a great interest in my work and over the next four years we met up when we could. He was very famous of course and travelled extensively himself, so finally he suggested the idea of establishing a permanent base for me. He knew the family of a gentleman who had owned a house in Falmouth before passing away. He told me he believed it would make a fine hotel and we bought it together, half and half. I was subsequently able to buy him out using the money from Valentine and George.

So that fills in some gaps for you. Must dash – as usual we're very busy downstairs!

All my love,

Your mother Gladys

Alma leaned back in the chair. It was like hearing her mother's voice from beyond the grave and she felt very close to her. Sleeping in the same bed, living in the same rooms. Holding a letter she had held in her hand. And there was little doubt now, about the source of her own talent as a clairvoyant.

Her mind drifted back to the previous evening. To a bereaved mother desperate for communion with her dead son, There was no doubt that Valentine Wragge was very convincing and Lady Watson had been deeply moved, joyful even. Alma now properly understood what a compelling offer the hotel made to its bereaved guests and why it was fully booked for weeks in advance.

But she also knew that Wragge, for all his undoubted abilities, was not a conduit for the dead. The séance had been theatre. Convincing and expertly delivered perhaps, but nothing more. Alma had participated in many séances at St Joseph's and knew how the energy swirled and her body reacted when a spirit was present. Although Alexander Watson had been in the entrance hall, he had not been in that room last night.

She frowned in concentration and tried to unpick what had happened. Wragge was clearly in possession of information about the Watson household and their lives before the young man's death, and he had skilfully introduced this into the session alongside more general remarks. It had been the mention of Mister Bones, a much-loved teddy bear and childhood toy that still lay waiting on his master's bed, that had first reduced Lady Watson to tears. But Wragge had also mentioned the names of pets and household staff, his favourite chair in the sitting room, their shared walks to the top of a local hill and even his preferred cocktail.

Did it matter? Alma wondered. There was no doubt that a bereaved and grieving mother had been given solace and would be looking forward to the next session. Miss Bede, the headmistress of St Joseph's and the woman who had first introduced Alma to clairvoyance, had been tolerant of the fakes that had permeated their world, believing they provided a service and a bit of entertainment. Alma frowned as her teacher's other observation came to mind.

'*Besides, they always get found out in the end.*'

With this troubling thought in her mind, she descended to the nook.

* * *

Later, James suggested a stroll into town and as they walked down the drive he told her that he and Hilda were going to return to London. Feeling rather bereft, Alma thanked him profusely for their help and said she hoped they would return soon. Then she decided to mention the German book concealed in the dresser.

The reaction in her friend and mentor was a surprise. He stopped walking and turned towards her, standing very still as he studied her with his heavy-lidded eyes. For once there was no hint of humour behind them.

'Shall I get it for you when we get back?' Alma asked, seeing his interest.

'No, leave it where it is for now.' His reply was quick and direct.

'It's curious though, isn't it. I mean why hide the book there rather than simply having it in one's room?' she added.

'Perhaps because if it were found in someone's room its owner would be identified. As would their ability to speak fluent German.'

Alma thought about this for a moment, then said, 'Well I know we are at war with Germany, but people do still speak the language. At the end of Whitton Road, there's a pork butcher whose family are from Essen. I know for a fact they speak German in the house and sometimes in the shop. It's hardly a crime.'

James nodded slowly. 'Not a crime, no. But your friend the pork butcher might be well advised to use English in public. I've heard reports of ill feeling in such cases as casualties mount amongst our soldiers.'

He added, 'Are you aware of any German speakers on the staff or connected with the hotel?'

She shook her head. 'No. It might be a guest or one of their servants, I suppose.'

'Possibly.' The man stared past her, clearly thinking hard. Alma had not seen this James Nascent before. Normally he was an urbane man who appeared to be slightly amused by life. She now realised there was steel inside him.

Then he said, 'You've got a lot on your plate at the moment, Alma. Perhaps it would be a good idea to keep the book to yourself for the moment.'

She looked at him. 'Yes, if you wish.'

Why are you really here? For the second time since she'd arrived at the hotel the intuitive thought came to her. Certainly, he was acting on the instructions of her late mother, but was there something else?

'James, is there another reason why you came with me to Falmouth?' The question was out before she could stop it and as it registered with him, she saw his attention snap back into the present. The penetrating stare melted into a familiar creased smile as he took her arm and they moved on.

'Not at all.'

There was a brief silence.

'How well did you know Gladys?' Alma asked.

'Quite well in the past, but latterly we rarely saw each other.'

'Do you know what was in the letter she left me?'

'Perhaps. Do you want to tell me?'

'She was my mother.' Then to her horror Alma burst into tears.

* * *

George Weaver climbed the stairs to the top floor of the hotel and then opened a door to reveal another uncarpeted flight. He ascended these and arrived in the tower room, high above the main entrance. It was ten feet square with a pair of pointed windows in an ecclesiastical style set into each wall. A door gave onto a narrow balcony edged with a decorative iron railing, which encircled the tower. It was from there that Gladys Timperley had fallen to her death, as all the staff were well aware.

He walked to one of the windows that overlooked the Fal estuary and the docks. The quays were crowded with freighters with more at anchor in Carrick Roads. The war had increased the traffic through the port and the local economy was flourishing as a result.

To his right the headland that guarded the channel to the sea was capped by Pendennis Castle, built by Henry the Eighth to defend the anchorage. Further out in the estuary, the lean grey outlines of navy ships waited and, as he stood there, another vessel hove into view. It was the *Lisbon Rose*, well known in the town and a regular visitor.

A powerful pair of German Zeiss binoculars normally lay on the window ledge but they were not there. Looking round he saw movement through the other window and realised someone was outside on the balcony. Curious, he crossed to the door, opened it and turned right along the side of the tower. At the corner he turned again, onto the section of balcony that faced the Fal river. Valentine Wragge was standing there, binoculars raised to his eyes as he studied the naval vessels out in the estuary.

'Anything interesting?' he enquired with a smile.

Clearly surprised by his arrival, Wragge lowered the glasses sharply, turned, and said with deliberate casualness, 'The usual array of armed might. It's nice to know our sailors are ready and waiting if the Kaiser's battleships come calling.'

'Very true.' Weaver nodded, then said, 'The usual array? You come up here often then? It sounds as though some of the ships are familiar to you.'

'I enjoy the view. Who wouldn't? I have no idea whose binoculars these are though. They've been here for a while now and they're very good ones. You'd think someone would have missed them.'

Noting he hadn't answered his question Weaver replied, 'Yes I'd noticed them too.'

There was a short silence as the two men looked at each other, then Wragge said, 'Well I'll go back down, I think. Care for a look?' He held up the glasses.

'I will, thank you.' Weaver took them and the two men parted. Left alone, he raised them to his eyes and had a long look at the port and then the vessels in the wide river basin. This complete, he returned to the corner of the balcony and looked down onto the road that led to the lower town. It was deserted apart from Alma Timperley and James Nascent. Idly he raised the binoculars to study them, rather enjoying the sense of power it gave him to watch them without their knowledge. They had only been in focus for a couple of seconds when, to his surprise the girl stopped, and her shoulders slumped. Weaver could see she was sobbing as she turned to the solicitor and he gently embraced her, distress and indecision showing on his face.

Interest mounting, he watched as Nascent produced a large white handkerchief, which the girl held to her face, then he took her arm and steered her off down the steep hill. He wondered what had upset her. As far as he could see she had been the recipient of considerable good fortune regarding her inheritance and was being well supported by the solicitor. He watched them disappear then replaced the binoculars on the window ledge and descended to the public rooms of the hotel.

In the entrance hall he passed Valentine Wragge, who was standing behind the reception counter perusing the register. Mrs Banks filled it in as bookings were confirmed, so it provided a handy guide to who was coming in over the next few weeks. The final column before the signature box contained the initials of the spiritualist the guest had chosen to see. If they had not indicated a preference it was left blank and under those circumstances the informal arrangement was that the spiritualists would select clients themselves.

'Don't take all the good ones,' Weaver observed to his colleague with a friendly smile as he crossed the hall. The men were not close but got on well enough, not least because they were both partners in a successful enterprise.

'There's plenty to go round, my dear fellow,' Wragge replied. As a result of Gladys Timperley's tragic accident, the boxes containing GT had been neatly crossed out by the assistant manager, leaving the choice open. As Weaver disappeared into the lounge, he traced his finger back along a line to read the guest's name. It was Lady Miranda Prior, and she was booked in on the third of March for a week. Making a mental note he climbed to his room and removed a well-thumbed copy of *Who's Who 1913* from a shelf. It was a moment's work to find Sir Gerald Prior and he read the entry with interest.

> PRIOR, Sir Gerald, CBE (1884) Chair War Refugees Society. b 1850 Winscombe Hants of Sir William Prior and Lady Jane Prior (nee Riley). Education: Eton, Cambridge. BSc (Hons) m Miranda Prior (nee Walker) 1880. Issue: Francis Harold Prior (b 1894) Residences Winscombe Hall, Hants and Primrose Hill, London. Clubs Atheneum, Whites. Recreations shooting, bridge. Address Greylands, Milford Road, Primrose Hill, London N.

Returning downstairs Wragge removed a fountain pen from his pocket and wrote the initials VW neatly alongside the crossed-out letters GT. Then he climbed back to his room and sat down at his desk. With the *Who's Who* open, he pulled a piece of notepaper out of a stand and wrote the following:

Sir Gerald and Lady Miranda Prior, Greylands, Milford Road, Primrose Hill, London. Son, Francis Harold Prior. By 28th February.

Adding nothing else he put it into an envelope, wrote a name and a London address on the front, and added a stamp. Then he put on his coat, left the hotel, and posted it in the box on the corner.

* * *

James Nascent returned to the hotel alone and met Hilda in their room. She was packing their suitcases.

'Alma has discovered that Gladys was her mother,' he said.

She paused, a shirt in her hand, and looked at him. 'I see. Was that entirely unexpected?'

He shook his head. 'No. I was aware of it and Gladys had said in her instructions regarding the will that she would leave a letter for Alma if she chose to take the hotel on.'

Their eyes met and she asked, 'Will she discover anything else?'

'Many things I would imagine,' he answered obliquely, then went on to tell Hilda about the German book.

When he had concluded, she said, 'Does that change your plans at all?'

'I wonder if it would be a good idea for you to remain here while I return to town and bring Vernon Kell up to date.'

'If you wish. I can keep an eye on Alma if nothing else.'

'Exactly.'

As this conversation was taking place the girl in question was entering Kimberley Park, a pleasant green space above the bustling town centre, which she had discovered as she wandered through the streets getting to know her new home.

The weather was improving and as the sun broke out from behind a cloud, she came up to a convenient seat overlooking the lawns and decided to rest for a few minutes. A man was sitting at the next bench not more than twenty feet away. On the pretext of looking round to enjoy the view, Alma glanced at his profile under the cap he was wearing. And she rather liked what she saw. In his late twenties she guessed, with a strong, clean-shaven chin and straight nose.

He was sketching something. The pad was on his knee and, pencil in hand, his attention was focused on the scene further along the path where two young mothers were sitting as their children played amongst the trees. A pair of older women walked past them and came up to the artist. To Alma's surprise they stopped, and she heard the exchange that followed quite clearly.

'Hello there,' one said as the other eyed him, hands on her hips.

'Good morning,' he replied politely. A northern voice, Alma thought.

There was a pause then the woman continued, 'Not in uniform then?'

'Pardon?'

'I'm just saying, our boys have volunteered to fight the Germans and you're sitting here enjoying a bit of winter sunshine.'

He put his pad down and replied, 'Well, yes, you're right. I . . .'

The other woman interrupted. 'You don't fancy it then?'

'No it's . . .' he started to reply, but she continued to speak over him, now addressing her companion.

'Doesn't seem right, does it, Rita? Strong British lads with a bit of heart and courage over there doing their bit, while others sit it out over here. Yellow, are you?'

'No, madam, I can assure you I'm . . .'

But she interrupted again. 'You'd better have this. And think about whether you're a man or a mouse.' She leaned forward and dropped something into his lap, then with a withering look took her friend's arm and they walked off, passing Alma without a glance.

All discretion gone she stared as the man reached down and picked it up. It was a white feather.

Sensing her gaze, he turned and looked at her, the pain in his face all too apparent. And when he spoke there was a degree of desperation in his voice. 'I'm not a coward. I tried to volunteer but they wouldn't let me.'

Alma stood up and joined him on his bench. 'I'm sure you're not. Women like that are just being very rude.'

He shook his head. 'No, they've got a point. A man should have to justify why he hasn't volunteered – I do believe that. I saw Lord Kitchener's poster and went down to the recruiting centre the next day, but they told me I had to stay in Cornwall. They should give you an armband or something if you're doing other war work. So people know.'

'I'm sure you're brave.' The words were out before she could stop them, and Alma blushed scarlet as he smiled at her.

'I hope I am, but you don't know, do you? Not until your mettle's tested.' He held out his hand. 'I'm Alan Bricken.'

'Alma Timperley.' They shook and she looked for any recognition in his eyes at her surname but saw none. 'What do you do, then?'

'I'm a telegraph operator. At Porthcurno down the coast. It's my day off so I've come into Falmouth for a change of scene.

There's not much where we are. My pal's doing a bit of shopping then I'm meeting him for a pint. What about you?'

'I work in a hotel. I've not been here long myself. I don't know anyone yet.' She saw him look at her again then. In a different way.

'Do you want to come for a drink? We can have a chat. Get to know each other a bit.'

She nodded, sure that she did. 'Very well, Mr Bricken. Lead the way.'

Chapter Six

James Nascent left his comfortable flat in Mayfair and walked to the Home Office in Whitehall where, ten minutes later, he was shown into the cramped office of a man called Vernon Kell. Energetic and casually handsome, Kell was the head of MI5 and responsible for internal security in Great Britian. Put simply, in 1915 his main job was to catch German spies.

'Come in, Mr Nascent, good to see you again.' He greeted the solicitor with a smile then gestured to another man who had stood up as he entered. 'My assistant Bright is here to take a note. If you'll forgive me, Mr Nascent, I'll just put him in the picture. For the record.'

'Of course.'

'Thank you. So here it is, Bright. One of Mr Nascent's clients is a woman called Gladys Timperley, a hotel owner from Falmouth. Sadly, she was killed in an accident last December, but before her death she wrote to him about her will. In the letter Mrs Timperley also made certain observations regarding someone she knew, who she believed to be acting suspiciously.'

Bright looked up from his notebook. 'Oh? With regards to the war, you mean?'

'Indeed. She didn't use the word "spying" but it was implied. You can read the letter later. We have it here now.'

'Did she name anybody?' the assistant asked.

Nascent himself replied. 'No, she didn't. It was a couple of remarks made as she was closing the letter. "You'll never guess what . . ." and so on. But Gladys was no fool, and her comments worried me, so I wrote back suggesting she have a word with the local authorities if she had any specific concerns.'

'And how did she respond to that?'

'She didn't. Two weeks later I received a letter from the police in Falmouth telling me that my client had died in an accident. An unlikely accident, frankly. It seemed she had fallen from the roof of the hotel during the night.'

Kell grunted. 'Falmouth is a defended port and a security area. The police down there were already uneasy with the circumstances of Mrs Timperley's death and when they became aware of her remarks in the letter, they pushed it upstairs and the matter ended up on my desk. Mr Nascent told me he would be spending time at the hotel while dealing with Mrs Timperley's will and I suggested that he could, acting incognito, see if he could discover anything. He agreed.'

Bright looked at him. 'That was good of you, sir. Who inherits?'

'A girl called Alma Timperley. She's moved down from London and taken over. I rather like her.'

'Any chance she's involved?'

'No, I'm certain she isn't.'

The solicitor went on to tell both men about the hotel, its unique purpose, and the people who were connected with it, before saying, 'I climbed up to the point from which Gladys Timperley is believed to have fallen. There is a waist-high railing and it's hard to see how someone would pitch over it accidentally, especially as there is a vertical drop to the ground of at least fifty feet. It's a place where one would naturally exercise caution.'

He added, 'I'd also make the observation that the view across the docks and Carrick Roads from up there is magnificent. One can see every vessel in the port and all the comings and goings. And someone had left a powerful pair of binoculars up there.' He gave them a look before continuing, 'There's one other thing, which I'd suggest is significant. Miss Timperley told me she'd discovered a German book concealed in a dresser in a room used by all staff as a dining room and rest area.'

'A book written in German, you mean?' Bright enquired.

Nascent nodded. 'Just so. *Der Antichrist* by Nietzsche. I sneaked a look at it when the room was empty and it is well used and certain passages are underlined in pencil.'

'As though someone is using it as a reference of some kind?'

Nascent gave a rather embarrassed little shrug. 'You're the experts but I thought it might be being used as a code key. To decipher and encipher messages.'

Bright and his superior exchanged a glance.

'Concealed, you said,' Kell observed. 'As though someone didn't want the book to be found in their room, for example?'

'That is what it looks like, yes.'

No one spoke as the sound of Big Ben chiming the quarter drifted through the windows.

Then Kell said, 'Have you been accepted down there? By the staff and so on?'

Nascent nodded. 'Yes, they know I'm helping Alma to get established, so my presence is justified.'

'I'm asking because I feel there's enough here to warrant further attention. Unlike the local police you're not known, and you have a valid reason for going back. If you are amenable, I must admit that's the way my mind is working. Could you find the time? I presume you have a practice to maintain here in town.'

The solicitor inclined his head. 'I do. However, Mrs Timperley was more than a client and if there has been foul play regarding her death then I am keen to get to the bottom of it. I have a reliable secretary and could source a locum to deal with routine matters for a month or so, without placing my affairs under undue strain.'

'Very well, let's have a stroll and agree the details. Bright, you carry on.'

Five minutes later he and Nascent emerged from the Home Office and made for St James's Park.

As they approached the gates, they passed a wrecked building. A crew of workmen were loading rubble onto a lorry. The house was in the middle of an attractive, red-bricked terrace and its four-storey façade had collapsed completely, leaving the interior open to the curious gazes of passers-by.

'A Zeppelin raid two nights ago,' Kell remarked. 'Four dead including an infant. They're trying to clear it up but the whole thing is so unstable they're not sure what to do.'

Stunned, Nascent stared upwards. On the second floor the brass frame of a bed hung over open space and he could see chintzy wallpaper behind it. The house almost seemed embarrassed to have its privacy invaded in such a violent way. Its inner workings brutally displayed to the gawping of the general public.

'It was just one, but there will be more. We Londoners will have to get used to it, I'm afraid. The Kaiser appears to think he can break British morale by bombing innocent women and children, but I doubt very much that he is right. The reaction has been one of fury, led by the press.'

He took Nascent's arm, and they moved off as he added, 'There is a blackout coming though. Or at least a dimming. People will be told to keep their curtains closed and public lighting will be turned off when there's a warning. From the air London must look like a great glowing bull's eye to the Hun bomb aimers.'

60

The two men passed between the park gates and Nascent asked, 'If there is a spy operating in Falmouth, what do you think they're after?'

'Shipping movements I'd imagine. And details about defences. Don't forget the German navy shelled Scarborough, Hartlepool, and Whitby, before Christmas. The public version is that they killed one hundred and thirty-seven people. Privately I can tell you it was a lot more. There's no telling when or where they might try the same thing again and Falmouth is a ripe target. Knowing exactly where our shore batteries are placed would be useful to them.'

Kell frowned and added, 'The big problem any spy will have is getting information back to Germany. We've got things locked down pretty tightly right across the country. The Post Office are on high alert and any suspicious telegrams are being intercepted. We also open letters from people with known German connections. You remember Carl Lody last year?'

'Yes. Shot for spying in the Tower of London in November, wasn't he.'

'Indeed. He'd been operating near our naval bases in the Firth of Forth and we first got onto him when he wrote to a contact in Stockholm. My colleagues in M16 knew the address was a cover for German intelligence. By the time we caught up with him, he was in Ireland, but he was arrested and charged under the Defence of the Realm Act. And, as you say, he was executed.' Kell paused for a moment and stared at the ducks on the lake before adding, 'I met him. He was a brave man and an honourable one in his own way.'

The men moved out of the way to let two Norland nannies pushing perambulators go past, then he turned to Nascent, his tone of voice hardening. 'But we cannot have these people swanning about giving away our secrets. If someone is spying for Germany in Falmouth, I want him caught. Once your office arrangements are in place, I suggest you return to the hotel and stay for four weeks to see what else you might find out. How does that sound?'

Nascent nodded. 'Yes, that will be acceptable. I'll admit I've rather got the bit between my teeth.'

'Good, but be careful. In her letter Mrs Timperley must have been referring to someone she knew, and now it appears she was deliberately killed. Please ensure you are not next on the list. And keep an eye on that German book; it could lead us straight to the man we're looking for.'

* * *

For Alma the next week passed in something of a whirl. There was so much to learn that she felt overwhelmed at times but Gracie's patient explanations and Hilda's insistence that 'you don't need to know it all within a week' provided some balance. Nevertheless, she went to bed exhausted each night and with her head buzzing.

The most recent development had been a visit by a police constable who had handed over a copy of the new blackout regulations. From now on they were to ensure that every window was curtained at night. Southampton had been bombed by a Zeppelin three nights earlier and the Falmouth port authorities were taking measures to reduce the port's visibility from the air.

'Don't worry too much, miss,' the constable had remarked, 'we're a long way from Germany here, but it's better to be safe than sorry. If there's any danger of a raid, you'll hear me and my colleagues in the street blowing whistles. They'll turn the gas off so the streetlights will go out as well.'

Thinking of her guests, she'd asked, 'And what should we do then?'

'Stay inside and take cover.' And with this he had departed.

Alma discussed the matter with Gracie Banks and the result was that each room received a note asking them not to open the curtains when it was dark and to get under the bed if they heard police whistles in the night. This caused a frisson of excitement and was much discussed over dinner, but her clientele were not ones to panic, and they stoically carried on.

In her mother's notes she'd discovered more useful information, including her thoughts on her two business partners, which Alma read with interest. Her comments regarding Valentine Wragge matched her own feelings.

At my insistence I occasionally sit in on the sessions they have with their clients. Both of them hate it, but I just sit quietly in the room and do not interfere in any way. I must ensure that the reputation of the Timperley Spiritualist Hotel remains high and that is one way to ensure that it does.

Valentine is rather highly strung, and something of a loveable rogue. He is not, I'm sorry to say, a medium, although somehow he does manage to provide a remarkably effective service and his clients adore him. He does have one curious rule, which is that he will only ever see people for one visit to the hotel, whereas George and I encourage people to return because it's good for our income. He told me once that this was because he wanted to keep his mind clear for new clients, but that seemed unlikely to me. So there must be another reason, although what it is escapes me.

George Weaver is a different matter altogether and can commune with the spirit world. He is an intense man, as you have probably realised, and brings a great sense of purpose to his work. There is no doubt his clients believe they are in the presence of a talented medium, and he seems able to capture them completely when they are here. Although as our clientele is almost exclusively female and George is a very handsome man, he does have certain advantages in that respect!

* * *

When Alma got back downstairs she met Hilda coming through the foyer and, on impulse, suggested a cup of tea. She felt she wanted to talk privately about the two spiritualists and the older and very sensible woman was the obvious confidante. But in the event, when they were settled in the empty lounge, Alma surprised herself by taking the conversation in a different direction.

'Gladys Timperley was my mother,' she said, without preamble. 'You might have seen James give me a letter from her and in it she explained that she fell pregnant when she was unmarried. After I was born I was handed over to her sister Harriet to be brought up. My real mother, Gladys, was kicked out of the household and never returned.'

Hilda had paused in the act of pouring the tea and was staring at her. 'Well that must have been a surprise,' she remarked, then returned her attention to the cups.

'Not half. It does explain a lot though. Harriet wasn't the warmest of people and I now realise that she didn't love me in the way a true mother loves her daughter.'

Hilda added milk and passed a cup to Alma. 'I imagine children sense these things, without knowing the reason. I don't have children myself. My dear husband died of typhoid when we were both in our mid-twenties and I lived alone for many years before meeting James.' She gave a rueful smile. 'By then it was too late.'

'You haven't got married though?'

She shook her head. 'I'm not inclined to.'

Because you still love your dead husband. Alma could sense it quite clearly, as Hilda added, 'Although he asks me every Christmas Eve.'

'It was Christmas Eve when I met you both,' she said. 'My word a lot has happened since then.'

The older woman's eyes glowed and she said, 'Hasn't it just. Now tell me, dear, how are you feeling about everything?'

* * *

In amongst her burgeoning responsibilities Alma was pleased to receive a telegram from Alan Bricken saying he was coming into Falmouth the forthcoming Saturday and would she like to meet. She did, and pondered, the slip in her hand, whether she should ask him to come to the hotel. But in the end she replied, '*Yes. Same pub 12.30.*'

On Saturday she prepared with a care that surprised her, added her red beret as a pleasing final touch and set off. The hotel was situated at the top of Swanpool Street and from the corner a raised pavement led down the steep slope towards the junction with Arwenack Street and Custom House Quay. Halfway down on the right two tall stone pillars marked the start of a broad straight road called Arwenack Avenue, which ran into the open ground between the edge of the town and Pendennis Castle. She recalled Mrs Banks saying that the ruins of Arwenack House, the ancestral home of the Killigrew family on whose land Falmouth had developed, lay in that direction and resolved to have a look when she had time.

The original little harbour was crowded with fishing boats and tenders from the naval vessels out in Carrick Roads and Alma loitered for a while, enjoying the marine hustle and bustle.

She noticed a tall brick chimney to her left and as she stared an elderly man passing by in uniform glanced at her and stopped. She saw the words Customs and Excise on his shoulder.

'That's the King's Pipe.' He nodded at the chimney. 'We don't use it now but when I was a lad it was for burning smuggled tobacco. It used to smoke like nothing on earth. Falmouth was the only port licensed to import tobacco at one time, you see. And some of it wasn't on the ships' manifests, if you get my drift.'

'So it was confiscated and burned?' She stared, imagining thick smoke coming out of the chimney pot. 'When was it last used?'

'Oh, a good while ago now. It was part of the Customs House in those days.'

They chatted for a short while before parting, and she made her way along Arwenack Street to the Blue Boar Inn, which stood in the heart of the old town. Alan Bricken was standing outside. He smiled and said, 'Hello, I thought I'd wait here so you didn't have to come in alone.'

She liked him for that. They went inside and found a table in the lounge bar. He bought her a lemonade and had a pint of bitter himself, and they chatted easily for a few minutes.

'Will you tell me about your job, Alan?' she asked.

'I work for the Eastern Telegraph Company. I'm a telegraphist by trade and I send and receive messages from all around the world. There's a good few of us further down the coast beyond Penzance, but there's a regular bus and I like Falmouth.' He gave her a grin and added, 'I like it even more now, as it happens.'

Smiling gently at the compliment, she asked, 'Where are you from?'

'Burnley in Lancashire, but I've travelled a bit. They send us to the relay stations, you see. There are postings all around the world. The telegraph signal fades over distance so it has to be received and resent and the relay stations do that. A telegram going to Australia will be relayed four times.'

Alma listened, fascinated. She had no idea that men were sent around the empire to do work like that. 'How long do you stay in a place?'

'It depends, two years is a normal posting, but last time I came back early. A spot of bother with the Huns as it happens.' He raised his eyebrows.

'The Germans? Crikey, what happened?'

Alan took a pull on his beer and told the tale.

'In 1913 I was sent to the Cocos Islands in the middle of the Indian Ocean. There's a relay station there for the Australian cable line and it was our job to receive telegrams and send them on, in both directions. It's just a small place, very isolated and tropical. Palm trees, a coral reef and a warm turquoise sea, and all that. And nothing ever happened there, although it was hot, I'll tell you that.'

Alma listened to his casual description of what sounded like heaven on earth to her. A place you only dreamed of. And the young man in front of her had lived there. It was astonishing. Something of it must have shown on her face because he smiled.

'Sounds lovely doesn't it. And it was in many ways. Paradise on earth. But it was boring too. We weren't allowed to mix with the natives and after a while you don't half miss a pint of bitter and the newspaper. We even had a drama group and put on plays. Anyway, I'd been there a year when war broke out and at six o'clock one morning we suddenly found the camp was full of Hun sailors with rifles. They'd landed off a German cruiser called the *Emden* and were intent on wrecking our gear so we couldn't pass signals.'

'Good Lord, what on earth did you do?'

'Our main business was the telegraph, but we had a radio too and we got a distress signal away on that. Then we just had to watch as they smashed our cable with axes. But that radio signal was picked up by an Australian navy cruiser called the *Sydney* and, as luck would have it, she wasn't far away. She must have had a turn of speed too because at just after nine o'clock a sailor comes running into camp shouting something. They all turned and ran down to the beach, and we followed. Well, there's the *Emden* hauling up her anchor and, in the distance, we can see another ship. That was the *Sydney*. We all sat down on the beach, us and the Huns together, and watched as they went to it out in the bay.'

'What happened?'

'The Aussies won. They took some hits, but they didn't half beat up the *Emden*. The skipper had to run her ashore on another island and then they sank the collier that was with her.' He chuckled and said, 'And here's the thing. Our man in charge was Mr Trent and he was a fly one and no mistake. He must have been expecting trouble because he'd had us build a dummy telegraph cable and that was the one the Huns smashed up. The real one was buried deep in the sand fifty yards away. So we had the last laugh anyway.'

Alma clapped her hands, delighted by the story. 'That's wonderful. What happened to the sailors on the island?'

'They pinched a schooner and sailed off. Fifty of them, there were. I've no idea where they ended up. Anyway, I was ordered home and I'm at Porthcurno now, doing some training for the new lads and taking a shift as well. They brought Mr Trent home too and promoted him. He's the superintendent at Zodiac House.' He shrugged. 'I'll be off again at some point, I expect.'

There was a short silence as this casual remark hit home. Then he said, 'What about you, anyway. What's the hotel you work at?'

'Well there's a bit of a story to that.' Sitting there with Alan she had decided to tell him the truth if he asked, so she did.

Although she kept quiet about how grand the place was and its purpose.

He was delighted and slapped his thigh with pleasure. 'Well that's a fine story too. I'm pleased to hear of your good luck, I really am.'

Alma watched closely, alert for any signs of avarice in his eyes, but he seemed genuine. Nevertheless, she remained cautious. She was a wealthy woman by Falmouth standards and wanted her relationship with Alan Breckin, if there was to be one, to develop alongside her good fortune, not because of it.

When she got back to the hotel she knew she had put off a decision for long enough. After a lengthy bath she sat down at the little table in her room and wrote to Jack Waring in France. It was a *Dear John* letter, and she was sorry to send it, but her conscience gave her no option. Even if things did not proceed with Alan Breckin, her interest in him meant that she could not, in all decency, continue to let Jack believe they had a future. It was a culmination of the thoughts she had been having since before she'd heard about the hotel, although she recognised that had been a catalyst of a kind.

> . . . *I know you might think it's a poor show writing to you in this way when you're over in France doing your bit and I'm very sorry about that. But in the end, honesty is the best policy, Jack, and I can't have you coming home thinking I'm waiting for you, when I am not.*
>
> *You look after yourself now, and you can believe that I respect the courage you have shown in joining up and fighting. You are a good and decent man who will find someone who loves you. I am sure of that.*

The letter concluded, she walked to the nearest post box and pushed it through the slit with no hesitation. The die was cast.

Chapter Seven

In their shared office overlooking the port, Captain John Hyde, the Royal Navy harbour master, and Harry French, his civilian deputy, stood at the wide window that overlooked Carrick Roads. It was half past eleven at night and they were watching a large tanker called the *Persian Knight* making her final preparations for departure, underneath the bright lights of the port. Soon she would sail, hoping to slip past the German U-boats that lurked in the Western Approaches like terriers waiting for rabbits to emerge from their burrows.

Out in the estuary HMS *Matchless*, a Royal Navy destroyer, was waiting. She would escort her all the way to the Arabian Gulf to load another twelve thousand tons of petrol from the refinery in Bahrain and then all the way back to Falmouth, providing protection from a submarine's deck gun but not from torpedoes.

The harbour master put his binoculars down and turned to his friend. 'Godspeed to the *Persian Knight*. She's fast and *Matchless* will help, but one hit from a torpedo and the crew are all dead. They're brave men, Harry.'

The other man nodded. 'I must admit, I'm always pleased to see her go, though. A single spark, especially when she's empty and full of petrol fumes, and the explosion would take out the entire docks. Quays, warehouses, dry dock, everything.'

'That's true. We'd lose the whole port. It would be a disaster.'

But Harry wasn't listening. Instead, he reached for the binoculars and muttering, 'What the Devil's that?' raised them to his eyes and focused on the sky over the eastern breakwater. 'Bloody hell, it's a Zeppelin,' he said quietly. 'Heading this way.'

Stunned, the harbour master grabbed the glasses. In the far distance a sliver of silver like a long cigar was clearly visible high in the night sky. As he stared two loud explosions reached them.

'They've seen her from the castle. That's their six-inch guns opening up,' his deputy said.

'Right. Action stations. Telephone the town gas plant and tell them to turn the supply off. That'll shut down the streetlights. Then we'll call the port engineers, and they can do the same with the electric lights on the quays.' But even as he said this the lights in the town slowly stared to fade and, shortly afterwards, as a second salvo sounded, the port lights died too. It was remarkable, he thought. Within a minute the whole town had been reduced to darkness.

'Not so easy for them to see us now, Harry,' he remarked.

'No. And the police will be out with their whistles dealing with any open curtains.'

They watched helplessly for twenty minutes as the airship approached the coast.

'She's taking her time, John,' the deputy remarked.

'The wind's dead against her.' The harbour master looked through the binoculars again. 'But she's getting closer. And losing height.' Ten minutes later the airship passed over the entrance to the estuary and he muttered, 'Coming in for her bombing run. All the ships have got their lights off. They'll only be able to see the coast.'

'They won't. Look at that!' Harry was pointing up the hill towards the town. A single bright light was flaring out into the darkness and, below it, between the town and the port, the harbour master could see the glow of two lights side by side.

'Who the hell's lit those?'

'They're pointing right towards the docks.'

The harbour master grimaced. 'They are too. They'll be able to see those clearly enough. Listen to that.' They could hear machine guns from the fort as the Zeppelin swung over the estuary and turned towards the lights, but the huge machine seemed impervious. The ominous vibrating thrum of her four engines reached them over the small-arms fire.

The deputy harbour master cursed in frustration. 'They must be hitting her at that range and damned thing's full of hydrogen. Why hasn't it blown up?'

'The bullets just go straight through. Nothing to ignite the gas. Here we go . . .'

They watched grim-faced as the first bombs were released.

* * *

As explosions rocked the lower part of the town, two police officers stared up Swanpool Street. 'Look at that! It's like a bloody lighthouse. The Huns must be using it as an aiming mark.' Sergeant Trewin pointed and shouted, 'Robinson, get up there and get that light off, whatever it takes!'

The young constable sprinted off up the steep hill. Halfway up, and blowing hard, he met a man standing staring up at the airship. A hundred yards beyond him, along Arwenack Avenue, a car was parked across the road, its lights shining towards the port. Indecision slowed him and he stopped then grabbed the man's shoulder and pointed.

'See that car with the lights on? Run over there now and turn them off! The Huns can see them!' Fortunately, the man didn't argue and dashed off. Robinson ran on up the hill. At the top he quickly ascertained that the light was coming from the top of the tower on the hotel that stood there. He ran down the drive and burst in through the front door.

A young woman was standing uncertainly in the foyer. She stared, shocked at his dramatic entrance as a further series of explosions sounded from the lower town.

'A light, you're showing a light.' He gasped and pointed upwards. 'From the tower. The whole town's darkened and you're shining over it like a bloody beacon.'

'What!' She frowned at him, then looked confused. 'In the tower?'

'Show me.' The constable was already on the stairs, leaping up them two at a time. The woman followed and a minute later they threw open the door to the tower room. The light was on. With a gasp of relief Robinson reached out and flicked the switch. The room was immediately plunged into darkness. As he leaned against the wall heaving for breath, Alma crossed to the window that faced the town and gasped in horror at what she saw.

Bombs were now falling in the port area, but three large fires were burning along Arwenack Street. By the old quay where she'd examined the King's Pipe she could see people running and bodies lying on the ground.

She turned away and addressed the constable. 'I checked the tower light myself at five o'clock when we drew the hotel curtains. It was definitely off. We have a rota, and it was my day to come up here.'

He eyed her, still breathing heavily. 'So who turned it back on?'

She shook her head. 'I have no idea.'

Robinson's thoughts were rapidly catching up and after a moment he said, 'When they turned the streetlights off it was dark everywhere. I don't know exactly when this light went on, but I'm guessing it was as the airship approached the town.'

There was a silence as the two of them looked at each other. Then he said, 'What's your name, miss?'

'Alma Timperley. I own the hotel.'

If he was surprised at her relative youth the constable gave no sign. He removed his pocketbook and made a note, then asked, 'Who else has access to the tower?'

She shrugged. 'Everyone. Staff and guests. People come up here to enjoy the view.'

He walked over to Alma and looked down at the town. The car lights were off, he saw, but it was too late now. 'Hell's bells, what a mess. I'll have to go back and report to my sergeant and he's going to want to know how that light came to be switched on. We'll be back, I think, but I'll take my leave for now.' With a nod he disappeared back through the door, leaving Alma standing alone, a confused and anxious expression on her face.

When she got back to the foyer, the bombing had stopped and people were starting to appear. Gracie was attempting to calm a hysterical maid and other people in dressing gowns were milling about in a state of high alarm. She climbed up a few stairs then called out, 'Ladies and gentlemen, please may I have your attention!' This had the desired effect and she continued, 'I can tell you that the Zeppelin has now departed. I saw it leave from the tower, so we are safe and can thank our lucky stars that no bombs fell close to us. If you have any immediate needs, please make yourself known to Mrs Banks or another member of staff. I am going to go down into the town to see what help, if any, the hotel can provide.'

Five minutes later, with the restoration of normality at the hotel in Gracie's capable hands, she set off down Swanpool Street.

The scene that met her eyes at the junction with Arwenack Street was appalling. Bombs had fallen diagonally across the road, hitting houses on both sides, and a fierce fire was raging on the seaward side. The house on the corner had been reduced to rubble, with only two walls standing, and a chain of men was steadily passing stone and wood away from the ruins. Valentine Wragge was in the line, working feverishly, hair awry and covered in dust.

'Two children not accounted for,' she heard a woman say as she stood, wondering what on earth to do.

'Miss Timperley!' It was a police sergeant. Constable Robinson was with him.

'What can I do?' she asked.

'Just pitch in. Maybe help with the wounded, God knows there's enough of them.' He pointed as a body, clearly dead, was pulled out from a tangle of steel and bricks thirty yards away. She stared in horror and recognised another man helping. It was George Weaver. *Doing his bit, like Wragge.*

'And, miss . . .'

'Yes?' Alma was already turning away.

'You own the hotel, I gather. I haven't forgotten that light. And neither should you. It gave them a reference point. We'll be up to talk to you about that.'

Face set, she ran towards a woman bent over a man lying in the street, giving Weaver a quick wave of recognition as she passed. He nodded back then returned to his work.

* * *

Earlier, the man who Felix Muller in Berlin knew as Excalibur was just drifting off to sleep in his bedroom on the third floor of the hotel when he heard the sudden crump of the six-inch guns below Pendennis Castle. The noise echoed round the town and for a moment he thought it was thunder, but there had been no sign of a storm coming in when he took a turn round the garden before retiring.

Donning his dressing gown he slipped along the corridor. As he climbed the stairs to the tower he heard doors opening below, and cries of alarm. Alma called, 'I'm going down to the guest floor, please follow the instructions you have and take cover under your beds.'

From the window of the unlit tower room, the town and port lay below him. Then as a second salvo sounded, it simply faded out of sight. With a shock he realised that every light had gone off and, even as he watched, the last of the lights on the ships out in the estuary died. He stared out to sea and saw the muzzle flash as the guns below the sixteenth-century castle fired again.

Is it a German ship? There doesn't seem to be any incoming shelling.

Raising the binoculars he scanned the moonlit water beyond the estuary entrance, but saw nothing and then, almost as an afterthought, did a quick sweep across the sky. There it was, distant in the moonlight. A long silver tube high above the horizon.

A Zeppelin! Coming to bomb the port.

He stared at it for a long moment then put the binoculars down and looked at the sky with his naked eye. There were no clouds out at sea, but they were building over the land. And from height, he guessed it would be difficult to locate the darkened town and docks. Eyes narrowed, he considered the merits of turning on the tower light.

He looked down over Swanpool Street and the old quay. To the left a car was coming to a halt on Wood Lane, its headlights brilliantly clear in the darkness. They suddenly died and he saw a

77

shadowy figure emerge and disappear through a gate in the high wall that bordered the pavement.

Mind churning, he crossed back to the other window and raised the binoculars again. The airship was making slow progress. He reckoned he had at least twenty minutes, probably more.

Is that enough?

Then, with a surge of exhilaration he crept down the stairs, leaving the tower light off. He stopped at the bottom and peered round the corner, listening carefully. The guns on the fort were firing steadily but all was quiet in the hotel, and he sensed no movement. He made it to his room, dressed in a frenzy of urgency and descended the back stairs. By the hotel's rear door he waited and listened again, then unlocked it and slid out into the night.

* * *

Kate Diss, the chambermaid from the hotel, was in the gardens of the ruins of Arwenack House, the old ancestral home of the Killigrew family. She was not alone. A young soldier with whom she had been walking out for a week or two was with her. They had been in the Eagle public house and were making their way along Grove Place down by the water when he'd taken her hand, gently pulled her into the grounds, and said, 'How about a little kiss then?'

She'd seen no reason not to and they were happily exploring this new element to their relationship when the first salvo from the guns fired. Shocked, they came to their senses and dashed back to the road.

'I'll have to get on up to the fort, Kate. Something's up for sure. Blimey look at that, all the lights are going out.' He took her hand. 'Sorry but I really do have to go. You'll be all right, just go straight back to the hotel.'

And Kate, who was a steady girl, said, 'I'll be fine. You go on now.'

He grinned. 'That was nice though, wasn't it.' He nodded towards the shadowy foliage.

'I liked it. And I like you. You let me know when you can get time off again, and we'll see what happens.'

They kissed again and would have stayed at it for longer but a sergeant running past shouted, 'That man! Get back to the fort!' And with another wide smile the young private was gone.

Kate stood by the great stone triangle they all knew as the Killigrew Monument and considered the quickest way back to the hotel. Then, decision made, she walked briskly in the same direction as the soldier. She could turn right at the end of Grove Street and climb up by the old fishponds. From there, long straight Arwenack Avenue would take her to Swanpool Street and the steep slope up to the hotel. Fifteen minutes at the most. With the young soldier very much in her mind she carried on. She wasn't one to gossip about her private life, even to Polly, but if things carried on the way she hoped they might, perhaps she'd mention him to her friend.

* * *

Excalibur walked along the hotel drive, keeping to the edge where moss had firmed up the gravel, so his feet made no sound. He emerged from the gates, walked the short distance to the top of Swanpool Street and stood for a moment, assessing the scene. To his left a police officer on a bicycle was coming along Wood Lane, blowing his whistle repeatedly, his gaze swinging from side to side as he checked the houses for any gaps in the curtains. There was no one else in sight. He stepped back into the shelter of some trees and watched the constable pass then glanced at his watch as the moon came out from behind a cloud.

It was eight minutes since he'd left the tower. The car he'd seen was thirty yards away. He crossed the road and withdrew a razor-sharp penknife from his pocket. As he'd expected, the door was locked and it was the work of moments to slash the canvas hood and stretch inside for the door release. He sat down and reached under the steering column, pulled out the ignition wiring and connected the two cables to complete the circuit. Then he peered into the passenger footwell. There was no sign of the starting handle, so he got out and walked to the rear of the vehicle, looking round as he did so. In the moonlit sky beyond the fort, the Zeppelin was clearly visible with the naked eye. It looked lower, he thought.

The starting handle was in the boot. He went to the front of the car, slipped it onto the crank and with a silent prayer pulled it round. The engine was warm and fired up immediately. He got in and threw the handle into the back then pulled away, leaving the lights off.

Less than two minutes later he was driving slowly down Arwenack Avenue. When he was halfway along, he stopped and got out. The tower of the hotel was visible above the top of the hill to his right. To his left he could see the bulk of Pendennis Castle, with the airship beyond.

Perfect.

He turned the car so it was facing diagonally across the street, pointing towards the fort and the docks below it. At that moment there was a knock on the window and Kate Diss's face appeared as she bent down to talk to him.

'Is that you? I thought it was. What are you doing?'

Shocked, but fired with adrenaline and utterly committed, the German made a split-second decision. He smiled and said through the window, 'If you let me out, I'll tell you.'

She stepped back and he clambered out, looking both ways along the avenue. It was deserted. By now the whole town knew that a Zeppelin was about to bomb them, and they were all inside, crouched under whatever cover they could find.

The girl looked at him. He grinned at her again and gestured. 'Come closer and I'll tell you. It's a secret, but I don't mind you knowing.'

And poor trusting Kate took the final two steps of her life.

Ten minutes later, panting for breath, the man re-entered the room at the top of the tower and turned on the light, then ran back down to Arwenack Avenue. The car was still there with Kate sitting motionless in the passenger seat. He pulled her body out and carried it over his shoulder into some bushes. Then he restarted the engine and turned on the headlights.

Exhilaration pulsed through his body as he settled down next to the girl and waited. He'd done it. The lights in the tower and the car pointed straight towards the port, giving his countrymen a clear signal. He was sorry about the girl, but there had been no time to work out another option. It was the second time he'd killed for the Kaiser. Gladys last year, and now the chambermaid.

Let's hope there are no more. But even as the thought struck him, he knew if the need arose, he'd take another English life without compunction.

The airship's engines could clearly be heard now. A terrifying pulsing rumble that vibrated the windows of the houses further along the avenue. Then a series of huge explosions sounded down near the old quay. Shouts and screams carried over the houses as he sat tight, huddled inside the bush.

In a lull he heard running footsteps and cautiously raised his head. A man was dashing towards the car, coming from the Swanpool Street direction. He hauled the door open and turned off the headlights.

'Bloody fool,' he heard him mutter. 'Bodies in the streets and some idiot's left their lights on.' With that he ran back the way he'd come.

Bodies on the streets. The words echoed in Excalibur's head, and five minutes later he emerged from the bushes, had a cautious look around, then unceremoniously hauled Kate's dead weight up onto his shoulder and set off along the avenue. The tower light was out now, he noticed. At the junction with Swanpool Street, he turned right and made his best pace downhill towards the firelit chaos below.

As he reached the bottom of the hill a hail sounded from behind. He turned. His colleague from the hotel was running down the road towards him. For a moment his heart sank.

Did someone see me?

The man caught him up and stared at his tragic load. 'What happened?'

'She was lying in the road back there. She must have been blown out of a house I think, poor thing.'

'Is she dead?'

'It looks like it.'

His friend grimaced and shook his head. 'What a mess. I've come to help. I'll see you later.' And with that he disappeared into the smoke and fire and noise. Shifting the girl's weight, Excalibur followed. Her face had been hidden over his shoulder; he just had to find a quiet spot to dump her now.

As he reached the corner of Swanpool and Arwenack Street a red-haired young woman in a nurses' uniform was bending over a woman with a bleeding leg. She glanced up and called over. 'Dead or wounded?'

'Dead, I'm afraid.'

'All right. They're splitting the casualties between the main hospital and Trevethan school. There's a muster point by the King's Pipe, or what's left of it. Take her there if you will, sir.'

'Certainly.' Fierce excitement ran through his veins. *It's all working out; I'm going to get away with this.*

Twenty minutes later, as he laboured with the others to extract a man from the rubble, he saw Alma. He paused for a moment and their eyes met. She gave him a quick smile and then hurried on.

Chapter Eight

By morning word was filtering out about the overall impact of the raid. Mrs Wilson's son Reggie worked for the *Falmouth Packet*, the main local newspaper, and she'd spoken to him on the telephone as dawn broke over the shocked town. Sitting in the nook with an audience of hotel staff and guests' servants, she brought them up to date. Wragge and Weaver were there, still in filthy clothes. Both looked exhausted.

'There were twenty bombs in total. They fell on the lower town and the docks, and one ship's lying on the bottom next to quay. There's twenty-three people dead or not accounted for so far, including five children. The houses along Arwenack Street took a terrible pasting and people were buried in the rubble. That's a dreadful thing, dropping bombs on innocent people in the middle of the night.' Sure of her audience, the cook paused to take a sip of her tea then continued.

'He says there was one mercy though. They didn't hit that big tanker, the *Persian Knight*. She was empty and full of fumes. The editor told my son if she'd gone up, the docks and most of the lower town would have been destroyed.'

'Good Lord, that was a lucky escape,' Weaver said to a stir of recognition from the others in the room.

'Do you think that was what they were after?' Wragge wondered aloud.

The cook shrugged. 'They say these airships are very susceptible to the wind. It might have been blown off course and the crew just saw the town and docks and thought they'd let the bombs go.'

'What about the tower light?' Gracie Banks asked. 'How did that get left on?'

Alma said, 'We're not sure. An oversight of some kind.' Keen not to dwell on that subject she glanced around. 'Where is Kate? Have you seen her this morning, Polly?'

The chambermaid shook her head. 'No, Miss Timperley.'

'I hope she hasn't been caught up in the bombing. Has anyone seen her since last night?' There was a general shaking of heads, so she added, 'Polly, run up and check her room, will you?'

The informal meeting broke up and when Alma returned to the foyer, she was greeted by a tired-looking Constable Robinson and his sergeant, who addressed her.

'We'll have that word now, miss. If you don't mind. My name's Trewin by the way.'

As she led the way to her office, Polly appeared with the news that Kate wasn't in her room and her bed was made. Shortly afterwards the three of them were settled in the small room and the door was firmly shut. Once the introductions had been completed, the sergeant took the floor.

'It's the light we're interested in. When the Zeppelin was spotted and the guns on the fort opened up, the whole town was darkened quickly, and the tower light was off. But by the time the Huns were close to the coast it was on. And so were those car lights. It may have been accidental but then again it may not.'

He let the remark hang in the air as Robinson took out his notebook and consulted it. 'A Mr Nancarrow of Wood Lane round the corner from here reported his car stolen this morning and that's the one that was found.'

Trewin nodded. 'So what we need to know, Miss Timperley, is what happened in the hotel in the period between the town being darkened, and the light on the tower going on.'

'What exactly are you suggesting, Sergeant?' she enquired cooly, but he ignored her and carried on.

'As far as we can work out, the timings are like this. The Huns were spotted at eleven twenty-five by the fort and the guns opened up five minutes later, at half past. Word was sent to the gas plant to turn off the supply and the port was telephoned to turn off the lights down there. By twenty-five to twelve the town was darkened, and the tower light was off.'

He nodded to Robinson, who took up the narrative. 'But when the bombing started at midnight the tower light was on, and the car headlights were shining out from Arwenack Avenue. It has been noted that the line of the two lights pointed directly towards the docks.' The constable paused meaningfully and raised his eyebrows.

Trewin nodded. 'So it has. We don't know exactly what time they went on, Miss Timperley, but we suspect that someone in your hotel lit the lights to act as a guide for the airship.'

'You mean in less than thirty minutes they realised what was happening, stole the car, got it into position and left it there with the lights on. Then went back and lit the tower light?' Alma sounded doubtful.

'The car's cover was slashed open, and it had been cross-wired to connect the electrics. The fellow was quick, I'll give you that, but it's not far to the avenue, less than four hundred yards. If they didn't hesitate and knew how to drive it is entirely possible.'

'Was it spontaneous, do you think?'

Trewin stared at her. 'Now there's a question.'

Wishing James was with her, Alma said, 'Are you suggesting that we have a German sympathiser amongst us?'

'It is something that we must consider. There's been an awful lot of talk of enemy agents in the papers and Falmouth is a place of interest. I'm going to have to ask everyone in the hotel to account for their movements during that half hour between half past eleven and twelve o'clock.'

'Well good luck with that, Sergeant.' Alma turned and rummaged on the desk until she found a copy of the directions they'd issued to every room in the event of an air raid. She handed it over saying, 'All the guests and staff have seen this. Once the fort's guns opened up they'd have been in their rooms under their beds. But you'll have a hard time proving it, I imagine.'

Trewin studied it gloomily then passed it to Robinson as Alma continued, 'I should also say that Kate Diss, one of our chambermaids, cannot be found this morning.'

'Do you think she got caught up in the bombing?' Trewin asked.

'I have no idea, but she should be here.'

'Well, they're making progress with a casualty list, so I suggest you check with the hospital. It's very possible she's just been wounded and kept in.'

'Yes, I'll do that.' Alma nodded and glanced at the clock. 'Look, it's eight o'clock. Why don't you catch all the guests at breakfast. You can speak to them and find out what you want. I don't imagine it'll take long. In fact most of the staff are eating in the nook at the moment. Come and talk to them now. We might even rustle up a bit of bacon and eggs. You look as though you could do with something.'

This suggestion produced a noticeable lift to the two policemen and Trewin willingly agreed.

Half an hour later, having given very similar accounts of the previous evening, namely being woken by the guns and dashing down to help with the rescue work, Weaver and Wragge turned in.

One fell asleep straight away but, despite his exhaustion, Excalibur lay awake for some time thinking hard about the earlier conversation in the nook.

* * *

At the outbreak of the war, Trevethan school on the Moor in Falmouth had been requisitioned by the military and turned into a hospital, and it was to there that many of the casualties from the bombing were sent. Dr Emmanuel Grant had been on night duty when they had started arriving. Some came by ambulance, others were carried, and some simply walked from Arwenack Street.

By one o'clock in the morning the chaotic, noisy, bloody scene in the entrance hall would have been only too familiar to the medical staff working in casualty clearing stations behind the British lines in Belgium. Casualties lay everywhere, some moaning and writhing, others ominously still, with more arriving all the time.

The doctor telephoned the main hospital in Falmouth only to hear they were overwhelmed as well, and he'd have to do his best, but gradually day staff arrived, and they began to establish a proper system. By three o'clock in the morning the flow of wounded had slowed to a trickle and Dr Grant was able to take stock.

Four bodies lay on stretchers covered with sheets and he went to double-check that they were definitely dead. In the chaos of the previous hours, mistakes were entirely possible. There was no doubt about the first one, a middle-aged man with a grievous injury to his chest caused by a wood splinter, most of which was still embedded. His face was covered with small cuts, and he'd obviously been caught directly in a bomb blast. He slipped his hand into his jacket and removed his bloody wallet. Three business cards were tucked in there. *Terence Gibson, Insurance Agent.*

Replacing the wallet, he crossed to the reception desk and added the man's name to the register they had established. Then he returned to the bodies and pulled back the sheet over the next one. It was a young woman wearing a plain black winter coat. There was a letter in the inner pocket and from that he deduced her name was Kate Diss. He looked but couldn't see any obvious signs of injury on her torso and pulled the sheet down to her ankles. Both knees were grazed, and her stockings torn, but beyond that the girl was unmarked. He checked for a pulse on her wrist and found nothing, then, because he was a good doctor and diligent, pulled down her collar and checked on her neck as well.

And what he saw gave him pause for thought. There was no pulse but there was something else.

At ten o'clock in the morning Dr Grant finally got off shift. He was exhausted and badly in need of his bed, but rather than walking straight home he first took a detour to inspect the damage in the town. Then he walked to the police station.

* * *

Having completed their enquiries at the hotel, Sergeant Trewin and Constable Robinson returned to the station. As predicted by Alma Timperley, the interviews with the hotel staff and guests had not been particularly helpful. At half past eleven when the guns on the fort had started firing, everyone had been in bed or claimed to be. And there was not a great deal that the police officers could do to confirm or deny their statements.

'At least we've got a starting point, Sergeant,' Robinson pointed out as they walked across the Moor. 'If we find any evidence to the contrary, we'll know someone has been lying.'

Trewin grunted in agreement as they pushed through the door. A dishevelled man in a tweed suit was sitting in reception.

'This is Dr Grant from the Trevethan School Hospital. He's come in to make a statement and I asked him to wait for half an hour in case you came back,' the duty constable said.

'Couldn't you have done it?' the sergeant muttered as he approached the desk.

The constable looked embarrassed. 'He gave me the gist of it, and I thought you ought to hear it yourself, Sarge. There's no one else here, because of the raid.'

Trewin looked across to the man who stood up expectantly. 'All right, come on then, sir. This way.' Five minutes later the three men were sitting in an interview room with three mugs of tea provided by the desk constable. 'What is it that you wish to report?' Robinson asked, his notebook at the ready.

'As your colleague said, I'm a doctor at the Trevethan. We started receiving casualties soon after the raid began, and I dealt with them as they came in. By the time things started to quieten down we had four dead and, before I left, I double-checked them for any signs of life.'

'And?' Trewin asked.

'Oh they're all deceased. No doubt about that. But one of them, a girl in her late teens called Kate Diss, wasn't killed by a bomb.'

'Eh?' Robinson looked at him. 'What do you mean by that?'

'When I checked for a pulse in her carotid artery, I saw clear signs of compression around her neck. Other signs confirm it.'

'Confirm what?'

'The poor girl was strangled. Concealed amongst the dead there is a murder victim, Sergeant.'

* * *

After some badly needed sleep, the two police officers visited Kate Diss's parents late in the afternoon on the day after the raid and reported the facts as they knew them.

'I'm sorry to tell you that your daughter has been identified as one of the dead by the hospital at Trevethan school,' the sergeant intoned gravely as they sat in a cramped but neat front room in a terraced house near Kimberley Park.

Understandably the news was received with shock and distress by her mother and father, but that rapidly changed to horror when he advised them that they were treating it as a case of murder. By the time he'd told them about the doctor's report, Mrs Diss was bent over with her face in her hands as great sobs wracked her body.

'It's one thing to lose her in the bombing, but to think about that . . .' Kate's father said, his face slack with emotion. 'What happened?'

The sergeant shook his head gently. 'At this point we don't know. The casualties were gathered together at the King's Pipe and I'm guessing that the murderer took the opportunity to add Kate's body to the others there. Or he might have left her in a dark spot to be found by someone else. In the chaos no one probably even noticed, and even if they did, someone carrying a girl wouldn't have seemed out of place last night.'

'But someone might have seen him doing it,' Mr Diss pointed out.

Trewin nodded slowly. *You are right.* It was the first time he'd thought objectively about what might have happened and the man had a point. 'That's certainly a possibility and we'll be looking at it,' he replied.

'You don't know anyone who'd want her dead, do you?' Constable Robinson asked. 'Did she have a young man for example?'

Mrs Diss shook her head. 'She wasn't walking out as far as I know. She was a quiet girl and I can't imagine her giving anybody a reason to kill her. I really can't.' She broke down again.

'What happens next?' her father asked.

Trewin hesitated, then said, 'I'm going to ask you something now. If it is murder, and it certainly looks like it, then we'll have a better chance of catching the man if he doesn't know we're after him. Do you see that?'

They both looked at him but neither responded so he pressed on. 'What I'm suggesting is that we say Kate was killed in the bombing, just like the murderer wants us to think.'

'Let him believe he's got away with it you mean?' Mrs Diss asked.

Trewin nodded. 'Aye, just for now. You can get on and bury her – we won't stand in the way of that – but let's keep quiet about her being murdered. Is that all right?'

The two bereaved parents looked at each other, then Mr Diss nodded. 'Yes.'

The policemen stayed for another ten minutes before taking their leave. As they walked back Robinson said, 'Do you think that's likely, Sarge? About a possible witness to someone leaving her body?'

'Well you'll be the first to know because I want you to get down there in the morning and start talking to people. You can tell them it's just clearing up where people were injured and killed to help piece together what happened. But try and find anyone who was working with the wounded by the King's Pipe. I saw a couple of nurses there for a start. It looked like they were

93

wearing Queen Alexandra uniforms. Get yourself up to the hospital as well and ask who they were. See what I mean?'

Happy with the task Robinson willingly agreed. Then he said, 'What about the lights up at the hotel and the car?'

'I think we'll focus on the murder for now. That trumps anything else and there's a wheelbarrow load of paperwork to get through as well. We can't prove anyone in that hotel was doing anything other than hiding under their beds. For now, we'll just note the fact that there's been some suspicious behaviour and keep an eye on the place.'

'Right you are, Sarge.'

* * *

The following morning Constable Robinson decided that the prospect of conversing with the nurses at the main hospital in Falmouth was more interesting than pursuing his enquiries in the cold drizzle of Arwenack street and directed his bicycle accordingly.

At the main reception he explained that he'd like to speak to anyone who'd been down on Arwenack Street during the bombing. The receptionist asked him to wait and fifteen minutes later two young nurses arrived, wearing their Queen Alexandra uniforms. He introduced himself and they went to the cafeteria and collected a pot of tea.

'We can't be too long,' the older one warned in a broad Irish brogue. 'Matron will be after us. She wasn't happy letting us come down at all, with the doctor on his rounds and due on the ward any minute.'

'I'll be as quick as I can. What are your names for starters.' It transpired the girls were called Nell McGuigan and Sally Regan and they were both from Sligo. Sally was older and tall, with red hair and freckles. Nell was plumpish and dark.

'We joined up together and finished our training last month,' Nell added.

'Will you be staying in Falmouth?' the constable asked, noting the girl's gentle voice and soft eyes with interest.

'We don't know yet. There's a good chance though. The hospital has been put on the list to receive casualties from the front. Trains will start arriving soon and we've cleared out four wards to take them, so we'll be needed.'

'Right.' Tucking this information away, he said, 'So you were both involved in the bombing down on Arwenack Street the other night?'

It was Sally who answered. 'Yes, our flat is in a house on Bond Street off the main road. We'd been on a late shift and got back just as the guns started. When the bombs began to fall, we went out to see if we could help. It was pretty nasty. You get used to blood and gore during the training, but even so . . .' She trailed off, eyes suddenly distant.

'It was raw all right,' Nell confirmed quietly.

'You did well,' Robinson said. 'I was down there too, and it was frightening. So were you by the King's Pipe?'

'We ended up there.' Sally nodded. 'It became the muster point for the casualties. A military doctor turned up and we helped to try and prioritise people as they arrived.'

'Thinking back to that night, do either of you remember seeing a man carrying a youngish girl in a black coat? We're just trying to find out what happened to her. Does that ring any bells?'

'She was injured, was she?' Nell asked.

'Definitely. Sadly she died.'

She shook her head. 'It was madness. The light from the fires, explosions and people running and shouting. It's hard to remember anything in particular, somehow.'

Sally watched Constable Robinson staring intently into her friend's eyes over the table. *Another conquest, Nell*, she thought wryly. Then a thought struck her.

'Not when I was at the King's Pipe but before then, not long after we'd arrived. Bombs were still falling, I think.'

Robinson looked at her, suddenly alert. 'And?'

'I was in the middle of the street helping a woman with a broken leg, and a man came past. He was carrying a woman in a dark coat slung over his shoulder. I asked him if she was dead, and he said yes. I told him to get along to the King's Pipe with her and I presume that's what he did.'

'What time was this?'

She shrugged. 'I've no idea. I wasn't thinking about the time, and he was just one of many people helping the injured.'

'Did you see his face?'

She paused and thought. Robinson waited. Then to his immense disappointment she shook her head. 'Only a glance. He had a hat on, and his face was shaded. It was just a fleeting encounter in amongst all the chaos. He moved well for someone carrying a deadweight. I will say that.'

'Would you recognise him again?'

She shrugged. 'Maybe, but I doubt it.'

They continued to talk for another five minutes then Constable Robinson departed, having first ensured that he had the address of the girls' flat in his notebook. Further enquiries with Nell McGuigan could not be ruled out, he thought.

From the hospital he cycled down to Arwenack Street and along to the area by Custom House Quay where the greatest damage had been done. He counted four houses with shops on the ground floor that had taken direct hits and were ruined. Many more had their windows broken and bore other signs of being in the range of the blasts.

Work was taking place to shore up damaged walls and clear rubble, and the constable could see many of the working gangs were in army uniform. He tried to make enquiries with some of the passers-by and shopworkers, but it rapidly became clear that he couldn't expect much in the way of useful intelligence. Most people had remained under their beds or tables as instructed, and those who had ventured outside could only remember a terrifying kaleidoscope of noise and flames and screaming. The idea of them remembering a single man carrying a woman was remote. He started to realise just how lucky he'd been with Sally Regan up at the hospital.

Down by the quay a lieutenant from the Duke of Cornwall's Light Infantry was directing a working party of soldiers, and he glanced up as the constable stopped to watch for a moment.

'Care to give us a hand?' he enquired with a smile.

'Sorry, I'm on a mission myself,' Robinson replied. 'Good to see you helping out though.'

'We've got the town, the navy's got the docks. They're trying to refloat that coaster and get her off the quay. There are divers down, I believe.'

'Really?' As if by instinct they both stared across the water to the breakwater below the fort. As they watched, a tender appeared from the inner dock and headed out towards the ships moored in mid-stream.

A cry of alarm brought their attention back to the scene in front of them as a sergeant shouted, 'Watch out, lads.' The soldiers scrambled back as a section of the upper floor of the building crashed down where they had been working moments earlier.

'Are we likely to find anyone else in there or is everyone accounted for now?' the officer asked. 'I'm only asking because I'm tempted to put some small charges below these standing walls and bring the lot down before we clear it. Otherwise, someone's going to get hurt.'

'I think we've got everybody but it's hard to be sure.'

The man opposite grimaced. 'That's not the answer I was hoping for. This really is dangerous work.'

Robinson nodded. 'I see that. I'll get back to the police station and see where we are. Explosives would need to be authorised by the inspector. Give me an hour and I'll try to get back to you. I suggest you stand the men down in the meantime, and maybe have a word with your colleagues up the road.'

'Thank you, I will.'

The two men parted, and the constable made his way back to the police station where he reported the request regarding explosives to Sergeant Trewin. The inspector was summoned and reluctantly decided he'd better go and have a look for himself. As they watched him depart, Trewin said, 'Well that's winkled him out. How did you get on anyway?'

He explained about the two nurses and how Sally Regan remembered seeing a man carrying a woman but couldn't say she'd recognise him again.

'Well it's helpful anyway. It supports the theory that the murderer dumped the body during the chaos, even if we don't know who he was.' He thought for a moment and then said, 'Of course this is where our scheme to keep the murder secret works against us. If it was public knowledge we could appeal for anyone who carried a young woman that night to come forward and we could see who we've got.'

'The murderer wouldn't speak up though would he.'

'No, but if someone else did, we'd know the man Sally Regan saw was innocent. Do you see my point?'

'I do, Sarge. Was it him, do you think?' Robinson asked.

'It's a clear possibility I'd say. You'd better get back over to the hospital and get a formal statement from her.'

'Right you are. She finishes at half past four so I might drop in on her at home, later. I've got the address.'

'All right, but either way get it down and signed, Constable.'

Happily anticipating another encounter with Nell McGuigan, Robinson nodded and went off in search of a cup of tea.

Chapter Nine

In the event it was longer than expected before James Nascent was able to clear his desk in London and return to the hotel. Hilda came back to town, summoned by a telephone call, and he briefed her on his plans over dinner. She suggested a suitable locum and they met him together and agreed terms, but then various pressing matters that required his personal attention arose and a delay became inevitable.

Therefore it was not until the first of February that he breakfasted with Hilda, kissed her goodbye and took a taxi to Paddington station.

He arrived at Falmouth at five p.m. and, after passing through the station checkpoint, took a horse-drawn cab to the hotel. As the crow flies it was less than half a mile but the steep hill above which the hotel lay meant the driver had to take a more indirect route in order to 'give old Mary a fighting chance', as he put it, nodding towards the elderly mare that stood blowing between the traps as the solicitor alighted in front of the hotel.

He checked in with Mrs Banks and had a cup of tea as she told him about the raid on the town. He'd been shocked to see it reported in the London papers but was horrified to hear that the hotel had lost one of its own.

'Poor Kate, she was such a quiet little mouse of a thing in some ways. Her mum and dad are devastated. The police said she must have been caught in a blast when she was coming back up to the hotel.' The assistant manager shook her head at the vagaries of fate.

'It's appalling,' he agreed.

'Mr Weaver and Mr Wragge worked all night in the rubble like most of the men. In fact we all did our bit.'

'Yes, I'm sure. I'll go down and have a look at the town in the morning. Was there much damage to the port?'

'They sank one ship and knocked down some warehouses. The railway was blown up too, I think. They've been working to fix it, I know that.'

He unpacked then went in search of Alma. It appeared she had gone out and was expected back later in the evening, so he resigned himself to dining alone. But then he found Valentine Wragge sitting with a drink in the nook.

Trying to avoid staring at the dresser and making a mental note to check if the book was still there later, he said affably, 'Evening, Wragge, not mixing with your clients in the lounge then?'

The man smiled. 'Not this evening. I'm happy to normally, but I'm having a night off tonight, to be honest. Here you are back again, Mr Nascent. I'd imagined you had finished your work in Falmouth.'

'No, no,' he said evenly, 'my client asked me to ensure that Miss Timperley is well supported in these early days, so I'll be here for a week or two yet.'

They chatted for a few minutes about the raid and then, at the solicitor's suggestion, went into the dining room together. The room was nearly full, but Maisie put them at a table for two by the window and left a menu. Nascent looked around. A pleasant hum of conversation carried to him and as before he was struck by the general air of wealth and position that the hotel's clientele exuded.

'Observe the two ladies in the far corner,' Wragge said quietly. 'On the left is Lady Buchanan of Rannoch and, on the right, Countess Wight. They've made friends since meeting when they arrived and are most definitely the senior table in the room. They've dined together every evening.'

The solicitor looked over. Lady Buchanan was a red-headed woman in her mid-forties. The countess was perhaps ten years older, and her hair was greying. They were talking quietly. 'Clients of yours?' he enquired.

'The countess, yes, but not Lady Buchanan. She's with Weaver. Her husband is a brigadier general in the army and is over in France. They lost their son early on. Isobel, that is the countess, is a widow and her second son was killed in the navy.' He smiled and nodded as the older woman looked over and met his eye.

Nascent enjoyed dinner. Wragge was an entertaining companion and regaled him with a range of stories from his early days as a stage actor. In turn he responded with some amusing anecdotes from the law courts, which had Wragge chuckling. His dining partner had charm and no little intelligence. And there was depth there too. The solicitor imagined he'd probably be a man of action if circumstances required it.

But is he a spy? During the meal he had manoeuvred the conversation around to foreign travel and the tricky issue of discourse with a foreigner in their own language. In response to a direct question Wragge had said that he spoke a little French and German. 'Just enough to get into trouble', as he put it with a smile.

Only a little? Nascent wondered if that was true. But when he gently pressed his companion, he dissembled and made vague references to being part of a European family with 'a branch in many cities'.

Having spent two hours with the man, he was certain that, if it were called for, Valentine Wragge would be a very good liar indeed. And by his own admission he'd been a successful actor before becoming a spiritualist. It was a lot to think about.

On his way up to his room he checked the dresser in the nook. The book was still there.

* * *

Just before nine that evening George Weaver entered his consulting room. It was simply furnished with two comfortable chairs facing each other across a small table. Against the far wall a floor lamp cast a warm glow onto a settee that stood in front of the heavy curtains, and a thick rug covered the floor. And that was all. Compared to the Edwardian opulence of the rest of the hotel and the rather theatrical setting in which Wragge conducted his séances, the room was positively monkish.

A large candle stood in the centre of the table. Weaver was a man who needed to observe his clients' faces when he was working.

As the grandfather clock in the foyer struck nine, Lady Buchanan arrived outside the door, her heart beating fast at the prospect of their second session. During the first, the medium had managed to make faint contact with her son, 'to make him aware that we are here and wish to commune with him', he had explained, adding it was a good start and not unusual. He had given her to understand that there was every chance of a more direct and personal engagement this evening.

'We have sent him a spiritual telegram, my lady, and we must hope he will respond to it. Beyond that we cannot know until we try.'

Fervently hoping that her son had heard the call of his beloved mother, she knocked on the door.

'Good evening, Lady Buchanan. Come in,' came the reply from within.

His voice sent a pulse of excitement through her and with a shock she realised that her sudden giddiness was not just due to the imminent reconnection with her dead son. It was George Weaver too. She had been apart from her husband for eight months, and the prospect of an intimate hour staring into George's eyes as they held hands in the semi-darkness was intoxicating.

He was sitting at the table. As he turned towards her the candle glowed on his face, as she knew it would glow on hers when she sat opposite him.

'Good evening, Mr Weaver.' Her soft Perthshire voice sounded in the room and a shiver rippled through her as she crossed the floor and slipped onto the chair.

He smiled. 'Perhaps you would call me George during these sessions. Would that be acceptable?'

She inclined her head. 'And I am Fiona.' He was wearing a loose white linen shirt, as before. Two buttons were undone below the collar, and she could see the beginnings of his chest. He stretched out his hands and she responded automatically, taking his warm grip.

His voice was quiet and purposeful. 'Look at me now, Fiona. I have been doing some preliminary work and I am very hopeful that we will be able to reach out to Iain tonight. But for that to happen you must give of yourself completely. Do you understand me? I will be doing the work, but you must follow me wherever we go.'

When she was a young woman Fiona and her ghillie had been caught in an electrical storm high on the Black Cuillin mountain range on Skye. The man had pushed her into a fissure in the rock and there they had waited as the air fizzed and crackled around them. She remembered her hair standing on end and pins and needles running through her arms and feet.

She was reminded of the intensity of that moment now, as he stared over the table and squeezed her hands.

'You do trust me, don't you, Fiona,' he said quietly.

His eyes were extraordinary, she thought. It was as though he was seeing right into her soul. And his voice. So reassuring and calm. But powerful. A warm feeling of peace and anticipation drifted over her and when he spoke again his words seemed to come from far away.

'Will you let me lead you? Will you come with me?'

'Yes,' she said faintly, her eyes slowly closing. 'Yes, I will.'

'Then let's talk about your family, Fiona.'

* * *

As she strolled along Cliff Road above the beach with the Countess Wight next morning, Fiona Buchanan was in a state of grace. The second séance had been wonderful. Remarkable. Her beloved son Iain had, as she had so fervently hoped, spoken to her through the medium. And the things he had said had convinced her that he truly was there in the room with her.

Later on, the intensity of the session had led to certain other developments on the settee in the darkened room and as they lay there afterwards the dear man had been appalled at his loss of control. But she had kissed his forehead and told him it would be their secret. They had talked long into the night as she, wrapped in a warm cocoon of emotion, revealed details about her husband and family that were only known to her intimate circle. And now she was looking forward to their third consultation with a giddy excitement that was reminiscent of her teenage years.

'It wasn't just what he said, Isobel,' she explained as she linked arms with her new friend, 'it was the way he said it. The phrases he used and particular words. So familiar, so like my Iain. It was wonderful. Utterly wonderful. I feel as though a great weight has been lifted from my shoulders.'

Thirty years earlier Lady Isobel's husband had chosen his bride for her looks not her brains, and she missed the subtle point that her friend was inadvertently making. And thus also failed to appreciate it was not one she could not have made herself.

'I'm so pleased for you. Dear Valentine is the genuine article too. He just knew so much that only my darling Randolph could have known about our lives at home.'

But Fiona was barely listening. 'George was so very thorough. The highlight was Iain of course, but I vaguely remember talking about my husband in France. What he was up to with the division and all his officer friends. He absolutely made sure he had the full picture.'

'The Timperley Spiritualist Hotel really does live up to its reputation, even though Mrs Timperley herself is no longer in residence. What do you think of Alma, the girl who has inherited?' the countess asked.

Lady Buchanan thought for a moment then said, 'They say she has some ability herself. I was told that when Lady Watson visited in January, Miss Timperley conjured up her dead son's name out of thin air as she was registering. She even sat in on one of the sessions that Mr Wragge had with her. Perhaps she'll consider filling in the vacancy left by her poor aunt's demise.'

'Yes, I suppose that's a definite possibility. When's your last session?'

'In two days' time and I simply can't wait. I'm already thinking about booking again. It's not cheap staying here but you cannot put a price on what the hotel does. My dear husband likes to keep an eye on the purse strings, but when he hears about what's happened, I really can't see how he can stand in my way. I really do need to keep my son in my life.'

* * *

Lady Buchanan wasn't the only person feeling rather happy that morning. Constable Robinson had paid a visit to the nurses' small flat the previous evening and taken a statement from Sally Regan. Nell had been there too, and she'd offered to leave them in private but, to the older nurse's amusement, he'd hurriedly made a point of saying she should stay, 'just in case something jogs your memory'.

It took fifteen minutes to get the thing down on paper and have her sign it, but the policeman had not appeared to be in any hurry to leave. A pot of tea was prepared and consumed as he asked them about their lives in Ireland and chatted about growing up in Falmouth.

Finally, Sally took pity on him and announced she was going to finish her book, leaving the love-struck constable at the mercy of Nell's pretty face.

It was familiar territory to the dark-eyed girl from Sligo. 'Do you have any more enquiries you wish to make, Constable?' she asked innocently, hands on her lap.

'Well, I must admit I was wondering if you are walking out with anyone or if you are unattached?' he admitted with a grin.

'I see. And how will that help you find out what happened to that poor girl?'

'It won't really. It's more in the nature of a private enquiry.'

'And why would I be telling you personal matters like that?' The carefully calibrated note of surprise in her gentle brogue lingered in the room and for an alarming moment Robinson thought he'd overstepped the mark, then he grasped the nettle.

'Er, well, you're right I suppose, it is a bit cheeky, but if you were by any chance unattached, then I would like to ask you if you'd walk out with me.'

'Would you now? I'd have to have a think about that.'

Robinson wasn't a policeman for nothing. 'Ah, so you're not with anyone special at the moment?'

'Isn't that for me to know and you to wonder about?'

She waited. In an ecstasy of indecision, the young man moved uneasily in his seat. *What to say next?* He couldn't tell if she was serious or just amusing herself at his expense.

Finally he plumped for: 'Well I'm on my own myself, you see . . .' then petered out as her warm eyes held his gaze for an alluring moment.

'Wouldn't I hope so, if you're asking me out,' she observed.

Is that a smile? 'Well what do you say, Nell? Will you come for a drink with me one evening?'

She stood up without answering. He did the same and his face fell as she said, 'I'll see you out.'

At the door he turned and was surprised as she held out her hand. He responded automatically and she gave it a firm shake. 'Come and see me tomorrow and I'll give you an answer, Constable Robinson.' And with that she closed the door. But not before she'd given him one last look. And that had been distinctly encouraging.

Chapter Ten

A quarter moon shone down onto Primrose Hill in North London, as a man emerged from a stand of leafless trees and eyed the garden wall of Greylands, the London residence of Sir Gerald Prior and his wife, Lady Miranda. It was six feet tall and cleanly faced with limestone, but he was nimble and strong, and it was the work of moments to pull his head up to the capstones and peer over.

The scene was deserted. Immediately below him a wide flower bed lay dormant, the winter skeletons of a few plants lying on the bare earth. Beyond it, a lawn ran slightly downhill for a hundred yards, an early frost dusting the grass like icing sugar on a cake. At the far end a veranda stretched across the rear of a substantial, detached townhouse. As he watched a maid appeared in the French windows and drew the curtains, blocking the light cast onto the flagstones outside.

Diligent, he thought. Because the master and mistress were away for the weekend and the staff would not be using the upstairs rooms. Arms aching, he slipped back down the wall, made his way round to the front, and positioned himself under the trees opposite the drive. There he waited until the same maid and the housekeeper appeared and set off for the bright lights of Camden Town, leaving the dark bulk of the house alone and unlit.

The man made to move but then stopped as the melancholy clop-clop of a horse's hooves sounded in the still, cold air. A hansom cab was approaching. It came to a halt thirty yards away and a couple emerged, their voices carrying to his position in the shadows. He shivered as their breath showed under a gaslight before they disappeared through the gate in the hedge next door.

He watched the cab depart, then crossed the deserted road and walked up the drive.

At the back door he knelt down and removed a set of lock-picks from his pocket. Tools that would earn him five years inside if they were found in his possession. But they did their job and shortly afterwards he eased the door open. Then the man, who was an experienced housebreaker, simply stood there for a full five minutes, alert for any noise or movement. A dog perhaps, or another servant curious about the sudden draught below stairs. But there was only a velvet silence, as though the house was daring him to creep inside.

He duly obliged, shutting but not locking the door before walking down the corridor, a familiar thrill rippling through his body. He glanced into the kitchen. It was warm and lit with pale light from a high window. At the far end a tamped-down range glowed and murmured quietly. The smell of fried bacon lingered in the air. Walking on, he climbed the backstairs and emerged into the entrance hall.

Again he paused. *Nothing.* Every sense told him the house was empty.

He moved across the Turkish rug and ascended the main staircase. The landing formed a square around the stairwell and in the light from the skylight he could see doors leading off on each side. He cautiously opened the nearest one. It was a bedroom but the gloom from the uncurtained window showed him that it was not in use. He moved on, silently checking each room until, at the fourth door, he found his objective: the mistress's bedroom. He crossed to the window, closed the curtains then withdrew a small electric lamp from the bag he carried and turned it on.

The glow illuminated the room, and he looked around, noting the double bed, large wardrobe and chest of drawers. There were some photographs on a dressing table in the bay window and he went to look, holding the lamp close. One was of a mature man in formal dress and the other two showed a young man in his early twenties. In one he was wearing military uniform and in the second he was wearing a suit and relaxing in a chair, a wry smile on his face as he looked at the camera.

Alert for the slightest sound or change in the atmosphere beyond the wide-open bedroom door, he quickly searched the drawers of the dressing table. They did not contain what he was looking for. He moved across to the chest of drawers and looked through those, with the same result, although he did find thirty pounds in a purse tucked away under some underwear. He left it where it was. Pausing he held up the lamp and looked around the room, then issued a hiss of satisfaction. There was a single drawer in the bedside table. Seconds later he had it open and withdrew a handful of letters bound together with a blue ribbon. He took them over to the dressing table, sat down and opened the one on top. The paper was smeared with mud and had a military postmark. A single glance at its contents told him all he needed to know.

My dear mother . . .

The man put down his bag and withdrew a notepad and pencil. He laid it on the dressing table next to the lamp and settled down to read. Half an hour later he moved to the master's room and, sometime after that, their son's. He took nothing and was careful to leave things exactly as he found them.

By the time the maid and the housekeeper rolled home, a little the worse for wear, he was sitting in the public bar of the Horse and Groom on Camden High Street, writing up a detailed report from the notes he'd made. His client was particular and exacting, but in ten years of working for him he had developed a clear knowledge of what was required.

By the time he'd finished there were four sides of tightly written words. He put them in an envelope and wrote the address and added a stamp. Then he finished his drink and left the pub, dropping the letter into a post box on his way to the tram stop.

* * *

In Falmouth a couple of days later Nascent managed to catch George Weaver in the nook and suggested they had dinner together that night. The jury was definitely out on Valentine Wragge, and he wanted to make an initial assessment of his partner. On the face of it, Weaver was a much more closed-up personality. He was a quiet man who gave little away, but the solicitor felt that there might be a great deal going on behind his rather intense and handsome façade.

His enquiry was met with a moment's silence and then a positive response.

'Of course, Nascent. Will here do, or do you wish to try somewhere else?'

'The hotel is fine with me,' he replied. 'Shall we say six thirty for a drink in the lounge?'

During dinner, the solicitor broached something that had been on his mind. 'Do I detect the slightest of accents, Mr Weaver? Would I be right in thinking English is not your first language?'

The younger man nodded. 'You would be. I was born in Switzerland and spoke French until my late teens. I came to England in 1907 and have remained ever since.'

'What brought the move on, might I ask?'

Weaver sipped his wine, then said, 'My mother was a talented clairvoyant, but my father did not approve and forbade her from acting as a medium. However, she continued to work behind the scenes at home and introduced me to the art. I found I also had a facility and wanted to explore how far I could go with it.'

Nascent raised his eyebrows gently and smiled. 'But . . .'

'But indeed. When I was eighteen my father found out what my mother and I were up to and there was a great scene. I left the house and have not been back. I was determined to pursue what I believed was my destiny and settled down to work as a medium in Geneva. A few years later Gladys Timperley's growing fame reached our spiritualist community in Switzerland, and I ended up coming to England to seek her out.'

He stared towards the corner where the Countess of Wight and Lady Buchanan were eating, then made a gentle gesture that encompassed the whole room. 'I arrived in Falmouth aged twenty-three and presented myself to Gladys. Fortunately I spoke English quite well. She and I did a séance together and she recognised my abilities straight away and offered me a position similar to Wragge's. I had enough money to buy in and became part of our little family here.' He shrugged and added, 'I'm not sure I've spoken a word of French since then.'

'How fascinating. The twists and turns our lives take are unpredictable, are they not?' Nascent raised his glass. 'A toast, Weaver. To kismet, may it always be in our favour.'

'Indeed.' They chinked glasses.

But behind his guileless smile Nascent's mind was busy. Switzerland was a multi-lingual country. French was certainly common, but German was widely spoken as well. Was it possible that the man opposite had made a minor change to his story? Was his first language actually German? Gladys probably would have known, but she was dead.

How convenient, he reflected.

Later on in his room Nascent sat down with a piece of paper, intending to draw up a list of the occupants of the Timperley Spiritualist Hotel and review what he knew about them. But he quickly realised that was unnecessary. Alma was clearly not an enemy agent. She had been utterly unaware of the place before she'd walked into his office on Christmas Eve. The staff seemed unlikely spies too. They were all resolutely Cornish apart from anything else, and he simply couldn't see Mrs Banks or Polly secretly gathering information on behalf of the Huns. Nor Alf the odd-job man whose deafness rendered the idea ridiculous. That only left Mrs Wilson the cook and her daughter Maisie. He scratched his head. Again, their pride and patriotism shone through, and anyway, what information did they have access to?

He looked mournfully at the blank piece of paper. There were only two names, and he didn't need to write them down. Valentine Wragge and George Weaver. If there was a spy in the hotel it was one of them.

Further investigations were needed. Probably starting with a search of their rooms.

* * *

Nascent sought out Alma, who was in her office and asked if she had twenty minutes. She replied in the affirmative and he closed the door and sat down opposite her.

During his walk in St James's Park with the head of MI5, he had suggested that it would be wise to take the young woman into his confidence, and Kell had agreed. So now, sitting in the little windowless office, he came clean.

'Alma, do you remember when you asked me if I had another reason for accompanying you to Falmouth?'

'Yes, I do.'

'Well your instincts were correct, and I regret to say that I dissembled in my response at the time. But now I have had permission to tell you the truth.'

She frowned. 'Permission? From whom? And what truth exactly, James?'

He told her, starting with the letter where Gladys had made the allegations against an unknown person. Then he explained that it was possible that her subsequent death might be connected to her suspicions about someone in the hotel. Finally, he explained about his contact with Kell and their agreement that he would return to Falmouth to continue his search for a German spy. It took ten minutes, and she listened in silence, her face blank.

As he concluded, he saw she was struggling to hold back tears and a sudden sharp stab of remorse flooded through him. He leaned forward and reached over the desk for her hand, but she sat unmoving.

You fool, you deserve her approbation.

He attempted to make amends. 'Alma, let me say that I have always been completely on your side. I consider myself most fortunate to have met you and, if you will permit the remark, have grown fond of you during our brief association.'

He was quite genuine in this, but as a single tear made its way down the young woman's cheek, he mentally cursed Hilda's absence. She would have predicted Alma's reaction and warned him.

'I am alone and utterly reliant on your guidance. Have you taken advantage of me, Mr Nascent?' Her quiet voice sounded loud in the stillness of the room and its tone broke the solicitor's heart.

'I fear I have to some extent and am deeply sorry. My only excuse is that I loved Gladys and am intent on doing right by her.'

117

'Loved her?' Alma sounded surprised.

'We were close once. I believe I told you that.'

'Yes, you did.' She nodded vaguely, as though distracted.

He could feel her chilly anger and hated himself for it. The natural warmth in her eyes had been replaced by caution. *And I have put it there.* He took a deep breath and battled on.

'Gladys charged me with looking after you and I have done my utmost to ensure that you are encouraged and supported here at the hotel. Had your mother not mentioned her suspicions in that letter, then that is all there would be to our relationship. But she did, and from that point onwards matters seemed to develop their own momentum. Once Kell had been in touch with me I was sworn to secrecy. Quite literally as it happens. He made me sign the official secrets act.'

He smiled ruefully across the desk. 'When you asked me whether I had another reason to be at the hotel I lied to you. For that I sincerely apologise.'

To his surprise her face melted into a gentle smile. 'It seems to me that you were overtaken by events, James. You loved my mother and acted for her in the way you thought best. I should be a poor daughter to find fault with that.'

Relief flooded through him. 'Then I am forgiven?'

'I believe you are.' She pulled a drawer open and reached inside, withdrawing a single item, which she placed on the desk between them. 'I assume you have told me all this now because you need this.'

'What is it?' Although he'd already guessed.

'It is the hotel's master key. To all the locks.'

He nodded. 'That would be extremely useful.'

'To business then, James. We have a German spy to catch.'

He smiled at her sudden enthusiasm. 'No, Alma, I have a spy to catch; you have a hotel to run. Let's not confuse the two things.

I will pursue my enquiries and you continue to learn about your new role. That is the way things will be.'

He saw her bridle slightly at this. 'I do agree I have a great deal on my plate, James, but if I can help in any way I will. Whoever it is, it appears they have got the cheek to use my hotel as a base, and I'm not sure I like that at all.'

He smiled at this and took it as a good sign. If Alma was already feeling protective about the Timperley Spiritualist Hotel, she was surely the right choice to be its new custodian.

* * *

As luck would have it, the following morning Alma heard Valentine Wragge tell the cook that he was lunching with a friend in town. James was also out so, realising that this was an ideal opportunity to explore his quarters, she climbed the stairs to the top floor and collected the spare master key that Gladys had kept in a bedside drawer for her personal use. Wragge's room was round the corner from Alma's and, after checking the coast was clear, she let herself in and relocked the door. His window faced downhill over open ground and across the railway line to Cliff Road. Beyond that lay the statuesque Falmouth and Pendennis hotels and the stretch of coast that led towards Gyllyngvase bathing beach. In amongst the woods and fields, rows of tents were visible, evidence of the swollen numbers of troops in the area to train and to garrison the town.

Alma could also see the bulk of Pendennis Point and the castle to her left, but the docks themselves were obscured by the shoulder of the hill. Nevertheless, it was a magnificent view, and she wasn't surprised to see the man in residence had placed a comfortable armchair in a position to make the most of it. A pair of binoculars lay on the windowsill. Elsewhere there was a single bed, washstand, chest of drawers and a wardrobe. A desk stood at the far end with some bookshelves alongside it. She inspected the titles, noting the *Who's Who* amongst a range of popular novels.

Overall, it was exactly what one might expect of a confirmed bachelor living comfortably within his means. She opened the desk drawers and went through the papers but found nothing of great interest. Although she did wonder, to her own nervous amusement, what she was expecting to discover. A letter from Berlin?

She pulled the *Who's Who* off the shelf and flicked through the pages, finding nothing. Then she stood uncertainly and looked around, aching with tension.

What would James do?

Fired with purpose she walked back down the room and climbed onto the bed to inspect the top of the wardrobe. There was nothing up there, so she attacked the chest, pulling each of the drawers out entirely and searching each one. Again, she drew a blank. But as she was replacing the bottom one, she saw a corner of paper in the recess. A large envelope was lying on top of the base plate of the frame. With the drawer in normal use it would be entirely concealed.

Heart beating she reached into the space and lifted it out. To her surprise it was stuffed with smaller envelopes, all addressed to Valentine Wragge, post restante, Falmouth.

The one on top was postmarked Camden three days earlier and had been opened. She took out two sheets of paper. There was no addressee, date or signatory. Just four sides of neat and closely written sentences. She started to read.

Greylands is a large, detached villa that backs onto Primrose Hill. A stone wall with a gate separates the rear garden from the parkland. There are similar houses on either side,

Henleaze, facing to the left and Wyvern Lodge, facing to the right. The drive is gravel, and the front door is painted black.

Fascinated, she scanned down the page and realised she was reading an accurate and complete summation, not just of the physical aspects of the house but also a comprehensive briefing of its occupants, including the names of the servants. But it was on the second and third pages that a light began to dawn regarding the true purpose of the communication.

Francis Prior's letters reveal a close relationship with both his parents. His mother calls him Frankie. His nickname for his father is the Governor and his mother is Mater. The family dog, a corgi, is called Belle. The cook does not like her . . .

Alma read on until the end then replaced the envelope and briefly inspected another. It was in the same format, with three and a half sides in the same handwriting. The family were from Henley-on-Thames, the dead son's name was Charles Halliday and he had been a sub-lieutenant on HMS *Pathfinder*, torpedoed by a German U-boat in September 1914. The envelope was postmarked November.

So that is how you do it, Valentine. A secret partner in crime.

Then disaster struck. As she stood by the bed with the letter in her hand she heard sudden footsteps outside and a key enter the lock. The next moment the handle turned and the door started to open. Appalled, she simply froze. There was no time to do anything. Valentine was about to catch her red-handed. What on earth could she say to excuse herself?

The door swung open towards her, meaning she was granted a few extra seconds before they saw each other, but it merely gave her time to picture his confused and excruciating reaction.

'*Alma? What on earth are you doing in my room? Is that one of my private letters?*'

Face tight, eyes narrow, and heart pounding, she waited for the inevitable disgrace. Then a voice sounded outside. It was James.

'I say, Wragge, someone told me there's a way to get up to the tower room from this floor. Is that correct?'

His reply came from four feet away on the other side of the open door. Alma could hear him breathing. 'Indeed you can. It's that door there.' She pictured him pointing.

'Really? Would you show me?'

'You just go up the steps.'

The amateur burglar held her breath. James Nascent showed his brilliance by simply saying nothing. After an agonising moment she heard Wragge sigh with mild frustration. 'Very, well, I'll lead the way.'

The door swung shut again. After a few seconds Alma heard the door at the bottom of the tower stairs open and the men's footsteps on the wooden flight. Valentine said something about lunch being cancelled, then their voices faded. In a frenzied burst of activity she replaced the letters in the envelope, tucked it back into the chest and pushed the drawers in. Then with a quick glance round, opened the door and peered cautiously out. Nothing stirred. Leaving the door unlocked, she scuttled hastily back to the safety of her own quarters.

Twenty minutes later there was a quiet knock on her door. She opened it to see James Nascent standing there, a rather ironic expression on his face. 'I thought we agreed I was going to do the investigating,' he said quietly.

She let him in and shut the door. 'I'm so sorry, I just saw a chance and took it.'

'Well, you're damned fortunate. I came back early, happened to see you sneaking into his room, and decided to loiter on the landing and keep watch.' He gave her a look. 'Lucky I did, wouldn't you say?'

She felt awful, not least because she'd had to be rescued from disaster. Her embarrassment must have shown on her face because his expression softened into a warm smile. 'Well no harm done and it was plucky, I'll give you that. Did you find anything?'

Perhaps it was the intimacy of their shared secrets, but standing there, in her mother's old room, Alma felt a sudden and strong connection to James. It burst over her, as though she'd walked from shade into sunlight.

You are important to me.

She shook her head. 'Nothing at all to suggest he is a spy.'

He nodded thoughtfully. 'No, I'm not surprised. I think Valentine Wragge is a very careful man but it was worth checking, wouldn't you say?'

She nodded. 'Oh, yes. That's certainly true.'

When James left a few minutes later, Alma made two decisions. She'd discovered the secret of Valentine's success with his clients, but couldn't see any point in confronting him with it. As far as she was concerned, it would stay a secret. And she would steer clear of any further investigating. The hideous sound of that key turning in the lock as she stood there, letter in hand, would remain in her memory for a long time.

James could do the sleuthing from now on.

Chapter Eleven

Alma sat on the top deck of the bus and willed it onward as it climbed, with no great enthusiasm, up the hill out of Penzance.

'Fares please,' the conductor called out as he appeared next to her.

'Porthcurno, please. A return.'

'Certainly, miss.' He rang up the fare on his machine and she paid.

As she took the ticket she said, 'Would you mind tipping me the wink when we're there? It's my first trip and I'm not familiar with the area.'

'Of course. It'll be a good while yet though, so sit back and enjoy the ride. They call this bus the Happy Wanderer because we call in at nearly every village between here and Land's End.' He went on his way whistling cheerfully and exchanging remarks with a number of the passengers, whom he clearly knew.

It was Sunday morning and Alma was travelling in response to a luncheon invitation from Alan Bricken, who had written to suggest she came over to 'see the place and what we get up to'. She'd decided to go, partly because she wanted to see him again, and partly because she was keen to take any opportunity to get to know her new home better.

And the next fifty minutes were fascinating as the bus ground along, threading a line between the dramatic, rock-bound coast and secretive valleys where tiny villages lay buried in stunted trees and thick bracken. There was a strong wind blowing and at times she could see great white rollers crashing onto the rocks in an awesome display of natural power. The contrast with suburban Hampstead beggared belief and she shivered at the thought of just how far and how fast she had come. Less than two months ago she had been planning a quiet Christmas in Whitton Road and now here she was, heading deep into the unknown, to meet a man she barely knew.

It was both thrilling and terrifying, but Alma sensed that it was all happening for a reason. Gladys had always been waiting for her; it was just that she hadn't known it. But now she was determined to see it through and succeed, even if the constant stream of new things took some getting used to.

As the bus pulled to a halt next to a pair of low slate-roofed cottages she stared downwards, barely seeing the couple who got off as thoughts tumbled round her head.

She'd searched Valentine Wragge's room and had drawn a blank. There was nothing to indicate he was engaging in any unpatriotic behaviour. The next job was to do the same with George Weaver's quarters, which James had said he'd do, with a firm smile. She leaned her head against the glass and hoped that he wasn't a spy. Since writing the letter to Jack Waring, she had allowed herself to consider her future with regards to the opposite sex, and had decided that, in all modesty, she was in a strong position. Not least because, to her astonishment, she was well-off. Not wealthy in the way the guests in the hotel were; she had no great estate or stock market investments, but nonetheless, she had money behind her and that was most definitely a change.

And that knowledge made her feel different, even with strong, attractive men like George Weaver, who could probably pick and choose their romances. She'd raised her face to look the world in the eye and liked herself for it. Also, she better understood the education that she'd received at St Joseph's. Miss Bede's girls, she now realised, were expected to take their place in the empire and deal with whatever that involved, wherever they were in the world.

She smiled. *I'm only in Cornwall, Miss Bede. But it's foreign to me.*

'Here we are then, miss.' The conductor's voice interrupted her thoughts, and she stood up as the bus came to halt. 'We go back at three ten and four thirty from here. Don't miss the second one or you'll be waiting all night. And that's a very fetching beret if you don't mind me saying so.' He gave her a nod and a smile as she stepped down.

The bus pulled away and she saw Alan Bricken waiting at the top of a lane. His smile of welcome pushed any lingering thoughts of George Weaver from her mind.

'Hello. It's nice to see you. We're half a mile down this way – I hope that's all right.' He gestured to where the lane disappeared between high banks.

She smiled. 'A walk will be lovely. Are we near the coast?'

'Oh aye, there's a fine beach down here. We swim in the summer.' And with that they set off, as the Cornish wind hissed in the rowan trees above them.

Fifteen minutes later they emerged from the tunnel of the lane into an open valley about two hundred yards wide. On the left the hillside rose steeply in a jumble of granite outcrops and gorse, flecked yellow with early flowers.

'There's a path up there. It leads out onto the clifftop. We can have a look after lunch if you like.' Alan's voice was in her ear, and it needed to be, because the wind was stronger and there was an angry background roar that Alma couldn't identify.

'That's where we are,' he continued, pointing ahead.

She'd seen the building already. It stood on the right of the valley, backed by steep green fields that were divided by wide, stony banks. A large plain white structure, with a central block and wings on either side. To her surprise – and incongruous in that wild, almost primeval setting – a pair of tennis courts lay in front of the building. In one corner a flagpole was bucking in the wind, its straining flag showing the letters ETC.

A gust hit them, and Alma reached up to grab her beret as Alan continued, 'The smaller building beyond is the Exiles Club. It's our clubhouse. There's a snooker table in there. We live and work in the big house and spend our time off shift in the other one. There's nothing else here apart from a cottage or two and a farm on the hill.'

'Why is it all here?' she asked.

'It's where the empire's undersea telegraph cables come ashore. From all over the world. I don't know why they chose here, but once one was put in the others followed.' He shrugged.

'What's that noise?'

'The roaring?'

'Yes.'

'Come and see. Then we'll go in, and you can meet some of the other fellows.' He glanced at his pocket watch. 'We've half an hour till dinner, yet.'

He led the way past the house and on down the lane until suddenly they were standing at the top of a short, steep slope, looking out over a scene that took Alma's breath away.

Porthcurno beach lay before them, a sandy cove two hundred yards wide with sheer cliffs towering over either side. Huge waves were pounding the beach creating a maelstrom of blue, white and yellow and as she stared the sun came out, lighting the scene as though spotlights were shining down from the cliffs. Out on the point a huge aquamarine roller thumped into the rocks, throwing spray into the air. Caught by the wind it soared higher and splattered against the rock face near the top.

Alma was stunned. The combination of the roar of the sea, the salt in the air and the kaleidoscope of colour as the great slabs of water rolled into the cove were beyond her wildest imagination. She had simply never seen raw nature like this.

A wild exhilaration swept over her, and she turned to Alan, laughing. 'And you said you swim here?' They were holding hands, she suddenly realised.

He grinned and called back. 'It's different in the summer. On a calm day, I reckon it's the most beautiful place on earth.'

'Better than the Cocos Islands?'

He nodded. 'Oh aye. To my mind anyway.' A huge whump echoed across the cove, clearly audible against the background roar. They turned to look as a column of spray rose to the height of the cliff top and disappeared inland, borne on the gale. 'They have to wash the salt off the windows on our place after a day like this,' he said. 'And that's a quarter of a mile inland.'

Alma was utterly intoxicated. 'It's superb. Magnificent. Thank you for showing me,' she shouted.

They stood in silence for ten minutes, just watching, then he squeezed her hand and spoke into her ear. 'Lunchtime.'

They returned up the lane and stopped outside the white building. 'Zodiac House, it's called,' Alan said, 'and that's Mercury House, the superintendent's quarters.' He nodded across the valley to another building that Alma had missed earlier. 'I'll lead the way then,' he added and climbed the five steps that led into a high-ceilinged hall.

A few minutes later she found herself sitting with Alan at a table and fielding some good-natured joshing from the other six telegraph workers who were clearly excited to be entertaining a young woman. Glancing round she saw that apart from the superintendent's wife she was the only woman dining in a room full of about eighty men.

No wonder they're giving me some attention.

She noticed an army officer in a kilt enter and take his place at the top table.

'Who's that?' she asked Alan.

'That is the Highland Light Infantry,' he declared, the irony plain in his voice. 'Lieutenant Graham. They arrived not long after war was declared to guard the place. They're not that popular to be honest. Things didn't get off to a good start because one of the privates got drunk on his second day and threatened to shoot one of his fellow soldiers. A corporal shot him dead when he started waving a loaded rifle around. Justifiable homicide apparently.'

'Good Lord. What happened to him?'

'He's buried in the churchyard in St Levan, up on the hill. They're billeted in the theatre, which doesn't help as we can't use it for our reviews. Still, at least they're here I suppose, although if you watch them doing drill on the tennis courts it's obvious they're pretty green. And sometimes there's no one here at all. It's all very relaxed to be honest.'

'They're not the Grenadier Guards, that's for sure,' one of the other men remarked.

The meal was plain but substantial and well cooked. A joint of mutton, potatoes and vegetables followed by a choice of tapioca or fruit tart. She noticed the former, which they called frog spawn, had few takers and the reason behind this became clear when a large bowl of thick yellow cream was placed on the table by a serving girl to cheers of delight from the men.

Alan grinned at her. 'Our Sunday treat from the farm on the hill,' he remarked. 'Help yourself – there's plenty.'

Alma had never heard of clotted cream, never mind tried it, but encouraged by her fellow diners she scooped a spoonful onto her apple tart. It was delicious and she made a mental note to suggest to Mrs Wilson that it became a feature of the menu at the hotel.

Cheerful conversation filled the big room and at their table the talk ebbed and flowed noisily. One of the men was deeply tanned and it became apparent that he'd just returned from the West Indies. Other exotic place names rolled off their tongues, along with details of how they filled their time in the valley when they weren't working. There was a drama society and a rifles club. They shot on the beach at low tide apparently. And climbed the rocks, which they called 'spadging', and took photographs and went for walks.

Alma was left with an impression of an adventurous bunch of young men who worked hard at their training but managed to find the time to enjoy themselves. Seeing Alan clearly at ease in the merry group, she found herself increasingly drawn to him, but in the back of her mind the idea that he could be off to somewhere, anywhere in fact, around the world, remained a nagging doubt in her mind.

Because I am bound to Falmouth now, as surely as if I have a ball and a chain.

The thought came back to her as she sat on the bus on the way back to Penzance. They'd finished lunch and he'd shown her round Zodiac House and the machinery where the tiny electrical impulses that came from Australia or Bombay or anywhere else were turned back into words. She'd found it fascinating, and when they'd waited for the bus at the top of the lane, he'd given her a quick peck on the cheek. Nothing too pushy, just a sign of his interest and affection. And she hadn't minded at all.

She stared through the bus window at the darkening landscape for a long time, then picked up a newspaper someone had left on the seat. The headline was uncompromising: *Germany declares war zone around Britain*.

In the dim lights she read the article. The German High Command had announced that unrestricted submarine warfare would now take place and any vessel, of any national flag, that was found in British waters could be sunk without warning. She thought about what that meant and was shocked. *Surely the Germans won't attack neutral shipping?*

'Dreadful isn't it.' The voice came from behind her, and she turned to see a middle-aged man wearing a flat cap. He nodded at the paper and added, 'They mean to starve us out.'

'Really?'

'That's it for sure. We import most of our food from the empire. If the ships can't get through, then we'll get hungry pretty quickly. Up until now they've only been after our vessels, but now any ship is likely to be sunk if she's spotted by the Huns.'

'But surely they can't just sink an American ship for example.'

He shrugged. 'They're saying they will. Although I don't think the Yanks will like it.'

* * *

Later that night, as the grandfather clock in the entrance hall of the hotel chimed midnight, Excalibur quietly entered his consulting room and locked the door behind him.

Ironically, the news about the unrestricted war zone had infuriated him as much as the British, because he had spent time setting up the system to smuggle coded letters in both directions on the *Lisbon Rose*. But the danger of her being sunk was now very real and he was sure that she would stop running with immediate effect.

He needed a new way to communicate with Berlin and for the last hour he had been mentally preparing for what he was about to do. It had started in December when he'd received the dreadful news via Lisbon that Leo, his younger brother, had been killed. His grief had been intense, like a physical shock, and he'd spent hour after hour in quiet contemplation as his mind drifted and swirled around his childhood memories. They'd run wild in the woods and open fields of the estate, left largely to their own devices by a father who was high up in the government and a mother whose clairvoyance was the major purpose in her life. Even when they'd left home and gone their separate ways the bond had been there, but then the devastating news had arrived.

Just before Christmas, Excalibur had woken in his room in the middle of the night. His grief was still raw but even so he realised that the sweeping, soaring, emotional fireworks he was feeling were beyond normality. Intense memories of his beloved younger brother seemed to be bouncing around inside his head uncontrollably, almost to the point of pain. It went on for what seemed like an age but then suddenly, after the crescendo, there had been peace.

And silence. A profound, expectant silence.

Eyes closed tightly in the darkness he had tentatively whispered, 'Are you there?' and the great warm flood of love and affection that had washed over him had been all the answer he'd needed. Then, as he lay motionless and tearful, his brother had started to speak to him.

From that moment the kernel of an idea had slowly grown in his mind. But today's news about the submarines had crystalised his thoughts into a plan. A plan so astonishing that nearly everyone in Berlin would have laughed with derision at the very idea. But Excalibur wasn't laughing. Because, like Gladys Timperley, he was the genuine article.

He could connect with the spirit world like one of Marconi's radio sets. He could transmit and he could receive, and he could relay messages. And so could his dead brother.

He sat motionless, eyes closed in the consultation room and, after five minutes of silent contemplation, a gentle smile appeared on his face and he murmured, 'Hello, Leo.'

Half an hour later as he completed his task, something occurred to him. The code book was now redundant and needed to be removed from its hiding place and disposed of. This was the perfect moment. He left the consulting room and walked to the foyer. At the foot of the stairs he stopped and listened carefully for any signs of movement, but the hotel was as still as a crypt.

Making no noise, he entered the nook and crossed to the dresser. It was the work of a moment to kneel, open the cupboard door and remove the book. He stood up and flicked through it, a thin smile on his face.

You've served me well, Herr Nietzsche, in the battle against the arrogant British.

But even as this satisfying thought came to mind, he was appalled to hear sudden footsteps in the kitchen and three seconds later Alma appeared in the doorway.

'George!' she said, clearly rather aware that she was in her night attire.

'Good evening. This is a pleasant surprise,' he remarked. 'What a fetching dressing gown.'

But even though he sounded at ease, inside he was humming with tension. In the brief moments before she'd appeared he'd

134

kicked the cupboard door shut and dropped the book onto the seat of a battered armchair that stood with its back to the doorway next to where he was standing.

If Alma comes into the room she'll see it. No doubt at all.

He walked towards her, subtly blocking her way into the nook. 'Tell me, Alma how do you light the gas ring? I was just thinking a cup of tea would go down well, but to my shame I'm sorry to say I have no idea about the technicalities of the kitchen.' He delivered a warmly apologetic grin. 'Would you mind showing me?'

'Men!' Running her eyes over his handsome face, Alma returned his smile. 'You are all a bit hopeless when it comes to looking after yourselves, aren't you. That's what I've come down for. Come on.' She turned and led the way back into the kitchen. Weaver followed, eyes narrow, thinking hard.

Ten minutes later, having seemed to have rather enjoyed her unexpected nocturnal encounter, Alma headed back to her room, leaving him in the kitchen. He swiftly retrieved the book from next door and made sure the cupboard door was shut, then returned to his consulting room and reviewed the incident in his mind. Miss Alma Timperley had had a narrow escape, he mused. Had she seen the book, he would have killed her, there and then, but as it was she suspected nothing; he was sure of that. And there was no doubt she cut a very attractive figure with her neat features and short dark hair.

His smile was very different to the one Alma had seen. Germany needed him and he couldn't run the risk of another slip-up. The girl would have to be brought under his control.

And I'll do that the way I always do it.

* * *

The following night the same moon that illuminated the calm waters below Pendennis Castle was also shining onto the wide lawns of a fine country house thirty miles east of Berlin. Standing at her bedroom window, Fräulein Charlotte Weber stared out towards the leafless silver-lit trees that edged the grass three hundred yards away.

Charlotte had been a clairvoyant since her eighth birthday, fifty years ago. At least, that was the day it began. Because as she lay in bed drowsily reflecting on the delightful celebrations she had enjoyed during the day, she realised that there was someone else in the room. Someone she didn't know, but who had come to wish her happy birthday too.

At the breakfast table the following morning her cheerful observation that Uncle Rolf had come to see her in the night caused great consternation to her parents and to the serving maid, who dropped the coffee pot. Her mother's brother was the black sheep of the family and never mentioned. So Charlotte could not have known of him.

And there was also the consideration that he had been dead for seventeen years.

Nevertheless, Charlotte was adamant that he had been in her room, and she described him with such accuracy that her stunned parents could do little more than accept the child's account and hurriedly move the conversation on to more prosaic matters.

But Uncle Rolf came calling more than once and, as she passed through her teenage years, Charlotte explored these intriguing aspects of her life in increasing detail. She was never scared, just curious. Fascinated by the idea that bodily death was not the end and keen to know more about the other side, she found a mentor, a genuine medium, who helped her develop and channel her innate abilities.

By the time she married she was sure that the main focus of her life, new husband notwithstanding, would be the spirit world and life beyond the tiresome physical constraints of the earth. And that was how it had been. She had produced two sons but had to acknowledge that their upbringing had been a little looser than those of their friends' children. Her husband was climbing the greasy pole of German politics and spent much time in Berlin. She was sure he had a mistress tucked away in an apartment somewhere in the city, but he was discreet, and she found it easy to close her mind to such distractions.

Because Charlotte's primary interest was the spirit world. She worked privately as a medium for people she liked, helping them to deal with the death of loved ones, but much of her time was spent in solitary contemplation, drifting in another dimension that was boundless in its interest and potential. It was the place, she now understood, where the souls of the dead resided until they returned to the earth in a new life.

There were rumours of course. Conforming was expected in the tightly regulated society of the German upper classes, and Charlotte Weber became a byword for bohemian behaviour. At parties people eyed her, and spoke behind their hands, and her husband's career suffered for it.

And finally, inevitably, there were suggestions of madness. It was the women who started the rumours. The ambitious wives of her husband's political enemies, who saw an opportunity to clear the way for their own men and took it. Whispers circulated that what had once been seen as amusing eccentricity was, in reality, insanity.

And in the cut-throat corridors of the Kaiser's palace those whispers grew to the point they could not be ignored.

Her husband returned to their estate and warned his wife about the damage she was doing. He pleaded with her to desist.

But by then Charlotte was living in two worlds not one. Her sons had grown up and left home. She was lonely and isolated, and she refused.

Two days later, after a final shouting match in her bedroom, he had told her that he was moving permanently to Berlin. She would remain on the estate and not leave it or communicate with the outside world without his permission. It was that or the asylum, he insisted. And to back it up he introduced two new staff, a large middle-aged ex-soldier who would ensure her compliance with the new regime, and the man's wife, a grim-faced woman who henceforth would be her companion.

To his surprise, his wife accepted these new arrangements with little fuss. She loved her home and the grounds and had little interest in what happened outside its high stone walls. And in any event, she could float away to a place beyond his comprehension whenever she chose.

So Charlotte settled down to a life that was, in many respects, not much different from the one she had been living. By now her eldest son was living in England and the youngest had joined the army. They wrote to her, and she wrote back. Her husband returned to Berlin and started to repair the damage, giving out that his wife was ill and confined indefinitely to their country house. She was not expected to reappear in society, he made clear. And the wives of his enemies frowned in sympathy, and expressed their deep sorrow at her condition, and cursed quietly at his sure-footed solution to the problem they had worked so hard to create.

Denied newspapers, she was unaware of the assassination of Archduke Ferdinand and his wife in Sarajevo in June 1914. As events rapidly unfolded in July, Charlotte wandered the estate, cut off from the outside world and blissfully unaware of the cataclysmic rush to war that was engulfing all of Europe. When

Germany invaded France and Belgium on the 4th of August and Britain declared war on her country, she sat and read a book all day as the clock ticked comfortably in her sitting room.

And although she started to receive letters from her youngest son describing the conflict and his role in it, as she rode slowly along a snowy bridle path one morning ten days before Christmas, she had no idea that Leo had just been shot dead in a field not far from Ypres.

But twenty-four hours later she knew. Because in the middle of the night he came to her.

And now, as the moon slipped behind a cloud and the distant trees were suddenly reduced to shadows, she felt a shiver down her back and raised her head, sensing the air like a hunting vixen. It was a summoning. Like the distant ringing of a telephone bell. With a faint smile of anticipation, she left the window and made her way to the room where she worked.

There she calmed and focused herself, settling into the reflective state that made her receptive to the other side and its many opportunities. An observer would have thought that nothing happened for the next ten minutes as she sat, eyes closed, motionless and poised, hands clasped together on her lap.

Then she inhaled slowly, breathed out and reached for the Ouija board. Placing her hand on the worn planchet, she whispered, 'Hello, Leo, my darling.'

* * *

At the crack of dawn the following morning the house's elderly butler cycled unsteadily into the local village and caught the first train to Berlin, where he posted a letter given to him by his mistress. He understood he was breaking the rules Herr Weber had prescribed, but he did it anyway.

Charlottle Weber was a woman he greatly respected, and it was her house, not his.

The German postal service delivered it to an address just off Unter den Linden by six o'clock the same day and two hours later, thanks to the highly efficient internal postal system, it arrived on the desk of Captain Felix Muller, deputy head of the German overseas intelligence service.

It was on plain paper, unsigned, and handwritten on a single side. The writing was neat and cursive. An educated woman's hand, he guessed. And the contents were intriguing. According to the writer, the British General Sir John Buchanan and his Highland Division from III Corps were moving from Ypres to Armentières on the 10th of February. And it appeared the information had come from his wife, Lady Fiona Buchanan.

He leaned back and tapped his fingers on the desk. The Highlanders were developing a reputation as crack troops and the news suggested an attack near Armentières might be planned, so this was valuable intelligence.

But who was the source?

Muller was not aware of any female German agents working in Britain. The mass arrest and incarceration of German nationals by the British government at the start of the war had ensured sympathisers were locked away where they could do no harm. The one light in the darkness had been the regular reports from Excalibur, but with the declaration of unrestricted submarine warfare he knew the *Lisbon Rose* service had ceased and he was resigned to that channel being closed, at least for the moment.

Do we have another? Someone new? They must be highly placed to get hold of such gossip from a general's wife. How had they got the message out?

He examined the envelope. It was simply addressed to Military Headquarters in Berlin and had been postmarked at the central post office in Berlin, apparently by someone who wished to conceal their identity.

With a sigh he wrote a note to the German High Command advising them of the information he had received and asking to be told if subsequent events proved it to be accurate.

Chapter Twelve

Encouraged by Alma's successful visit to Porthcurno, Alan Bricken decided it would be fun to call in on her unannounced. So the following Saturday he caught the early bus to Penzance and was in Falmouth by half past ten.

He asked for directions to the hotel and followed the footpath from the town station across the open ground and up the hill. Surprised and a little intimidated by the building's high façade, he entered to find the foyer deserted and after a moment's hesitation rang the bell on the desk. As he did so a man in his early thirties emerged from a corridor to the side of reception.

'Excuse me, I'm looking for Miss Timperley,' Bricken said.

The man stopped and looked at him with clear blue eyes of alarming intensity. 'I'm not sure where she is, I'm afraid.'

'Ah, I've just popped in to see her. I was in town . . .' He tailed off, suddenly unsure of himself as a finely dressed woman and her maid appeared on the half landing.

'Where is Mrs Banks?' she announced, proceeding downwards.

'Here I am, my lady.' A woman came through the office door.

'I shall be lunching out. Will you summon a cab?'

'Certainly.' She turned to Alan and said, 'What can I do for you, sir?'

'I was hoping to see Miss Timperley?'

'You've missed her, I'm afraid. She won't be back until mid-afternoon.' Catching the woman's eye she lifted the telephone and called the taxi office in the town. A brief conversation ensued then she replaced the receiver and said, 'Ten minutes, Lady Antrim, will you take a seat in the lounge?'

Apparently curious about the visitor who was interested in Alma, the man said, 'It seems you've had a wasted journey. Will you join me for a cup of coffee?' He gestured towards the door through which Lady Antrim was disappearing.

'Aye, all right then, I'm Alan Bricken.' He offered his hand.

'George Weaver.' They shook and within five minutes were settled by a large window overlooking the front garden and the visitor placed a foolscap envelope on the table.

George didn't say anything, but looked at it, a question in his eyes. 'It's a picture I did for Alma,' Alan replied.

'Oh really? You're an artist then? May I have a look?'

'If you like.' He opened the envelope and handed over the contents. It was a sketch of Alma done in pencil and then skilfully filled out in watercolour. She was looking directly at the viewer, a small smile on her lips and, as he admired it, Weaver realised two things. Alan Bricken was a talented artist. And he had a rival.

'That is absolutely splendid,' he said with a smile and handed it back. 'I'm sure she'll be delighted.'

'Do you think so? I worried it might be a bit forward – you know.'

'Not at all. Now tell me, how did you meet?'

An hour later they parted cordially on the front steps of the hotel and Weaver returned to the table where he lit a cigarette and blew the smoke out thoughtfully. Bricken was a pleasant fellow and clearly keen on Alma, which was not ideal given his plans. It was time to move things along in that department, he mused.

But it was the chat they'd had about his job that had really caught Weaver's attention. Even though he'd been in Falmouth for some years, he had no idea that there was a telegraph station at Porthcurno. Certainly not one of such importance. It sounded like a fine job for someone young and keen to the see the world, and he'd laughed delightedly at Bricken's tale of the German raid on the Cocos Islands and the sinking of the Emden. The young man had been keen to show him his shiny brass lapel badge, which had been issued by the government to protect men doing essential war work from criticism for not volunteering.

'Brand new these are,' he'd said proudly. 'I've had a bit of trouble from one or two people about not signing up, but this will show them I'm doing my bit.'

And Weaver had congratulated him and agreed that there were many ways to serve the country's cause. But now, sitting alone in the beautifully furnished lounge, his eyes narrowed as he allowed his mind to wander over all kinds of possibilities.

* * *

When Alma returned from her meetings with various suppliers in the town, she found a note pushed under her door.

Miss Timperley, would you care to dine with me this evening? I suggest the Fleurs de Lys at 7.00 p.m. and will order a cab for six forty-five unless I hear to the contrary.
    Yours, George Weaver

She read it thoughtfully, sitting in her armchair with a cup of tea. The restaurant was reputedly one of the best in the town and she would be interested to see how it compared to the hotel.

And a change of scene for supper would be nice. But as she made these little justifications in her mind, she was also honest enough to admit that the prospect of dinner opposite handsome George Weaver was an intriguing prospect, whatever the venue. She decided to accept and then spent a pleasant half hour considering what to wear.

With her new wealth she had upgraded her wardrobe, not least because her status as the hotel's proprietor required a level of presentation that her existing clothes did not meet – the clientele did not expect to deal with a woman dressed as an office clerk. She had also decided that Mrs Banks, as the assistant manager, should be given a clothes allowance, so the pair of them had visited E J Reynolds on Killigrew Street. It claimed to be the premier ladies' outfitters in the town and the manager had been more than happy to open an account when Alma explained the circumstances. And he had been even happier when he waved them goodbye an hour later, promising to ensure their various new outfits were adjusted and delivered the following day.

Having finally settled on a burgundy dress and matching jacket she had a long bath, washed her hair, and thought about the evening to come.

Does George have romance in mind? And if so, how do I feel about that?

There was also Alan Bricken to consider. Gracie had mentioned that he had called in to see her and she thought that was sweet. And the picture he'd left was lovely. Really lovely. He obviously liked her and she liked him. The visit to the Eastern Telegraph Company had reinforced her feeling that he was a solid and likeable man, with a decent future before him. Jack Waring had been nice too, but she now realised that her lingering doubts about him were because, unacknowledged in the back of her mind, she knew

146

that he wanted a wife to look after him. *A mother with benefits, to ease his passage through life.*

He'd settled on Alma, but in some ways it could have been anyone.

She swirled the hot water around and reflected that Alan Bricken was not like that at all. He would not be a liability. But as she lay there, one scene kept coming back into her mind. After their lunch he'd shown her a big wall map, ten feet long, in the main instrument room. It was of the world with the empire marked in red, and black lines running across the sea to show the cable routes. Relay stations were marked in blue, and he'd proudly pointed out the Cocos Islands. But Alma's overriding reaction as she stood there had been the thought that in three months or even less, Alan could be anywhere on the map. And for two years. He might be an interesting man, but there was no getting away from that.

George Weaver, by contrast, was clearly well settled in Falmouth. And he was also an interesting man; there was no getting away from that either. Thoughtfully she stood up, dried herself, dressed, and went downstairs to see what was going on.

* * *

Two hours later Valentine Wragge appeared in the entrance hall just as George Weaver was holding the hotel's front door open for Alma. In the gloom a horse-drawn cab was waiting in the turning circle, and he watched them climb in before addressing Gracie Banks who was behind the counter.

'Are they going out together?' he asked in surprise.

'It looks that way, Mr Wragge.'

'On an . . .' he paused and reached for the appropriate word: 'assignation?'

'That's really not our business is it. And I can't say I know anyway.'

He stared at the door. 'They were dressed up though.'

She nodded. 'They were that.'

'Well really. It hasn't taken him long, has it. The woman's only been here a few weeks.'

She looked at him cooly. 'It takes two to tango. Perhaps she's keen as well.'

'But I understood she had a gentleman caller only this morning.'

'She did, and he even left a picture of her.' A smile appeared on Mrs Banks's face. 'Do you have an interest yourself, Valentine? Only there seems to be a queue developing, so my advice would be to make your feelings clear at the earliest opportunity.'

He drew himself up. 'I can assure you I do not. Miss Timperley is young enough to be my daughter.'

'Well then, we'll have to let them get on with it, won't we. Good evening.' With that she turned and disappeared into the office.

* * *

Alma enjoyed her evening. The food at the restaurant was delicious and it was very pleasant to have dinner without feeling she was being covertly inspected by guests as *the girl who had inherited.*

George was very different to both Jack Waring and Alan Bricken, but his intensity was tempered with considerable charm and, as their eyes met in the low light of the dining room, gentle shock waves rippled through her.

She briefly wondered if he would have felt the same had they met *Before Gladys* as she now characterised her former life in Hampstead, but decided such speculation was pointless. A door

148

had opened, she had gone through it and was rapidly becoming more and more absorbed in the life of the hotel. She needed to look forward, not back.

George told her about growing up in Switzerland and his increasing interest in spiritualism and eventual move to England, with the intention of meeting Gladys Timperley.

'What was she like? I've seen a photograph and read a magazine article about her, but in the flesh I mean.'

He thought for a moment. 'She was a remarkable woman. A genuine medium who could communicate with the dead. She had a spirit that made her unique, if you will forgive the pun' – he smiled across the table – 'although perhaps I see the same thing in you, Miss Timperley. Have you had any spiritualist experiences?'

'Yes, some.' She didn't offer anything further.

The man opposite watched her careful eyes for a long moment, then remarked, 'I thought that perhaps you had. And I wonder if you are considering a more active role in the work at the hotel?'

Put on the spot, she grasped the nettle. 'I was taught by a gifted medium when I was a teenager, but I drifted away from it.' She went on to explain the role Miss Bede had played in her life at St Joseph's school and the regular séances she had participated in. Then she told him about the jealousy she had experienced from the other girls in the group and the difficulties they had caused for her in the school.

'They did not like the favouritism that the headmistress displayed towards me, and the result was a rather unpleasant whispering campaign amongst my fellow pupils, orchestrated by them. Although the headmistress encouraged me, I decided in the end that it would be better if I resigned from such activities. And it worked by and large. The girls who were competing for her approval were satisfied to have a rival removed from the field and the unpleasant treatment stopped.'

She gave a little shrug, adding, 'Miss Bede was frustrated, but I think I made the right decision. And I carried on with it. Since I left school I haven't been to the Hall of the Dead.'

His eyes crinkled. 'Ah, yes, the Hall of the Dead. Gladys called it that too.'

Alma nodded. 'She mentioned it in a letter she left me.'

'A letter?' He was still smiling but she felt his interest quicken.

'It was amongst some notes about running the hotel.'

'Ah yes, of course.'

There was a brief silence and Alma had a strong sense he would have liked to know more about the letter, but instead he remarked, 'School can be a difficult place. I recall a very unwise attempt to discuss the spirit world with some of my fellow pupils, which led to a nickname that I did not welcome.'

'What was that?'

'*Der Spuk*, which I suppose translates as "the spook".'

'Oh dear.' A faint alarm bell rang in Alma's mind. She'd studied languages at St Joseph's and the word sounded German to her, but before she could question it, George moved the conversation along.

'Quite.' He nodded. 'From your rivals' reaction at your own school am I to infer that you displayed some talent during these séances?'

'Yes. I was a skilled clairvoyant during my teenage years.'

Her direct and unequivocal response made him raise his eyebrows in surprise. 'I see. You sound very sure, if I may make the observation.'

Instead of answering this directly she said, 'Gladys thought you were the same. Is that true?'

He nodded, his eyes fixed on hers. 'It is.'

'So we suffer from the same affliction, Mr Weaver. One that can only be discussed amongst those with open minds.'

'That is true, although the visitors to the hotel most definitely fall into that category.'

'Indeed.' Curious to see if he knew his colleague's secret she added, 'What about Mr Wragge. Is he talented in the same way?'

He grinned, genuinely amused. Alma thought it was like watching a wolf who'd heard a good joke. 'Valentine? He is certainly talented, but a genuine medium? I think not.'

Rather enjoying her secret knowledge she said, 'I sat in on his first session with Lady Watson. He was very convincing.'

'To the lady in question perhaps. But were you convinced?'

She shook her head. 'No. I felt nothing. When a spirit is present my body reacts.'

He eyed her and she felt his interest. 'How does your body react, Alma?' he asked quietly. 'For example, when Alexander Watson appeared to you in the hall?'

It was the first time he'd used her given name. She looked at him but said nothing, so he continued, 'That business with Lady Watson's son was all round the hotel in less than an hour. Please, Alma, I really am interested in your experiences. Gladys and I used to talk about it all the time.'

She found this believable. Genuine clairvoyants were rare creatures and she thought it was highly likely that, living and working together as they had, her mother and the charismatic Mr Weaver would have discussed their work.

'I imagine I am like you, George. I can visit the Hall of the Dead and commune with the souls that reside there.'

He nodded. 'The same. And young Mr Watson?'

'Sometimes I act as an unwitting conduit. It's rare, but spirits can appear without being invited, if I may put it like that.'

'And he was one such, keen to see his mother for the last time perhaps?'

'Perhaps.'

'You must be powerful.'

'So I have been told. I spoke the truth when I said I hadn't visited the Hall of the Dead since my schooldays, but there have been other Alexander Watsons, so to speak, and I've always tried to help them.' She took a deep breath. 'My word it must be getting late.' She looked around. The room was almost empty.

'Is it all right to call you Alma? When we are alone together?'

'Yes, George, that will be acceptable. When we are alone.'

'And do you think we might be alone together again before too long?'

'Yes, I think that might be arranged.'

'Then I am a happy man.' He gestured to a waiter. 'The bill and a taxi please.'

Later, as she lay in bed turning the evening over in her mind, his remark about *Der Spuk* came back to her. George had told James Nascent that French was his original language and he only spoke a few words of German. Was that true or was it a lie? Was he actually more fluent than he had admitted? She mulled the question over and decided that she would mention it again to him when a suitable opportunity arose.

And one would because, as they travelled back from the restaurant, she had agreed to have dinner with him again. He'd asked her when the cab was stationary under a gas lamp and its light had thrown his face into sharp relief in the darkness. His smile when she said yes had carried a degree of intimacy that even now, an hour later, sent little thrills through her.

There's something about you, Mr Weaver, that is rather hard to ignore.

* * *

The following morning in a gusting wind and spiteful rain, the man in question walked to the library. Since the discussion in the hotel kitchen after the bombing raid, he'd been wondering about the *Persian Knight* and wanted to find out more. At the desk he asked the bespectacled young man a question.

'I'm looking to identify the details of a particular ship. Its size and tonnage and so on. Would you have any reference book of that nature?'

'Indeed, we do, sir. That'll be *Lloyd's Register of Shipping*. You'll find it on the shelves around the corner.'

Weaver located the thick volume and took it to one of the tables. It didn't take long to find the *Persian Knight*. She was four years old and owned by the British and Persian Oil Company. Her gross tonnage was twelve thousand five hundred and her standard crew was seventeen.

Under the capitals P. K. he made a note of the salient details in his pocketbook and returned the volume to the shelf.

As he approached the door a voice said, 'Did you find what you needed, sir?'

He nodded to the assistant. 'I did. Thank you for your help.' Then a thought occurred to him, and he asked, 'Do you have a large-scale map of the coast between Penzance and Land's End?'

'We have the Ordnance Survey series. I'll show you.' He escorted Weaver to another part of the library and consulted a shelf of maps. 'Yes, here we are.'

Weaver took the map back to his table and unfolded it. Penzance and Newlyn lay on the right-hand side, and he traced his finger westwards along the coastline, through Mousehole and Lamorna, and finally Treen, unwittingly mirroring the route of the Happy Wanderer bus that Alma had taken on her Sunday lunch outing.

He peered at the map, unable to see a village called Porthcurno anywhere. When he got to Land's End with no success he went over to the helpful man at the desk and asked if he had a magnifying glass. This duly obtained, he returned to the table and began a careful examination of the coastline, working back towards Penzance.

And there it was. A narrow valley, steep-sided, he guessed by the contours, with a sandy beach at the bottom that was part of a wider bay. A hamlet called St Levan lay on the headland to the west and there were a couple of buildings shown in the valley but nothing more. It looked like a remote place.

Without realising, he put his finger on the exact place where Alma and her friend had stood as the rough sea poured into the cove.

So there you are, Alan Bricken.

With a lot to think about he returned to the hotel, hat pointed downwards, and coat tightly buttoned against the weather.

* * *

In his office in Berlin, Felix Muller received a telephone call from a colleague in the military high command.

'That note you sent last week, about the British General Buchanan and his Highland Division.'

'Yes, I remember.' Muller waited.

'I think you were right. Our units around Armentières report some clashes with Scottish soldiers and air reconnaissance seems to confirm it. How did you know?'

'Just part of our general intelligence-gathering activities, Major. It looked that way, so I thought I'd better tell you.'

A grunt of satisfaction came down the line. 'A lot of people here at headquarters don't hold with what you do, spies and the like. But I say anything that helps us win the war is worth it. You let me know straight away if you get any more titbits like that, you hear me, Muller?'

'I do, sir, and I certainly will.' He replaced the receiver and leaned back in his chair. *So the note was accurate.* He crossed to the safe, removed it, and took it back to his desk. Sadly it was as uninformative as before. There was nothing to indicate the author or where it had come from, beyond the Berlin postmark.

How does a German spy know Lady Fiona Buchanan well enough to gossip with her, and how did you get the message out of Britain?

He sat at his desk for a long time, with the piece of paper in his hand, but finally he had to regretfully conclude that he had absolutely no idea.

* * *

In the police station in Falmouth, Sergeant Trewin knocked and entered the office of his superior. It was well known amongst the local constabulary that the two men did not get on and he was not looking forward to the encounter. Inspector Luke had a few months to go before his retirement and had been anticipating that glorious moment for the previous decade. Long resigned to the fact that he would go no further in his career, the inspector was entirely focused on making his life as easy as possible.

The outbreak of war had greatly disturbed the regular and undemanding rhythm of his working days and the unwelcome news a fortnight earlier that there had been a murder on his patch was not seen by Luke as an opportunity to excel. Quite the reverse.

'What progress with the Diss girl?' he asked, mustering a semblance of interest as he stirred his tea.

Trewin stood to attention in front of the desk, stared past his shoulder, and made his report. 'We've been pursuing enquiries amongst people present in Arwenack Street on the night of the raid but I'm afraid there's precious little to go on. As you know we only have one witness, the nurse Sally Regan, who spoke briefly to a man carrying a girl in the immediate aftermath of the bombing. She sent him down to the King's Pipe, but we don't know what happened after that. Or how the body got to Trevethan School Hospital for that matter. It was pretty chaotic down there and we haven't found anyone else with anything useful to say.

'And the girl doesn't think she'd recognise him again, anyway,' he added, gloomily.

'No other suspects?'

Trewin gave a rather uneasy little shrug. 'I'm afraid not, sir. She lived a quiet life and her parents said she wasn't walking out with anyone.'

'What about putting out a public statement asking for further witnesses?'

The sergeant frowned and moved uneasily on his feet. 'As you know, sir, our plan is to keep the fact that the police know Kate Diss was murdered a secret, so as not to put the killer on his guard. Asking if anyone saw a man carrying her body would rather let the cat out of the bag.'

'Always assuming that man was the murderer and not a good Samaritan helping with the fallen.'

'Yes, I do take that point, sir. But for now we're working on the basis he is.' He made an unconscious and rather defensive gesture with his hands, adding, 'If it's not him then we're nowhere. He's all we've got.'

'Well it's your decision. I just hope it's the correct one.' Having absolved himself of responsibility, Inspector Luke leaned back in his chair and pondered, then remarked, 'I suppose there is method in your madness. If the public are not aware there is a murderer in their midst, then we cannot be accused of not catching him.'

Trewin hated to admit it, but his superior had a point. 'Very true, sir, although that was not the reasoning behind the decision not to go public.'

'Nevertheless, best to let sleeping dogs lie, I think. Give it another couple of days but if you and Robinson can't move things forward, we'll have to let matters rest. This war has stretched us to the limit, especially with men volunteering all over the place. If you've got nothing new by Wednesday close the file. Carry on.'

Shocked, the sergeant bridled at this. 'Sir, with respect, we need more time.'

Luke raised his eyebrows. 'Are you arguing with me, Trewin?'

'No, sir, but the poor girl was murdered. Surely she deserves our best efforts. There's always a chance we'll have a break-through if we keep at it.'

But, irked by his inferior's tone, the inspector was already beyond the wisdom of concession. 'By Wednesday, Sergeant. That's my decision.'

Visibly frustrated, Trewin muttered, 'As you wish, sir,' and turned away.

Luke watched him go. *That's the way to do it.* As the door closed, he took a sip of tea and reached for the *Falmouth Packet*.

Chapter Thirteen

It was Alan Bricken's day off and he was on the cliffs half a mile to the east of Porthcurno. His objective was a famous local landmark called the Logan Rock, which perched high above the sea on a rocky point that marked the edge of Porthcurno bay.

The landlord of the public house in Treen had told him the story. The rock had been one of the famous 'logans' of Cornwall, which meant it was so finely balanced that it could be rocked by hand even though it weighed eighty tons. But in 1824 disaster had arrived in the shape of a Royal Navy lieutenant who, upon hearing the local legend that no man could dislodge the great stone from its perch, set to work with some of his crew. It took them several hours of work with iron bars, but they finally sent it crashing down.

Well satisfied the men went back to their ship, with no idea of the storm that was about to break. The rock was a well-known tourist attraction, and the locals were outraged with the desecration of their headland. Harangued and pursued throughout Penzance, the lieutenant was reported to the admiralty who instructed him to return the rock to its former position. This he finally managed to do six months later, although the complicated engineering arrangements required in such a remote and exposed position broke him financially. And the locals insisted it had never rocked in the same way since.

Alan was intent on inspecting the site of this colourful tale and strode out through the gorse and low heather until he reached the headland. A great tower of living granite rose above him and on the summit he could see a block about six feet square, which he assumed was his target. To many people the climb would have been an alarming prospect, but he was nimble and fit, and ten minutes later he scrambled up next to it, breathing heavily from the ascent. But to his great frustration he couldn't move the rock.

Finally admitting defeat, he sat down in the lee of its bulk and stared back towards the cove at Porthcurno. Even in the steely light of midwinter it was a magnificent view. Pedn Vounder beach lay in the middle distance, its yellow sand and turquoise water showing their best at low tide. The men from Zodiac House had found a way down the steep cliffs and occasionally swam there, although their favourite bathing beach was a deserted cove called Porthchapel, which lay below St Levan's holy well, half a mile past Porthcurno in the opposite direction. They normally swam naked, blissfully unaware that two teenage sisters, who lived in a farm they passed through on the way, spied on them with great delight from a grassy shelf at the back of the beach.

He looked inland. The ground was gently undulating and treeless, broken into fields by Cornish hedges. Generally about five feet tall, these were stone-faced and filled with clay and sand, the width of the base being the same as the height. Over time they became covered in rough vegetation and settled immovably into the landscape. Many were hundreds of years old, built by men who understood that the unique, storm-bound landscape needed hedges that were more or less indestructible.

A movement caught his eye and he saw a single figure approaching across a field. To his surprise he recognised him. It was George Weaver from the hotel in Falmouth. He stood up and gave him a hail and a wave.

'Come up,' he beckoned and with a quick raised hand in acknowledgement, the new arrival disappeared out of sight at the foot of the rocks. Shortly afterwards his head showed over the parapet, and he scrambled onto the platform.

'Well met, Mr Weaver. What brings you to our remote outpost?' Bricken enquired as they shook hands.

'Your tale of Porthcurno intrigued me and I thought I'd come and see for myself. I left my motorbike at Treen and must have missed the path.'

'Aye, you did, there's a lane a bit further on. But it's not too far from here.' He pointed along the coast. 'That's us. The second beach you can see.' He told him the tale of the Logan Rock, concluding with: 'Come back with me if you like and we'll give you a cup of tea.'

'That sounds like a good idea, thank you. It's quite magnificent up here, isn't it. The view . . .' Weaver gestured across the horizon.

'You get used to it in the end, but I know what you mean.'

The two men descended from their rocky eyrie and headed back along the cliff path, chatting about the Eastern Telegraph Company. As they reached the lip of the valley, Zodiac House came into sight, standing stark and exposed, a quarter of a mile up from the cove.

'Fascinating,' Weaver said. 'So the cables come up the beach?'

'That's them over on the far side.' Alan pointed to the base of the steep cliffs where two thick black pipes were visible emerging from the sand and running into the bracken and gorse at the back of the beach. 'There could be a message from Bombay or Barbados running up one of the cables in those right now.'

Voices sounded behind them, and they turned to see two kilted soldiers armed with rifles emerging from a narrow path that led towards the cliff edge. An officer appeared behind them.

'Hello, Mr Bricken,' he said.

'Lieutenant.' He nodded back but didn't introduce Weaver as the three men squeezed past and headed down the rocky path into the valley. They watched them disappear then Alan said, 'They're posted here to guard the place. From Glasgow I believe, which may explain why we can't understand a word they say. They've got themselves a little spot up here. I'll show you.' He led the way through the gorse and dropped down to a flat area high above the sea where a small wooden hut had been built.

'A lookout,' his companion observed.

'Yes, although heaven knows what they're expecting. Or what they'd do about it. The last week of every month they all disappear anyway. Something to do with a training rotation.' He shrugged. 'How about that tea? There's a path that leads along the valley side and straight to Zodiac House.'

Weaver nodded. 'Lovely, lead on.'

The telegraphist turned and strode off, and he followed, but only after he'd stood for a moment staring over the cove. 'What's beyond the far headland?' he asked when he caught up.

'Another little cove called Porthchapel. It's our favourite swimming spot in the summer and only half a mile from the house over the fields.'

'It sounds like an idyllic life here.'

'Aye, it is lovely. But it's a bit boring. And man to man, Weaver, we're a bit short of female company. There's a pair of sisters at the local farm but they've not been blessed with looks, if you know what I mean.'

'Oh dear.' Weaver laughed. 'But Alma Timperley's caught your eye then?'

'I do like her. I'll say that.'

'Well good luck, Mr Bricken. I'll put in a word for you if I can.'

* * *

At the docks in Falmouth, work was continuing to repair the damage from the Zeppelin raid. The coaster that had been sunk was called the *Annie-May* and she still lay on the bottom alongside the eastern breakwater with her bridge and masts sticking out of the water. Attempts by the navy to refloat her had been unsuccessful so far. At the landward end of the western breakwater, a warehouse had been destroyed and the railway line that ran next to it badly damaged. Three people had been killed: two on the coaster and a stevedore who had been running for cover and got caught in a blast near the warehouse. Thankfully the dry dock was undamaged.

Captain Hyde stared at the scene through his office window. Despite the damage, he knew that they'd been lucky. People were saying if a bomb had hit the *Persian Knight*, they'd all be up in heaven looking down on the place where Falmouth used to be. They were right, but nevertheless he'd smiled with affection at their grim humour. The staunch people of Cornwall had sent their men to sea for hundreds of years and didn't scare easily. The sight of the great airship over the town had been shocking, but now there was just anger and frustration that the guns had proved so ineffective against the Huns.

As to the *Persian Knight*, if she successfully ran the gauntlet of the submarines, she'd be back in three weeks with another twelve thousand tons of petrol. And for the four days she was in Falmouth his nerves would be just a little bit more wound up.

And as he stared at her empty berth four hundred yards away, an alarming thought came to him. When she was in port the tanker moored on the outside of the mole, her long flank exposed to the wide sweep of open water that formed the deepest natural harbour in western Europe.

Could a U-boat get into the estuary? As he stared at the narrow entrance and the guns on Pendennis Castle he rapidly dismissed the idea as ridiculous. The Zeppelin raid had made him jumpy.

Damned war, he reflected gloomily.

* * *

On the hill behind the dockmaster's office, Alma and Valentine Wragge walked along Castle Drive in mild sunshine and a gentle breeze. Since the outbreak of war the road up to the fort was normally closed to the public but, on fine Sundays such as this, it was opened up so people could enjoy the magnificent view across the estuary to St Mawes.

And it was no accident that on such days the flat area opposite the old entrance to the fort, which was known as the Hornwork, was populated by troops drilling and exercising in the sunshine. The colonel in charge of the garrison was an experienced man and saw no reason not to boost the town's morale when opportunity beckoned.

'I noticed you went out with George the other evening. Did you have a pleasant time?' Valentine asked, in a neutral tone.

'I did, thank you. He doesn't give much away normally, so it was nice to have a chat.'

They walked on for a few paces. 'He's a good-looking fellow, they say,' the man next to her observed. 'At least that's the talk among the maids and the guests.'

'I'm not surprised to hear it,' she said, 'and I must admit I concur. He's rather charming as well, when he puts his mind to it.'

Valentine made a strange noise somewhere between a groan and a sigh. 'I'm sure he is. Very popular with the ladies, one might say.'

Alma slipped her arm through his and said with a smile, 'Are you trying to tell me something?'

He stopped and looked down at her. 'I've known George for some years, and I'd suggest you exercise caution. He is very discreet but is definitely a ladies' man. If you understand me.'

She realised that he was serious, and she was being warned. After a moment she replied, 'I shall certainly bear that in mind, Valentine.'

They walked on in silence as she considered this new intelligence. And it didn't take long for her to realise that it was probably true. George Weaver exuded an air of danger that left a rippling sense of excitement in the air. After their dinner date she had lain in bed with the image of him across the table in her mind for a long time, and if she felt like that about him, then perhaps others did too.

Ruefully she realised that Valentine's remarks were very timely. She'd only had one assignation with the fellow, but another one was coming up in a couple of days' time and in the back of her mind she'd been quietly fantasising about life with George Weaver without even realising it. She squeezed his arm again. 'Thank you, Valentine.'

He glanced down at her and murmured, 'My pleasure.'

Five minutes later, as the road steepened, Alma stopped to catch her breath and looked towards the beacon that marked Black Rock, the notorious reef in the middle of the estuary's entrance.

'That's sunk a ship or two over the years,' her companion remarked, 'before they finally got a marker on it. On a spring tide it's nine feet underwater, but when the tide's out there's clear rock all round it.'

'Yes, I can see.' She stared, imagining a ship feeling her way in at night.

Her companion cleared his throat. 'There's an amusing story about it. I'm not sure if it's true but many years ago a fellow from Trefusis on the St Mawes side was supposed to have suggested to his wife that they picnic on Black Rock at low tide. Rather unwisely as it turned out, she agreed, but when they reached the rock, he assisted her ashore then promptly rowed off again, shouting that he was tired of her, and she could take her chances with King Neptune.'

'Good Lord, whatever did she do?'

'The water was up to her knees when she was spotted by a fishing smack and rescued. They brought her back to Trefusis and claimed a reward for saving her, but her husband was apparently furious and refused to pay them a penny. I'm not sure what happened after that.'

She looked at him and he was smirking. 'Don't laugh, it's a dreadful thing.' But the urge to giggle suddenly engulfed her and she sniggered. Moments later they were both roaring with laughter. And the nature of such things being infectious, other couples and family groups looked at them and smiled as they walked past.

Arm in arm they made their way up the hill to the Hornwork. At the top a little crowd had gathered to watch the men exercising. They were mainly young and female – shopgirls and factory workers, Alma suspected – and the odd ribald remark carried across the grass to where a squad of perspiring men in vests were drilling with Indian clubs.

''E's a big strong one at the end, Molly,' a girl of about seventeen in her Sunday coat observed to her friend.

'Ain't he so,' she replied thoughtfully, and bellowed, 'Oi! You can save me from the Huns any time!'

A ripple of laughter passed through the crowd as the sergeant turned and shouted, 'That's enough of that.'

'I'll let you know when I've had enough,' the girl called back. 'Until then, you can carry on, my lover!'

This retort was received gleefully by the other girls. 'When do you get some time off then?' someone else called.

'Don't tire yourselves out too much,' another voice carried to the soldiers who were openly grinning.

Valentine said, 'This has become rather a ritual. The girls know the men will be up here because the colonel insists on it. So they come up too. I think the only one who doesn't enjoy it is the sergeant.'

To whooping catcalls of approval from the crowd, the men put the clubs away and started to run in a circle round the edge of the field. As they approached the waiting girls Valentine murmured, 'Here we go . . .'

'Stop me and buy one,' a plump and pretty girl next to Alma called out, and many invitations, in vary degrees of salacity, followed as the sweating men in singlets trotted past.

'Eyes front,' bellowed the sergeant.

The girl next to her had a note in her hand and Alma clearly saw one of the men reach out and take it. He gave her a quick grin. She turned and met Alma's eye, then shrugged. 'Well I like the look of 'im and I thought I'd move things along a bit.'

Alma smiled. 'Fair enough,' she said, rather envious of her uncomplicated opinion.

Alan Bricken is lovely and I like him, but he might disappear at any moment. And George Weaver could be a German spy and a womaniser, but he keeps popping up in my head. Oh dear. Maybe I should have stuck with steady Jack Waring after all.

* * *

James suggested that they eat in the dining room that evening. There was a free table near the fireplace, which wasn't unusual. She'd noticed that the bereaved women formed friendships quickly and as most of them were travelling solo apart from their maids, they often ate together in twos and threes. It was almost like being in a special club, she thought, and sensed that some relationships were starting that would endure way beyond their shared time in Falmouth.

Her friend had news to impart. 'I heard Mr Weaver tell Gracie that he was going to be out all day today and I took the opportunity to investigate his room.'

'Oh really? Did you discover anything?'

'Not really. The room is comfortable, and he's got it set up in a way that suits him, but there's nothing to raise any alarm bells. Certainly no concealed German books.'

'Nothing at all?'

He shrugged eloquently and said nothing. But his silence hid a lie. There had been something, but he had taken the view that it was not relevant to his enquiries. Beneath the headboard of the bed, he'd found a wide four-tooth comb of the type women use to pin up their hair. He'd left it there, but the implication was clear. Weaver had shared his bed with a woman.

Before dinner Nascent had spent some time wondering who that might be. Perhaps it was a spontaneous assignation with a guest at the hotel or one of their maids, in which case the thing would be fleeting. But there was also the possibility that he was a serial offender. The work ensured a regular supply of bereaved mothers, wives, and sisters, who were obviously vulnerable.

Is he a predator?

If Hilda had been with him, she would have known about Alma's nascent interest in George Weaver and their dinner together. And she would have insisted that James reveal what he knew for the girl's own protection. But she wasn't there, and he let the moment pass.

Feeling an undeniable sense of relief at James's news, Alma asked, 'What will you do next?' before taking a mouthful of roast lamb.

'Do either of them have any friends? I see them around the hotel but know little of their lives outside it.'

'I haven't been here long enough to know myself. I suggest you talk to Gracie, or maybe Mrs Wilson in the kitchen. Or even Polly,' she added as an afterthought. 'She likes a gossip.'

This seemed like a good idea so the next day he found the assistant manager in the office and instigated some general enquiries. And he could see no great harm in being direct.

'Tell me, Gracie, what do Weaver and Wragge get up to when they're not working? Do they socialise together?'

She thought for a moment and replied, 'Valentine plays bridge and is a member of a club in town. He tries to play two or three times a week, I think.'

'Does he entertain friends in the hotel at all, or have any female companions?'

'I'm not aware of any particular associations with regard to the opposite sex, but he does host a dinner table here from time to time. Bridge club people, I think.'

The solicitor nodded. 'And Weaver?'

'George isn't quite as highbrow in his tastes. He has told me he enjoys a pint of beer and frequents some of the public houses down by the docks. He has a few friends and acquaintances in one or two of them I believe.'

'No other hobbies?'

'They both walk on the cliffs in the summer and bathe over at Swanpool, like a lot of people. George has got a motorbike as well and rides it around exploring. He keeps it in the garage round the side of the hotel but doesn't use it much in the winter.'

'That sounds adventurous though. And how about you, Gracie, what do you do in your spare time?'

She laughed. 'There's not so much of that. I have a cottage a step or two away through the back gate in the garden and I sleep there. My husband was in the merchant navy, but we lost him in a sinking eight years ago, so it's just me. My two girls are both married now and live in the town.'

They chatted easily for another fifteen minutes and afterwards James reflected that sometimes the easiest way to gain information was simply to ask.

Chapter Fourteen

George Weaver sat in his room nursing a whisky. It was eleven o'clock in the evening, and he had a decision to make.

He felt it was time to grasp the nettle and be more proactive. So far, his espionage work in England had mainly involved passing on information gleaned from the wives of influential people during their séances. Sometimes this was surprisingly easy to obtain. Indeed, the idea for the whole business had started very early in the war when he'd met a woman whose urge to communicate the importance of her husband's position was only exceeded by her lack of discretion about his work.

'He tells me everything and often asks for my opinion when something big is happening,' she'd blithely remarked, and it had been simple for Weaver to mine this rich source. As a result, he'd sent a letter to the private address of an acquaintance in the German diplomatic service in Portugal and the *Lisbon Rose* system had rapidly been established. And as he passed more and more information to Berlin he found he enjoyed being a spy. Although Gladys had been a close friend and he enjoyed the company of the fishermen and other artisans in the Rook public house, in general he found the British were an arrogant race. Especially the newspapers. Full of the empire and boastful about their great naval battle fleet. Secretly getting one over on them had added salt to his soup, as his mother's favourite expression went.

But the really big targets, including the bereaved wife of a cabinet minister and the grieving sister of the First Sea Lord, had known how to be discreet. In an effort to unlock their secrets he'd started experimenting with hypnotism and found he had a natural facility for it. In the dimly lit intimacy of the consulting room with the women's entire attention focused on him, it had been surprisingly easy to reach deep into their psyches and build their trust. And once they opened up, there were few barriers to what was discussed.

The result was that George Weaver knew many secrets about the intimate lives of the upper echelons of society and he kept them written down in a notebook that was secreted with a quantity of cash under a floorboard in his room. But that was not all. Married or not, in the warm intimacy of the consulting room, some of his clients had surrendered completely to his overpowering presence and handsome features. And as his skill in mesmerism had grown, he'd found he was able to pick and choose his conquests more or less at will.

Afterwards he always professed his regret and embarrassment at the incident and suggested that their mutual recklessness had been brought on by the overriding emotion of the séance. Assured of his utter discretion, in the cold light of day, most of the women were only too happy to accept this convenient explanation for their unfortunate transgression and pretend it had never happened. There had been one or two who had clung to him, but he had managed to disentangle himself on each occasion.

He sipped his scotch and pondered the events of the last month, including his visit to Porthcurno and the meeting with Alan Bricken. He'd professed amusement at the tale of the German raid on the Cocos Islands, and their work at the cable station sounded fascinating. No wonder the British had soldiers stationed there; it was clearly a vital communications centre. Then there was the conversation in the nook the morning after the Zeppelin raid. It appeared that the tanker *Persian Knight* was a floating bomb and the town had been extremely lucky that she had not been hit in the raid. He'd seen her moored on her berth from the top of the hotel's tower many times, but the thought she might be dangerous had never occurred to him.

He stared out over the dark garden and turned various ideas over in his mind, calmly considering the relative merits of each one. Half an hour later he'd settled on a plan that was audacious to say the least, and worthy of the British themselves. As the hotel slept, and with a few notes in his hand, which he would burn later, he descended to his consulting room.

Twenty minutes later, in the silence, he slowly exhaled, opened his eyes, and said quietly in German, 'Welcome, Leo. I have a message for Mother.'

* * *

Two days later, in Berlin, Felix Muller was intrigued to receive another letter from his secret correspondent. As before the letter was simply addressed to the High Command in Berlin and had been opened by the sorting staff in the office. But this time the contents were even more of a surprise.

> *It would be appreciated if someone who deals with war matters could attend Eastwood House in the village of Esten at their earliest convenience. Ask for Herr Weiss at the lodge.*

He stared at the two sentences for five minutes, turning things over in his mind. Because he knew of Eastwood House. Everyone in Berlin society knew of it – the home of the Weber family and the place where Charlotte, wife of the German economics minister resided. It was said she was mad, and rumours abounded that she was a virtual prisoner on the estate. And yet here was an invitation to visit. It was interesting at the very least and there was no doubt it was from the same source that had provided such useful information on Sir John Buchanan and his Highland Division.

Deciding to act immediately, he stood up and reached for his cap and thick coat. Calling to his aide that he was going out for the rest of the day, he left the office, walked to the station, and caught a train to Esten. It was late morning by the time he arrived and was snowing heavily. Noting he was the only passenger to get off, he emerged onto the station forecourt to find a solitary horse-drawn cab waiting. Congratulating himself on his luck, he instructed the driver on his destination.

'Is it far?' he added.

'Fifteen minutes,' came the laconic reply from above.

'Very good. Stop at the lodge.' And with that they set off.

As promised, they arrived a quarter of an hour later and a burly man appeared behind the wrought-iron gate in response to the coachman's hail. 'Yes?' he enquired.

'My name is Muller, from Berlin,' Felix called from the cab window. 'To see Herr Weiss.'

'The butler?' The doubtful note of surprise in the lodge-keeper's voice was obvious.

'Indeed.'

'What do you want with him?'

'None of your business. Now let me through.'

'How do I know you're invited?'

Cursing quietly, Muller got out of the cab and walked to the gate, head bent against the gusting snow. 'Because I am telling you,

you damn fool. I'm with the government and I'm here to see Weiss. So open the gate or I'll have you in the village lock-up before you can get back inside your lodge.'

'All right. No need for that. It's my job to be curious. Mr Weber told me.' Keen not to offer any further information to the lodge-keeper, Muller simply turned on his heel and crunched back through the snow to the cab. Moments later they were on the way.

The drive led slightly downhill and was edged with thick woods on the right, but to his left the man from Berlin could see wide parkland dotted with clumps of trees. A herd of deer were grazing, apparently immune to the weather.

'Front or back?' the driver called.

Muller hesitated for a moment. Weiss was the butler apparently. 'Back,' he replied.

They swung through the turning circle, and he caught a glimpse of a large brick country house and shortly afterwards entered a stable yard to the rear. 'Will you wait, please,' he said to the coachman and received a nod in return. As he stood and looked around, a door opened twenty feet away and an elderly man in livery appeared.

Muller addressed him. 'Good morning. Herr Weiss?'

'Yes, sir. Come in out of this weather.' The butler held the door open in invitation and he walked over and entered a stone-flagged corridor, which he assumed was the rear entrance to the house.

'My name is Captain Muller. From Berlin,' he said quietly as the man helped him remove his coat.

'Welcome to Eastwood, sir. I thought you might be. Fräulein Weber will be pleased you've come so promptly.'

'She sent the note?'

'Indeed. This way, please.' They climbed the back stairs and emerged into an entrance hall with a fine oak staircase and a blazing fire. 'If you'll just wait, I'll tell Fräulein Weber you're here.'

He disappeared through a door and a minute or two later reappeared and addressed the new arrival. 'Would you like to come through?' Increasingly curious, Muller crossed the hall and entered a comfortably furnished sitting room.

Charlotte Weber was in her mid-fifties he guessed, with chestnut hair styled high on her head. She was wearing a simple but expensive day dress, and her only jewellery was her wedding ring. But it was her eyes that caught his attention. They were a deep brown and sensitive, but there was a maturity there that belied her slightly anxious expression.

He clicked his heels and kissed her hand, then she indicated a seat in front of the fire and said, 'Something warming after your journey, Herr Muller?'

'That would be most welcome.'

She looked at Weiss and said, 'Coffee and brandy, Gert. And some of that apple cake.' He nodded silently and left.

Alert for any signs of madness or instability, the next few minutes were something of a disappointment to the new arrival. His hostess made small talk of the most normal kind, asking for news of people in the capital and bemoaning the fact that she got up to town so rarely.

She asked if he was married and did he have children, and their polite discourse continued, as she clearly intended, until the butler returned, served coffee, cake and brandy, left the bottle on the table and departed without saying a word.

Then they got down to business.

'It was good of you to respond to my note so quickly. I had no idea if the previous one had found its way to somewhere useful,' she remarked.

'I got your first message regarding General Buchanan and passed it on to the army high command. I've subsequently heard that the intelligence in it was accurate, so may I first of all thank you. Your contact is obviously well connected.'

She made a vague gesture with her hand. 'There's no need for thanks. I'm only the messenger.'

Well that was something. Muller groped momentarily for what to say next, then asked, 'Is there another message? Is that why you wanted to see me?'

Her eyes met his and he was again struck by their depth. 'There is another message. The reason that I broke my anonymity is because it will require a reply.'

'A reply to England? And you have the means to achieve that?'

'Yes, if it isn't too complicated.' She stood up and crossed to a side table, returning with a single piece of paper. 'This is the message. Have a look.' She passed it to him and sat down.

Utterly absorbed, Muller bent his head and began to read. It was written in the same clear hand as the others and its contents were astonishing. He looked at her, but his mind was so full he couldn't think of anything to say. She filled the silence.

'I'm no expert but the case seems well made, would you not say?'

Mind racing, he nodded. 'I would, Fräulein.' Another brief silence filled the room as the clock ticked gently on the mantelpiece.

'Ask your question, Herr Muller,' she said.

'In fact there are two. How did you receive this message and who has it come from?'

'I'm not sure I can answer the first in a way that is comprehensible to you. And I would rather not give you the name of the person involved on the other side, so to speak.'

Muller noticed she seemed amused by this remark. 'As you wish. With your permission I'll just read this again.' He did so, his agile mind rapidly getting to grips with what would be needed.

When he'd finished, he said, 'You mentioned the need for a reply. I assume that would be a yes or no and a date.'

'I'd imagine certain things would need to be put in place over there,' she replied, 'given what is proposed.'

He nodded. There was something nagging in his mind, and he voiced it. 'This will require resources and commitment. With the greatest respect, Fräulein, I have only received a single message before this. It was accurate and useful, I grant you, but that is a small foundation on which to initiate such a plan. It would be a considerable leap of faith.'

'I understand. There was a final part of the message, which I didn't write down. A single word. It is Excalibur.'

He sat up. 'Your contact is Excalibur? Our agent in Cornwall?'

'That is my understanding.'

'You're saying he's found a new route for messages, with you at the end of it here in Germany?'

'Yes.'

* * *

The headquarters of the German high seas fleet in Wilhelmshaven on the North Sea coast was a modest building from the outside, but that was deceptive. It extended a considerable distance from the street and hosted all the departments necessary for the successful operation of the world's second most powerful navy.

On the third floor a series of offices housed the senior commanders. The largest of these was the base from which Grand

Admiral Tirpitz operated when he wasn't in Berlin. Tirpitz ran the navy and reported directly to Kaiser Wilhem II, the man who ruled Germany and at whose direct order Germany had invaded France and Belgium the previous summer.

A meeting of senior officers was concluding and as the men were leaving one approached the admiral and asked for a private word. Five minutes later they were alone.

'What can I do for you, Muller?'

'I have an idea, sir. I wondered if I might present the bones of it to you.' He held up the rolled-up chart he was carrying.

Tirpitz glanced at the clock. He was due back in Berlin that night. 'You have five minutes.'

Muller unrolled the chart and weighted the corners down. It was a British Admiralty chart showing west Cornwall from Falmouth to Land's End.

'A message has come through from a friend we have in this area.'

'A friend? You mean a spy?' The distaste was all too apparent in the great man's voice and Muller hurried on.

'They have made a suggestion for an operation. One that could have a significant impact on the British.' He paused and added, 'Especially with regard to their fleet.' Muller knew his business

The grand admiral eyed him sceptically. 'Really? Where?'

'At a point of vulnerability.' The captain put his finger on the map. 'Just there, sir.'

The senior man leaned forward and studied the location for a full ten seconds then asked, 'What is the proposal?'

And Muller told him.

Later, as he sat in his own office, Captain Muller reflected that if Admiral Tirpitz knew that the message suggesting the operation had come from a woman widely believed to be insane by Berlin society, he'd probably have thrown the intelligence officer out of his office himself. Nevertheless, he picked up the telephone and asked for a number. Thirty seconds later the call was answered.

'Weber residence,' the voice came down to the captain.

'Good evening, it is Muller. I have a message for Fräulein Weber.'

'Very well, I will take it.' The butler was loyal to his mistress, and discreet.

'Tell her Muller says the great man likes the idea and a plan is being prepared. She may communicate that to her contact.'

As he replaced the receiver the captain sat back in his chair with satisfaction. Tirpitz had been so taken with his proposal that they had discussed it for twenty minutes. The end result had been permission to work things up into a fully operational plan and to return with that in a month. It would be reviewed by the same men who had attended the meeting earlier and, if approved, resources would be allocated.

Muller unrolled the map of Cornwall again and studied it, his mind racing. A successful operation would make his reputation and do great damage to the British. He pulled a notepad into the pool of light on his desk and started to make notes.

And the first thing he wrote down at the top of the page in capital letters were the initials P. K. Then he underlined them.

* * *

In Falmouth Sergeant Trewin was also staring at a notepad. It was his own private summary of the events in the Kate Diss murder, and it made depressing reading, not least because of its brevity. Despite his and Constable Robinson's efforts, he had to reluctantly concede that they had made no progress since the early interview with Sally Regan.

He'd convinced himself that she had seen the murderer, but they simply hadn't found anyone else who had any useful information. He was also aware that he had stretched the investigation way beyond the two-day limit Inspector Luke had given him three weeks earlier, and they still had nothing. If, at this late stage, he proposed changing tack and putting out a statement asking for witnesses, he was certain his superior would refuse and haul him over the coals for disobeying a direct order.

Sergeant Trewin was forty-two years old and hoped one day to be an inspector himself. And, even more pertinently, so did his wife, who found the idea most appealing, especially with regard to her own reputation in the town. Inspector Luke was retiring soon, and a vacancy was coming up, so it was not the moment for a misstep that might come to the attention of the senior officers who held his future in their hands.

It is time to let poor Kate Diss go. He'd tell her parents they were still looking but, in reality, he'd stand Robinson down and quietly shelve the file. Very few people knew that the girl had been murdered and it was better that it stayed that way. He'd been a police officer for many years and knew that sometimes things popped up out of nowhere to give new impetus to a case. Perhaps they would be lucky, but for now, he reluctantly conceded that the murderer had got away with it.

Chapter Fifteen

The *Persian Knight* arrived back in Falmouth on the first of March, having steamed the three thousand sea miles from the Persian Gulf in nine days at a steady fifteen knots. Thankfully there had been no incidents involving the enemy although the captain and crew were aware that they were playing a vicious game of cat and mouse, in which the cat only needed to win once. The sustained strain on the men was appalling and once she had berthed on the outside of the mole, most of them went ashore and headed for the pubs along Arwenack Street. She would be in port for four days before leaving again for the Gulf.

George Weaver noted the tanker's arrival from the tower of the hotel and, one floor down, James Nascent wondered what else he could do to further his investigation into both Weaver and Wragge. Bereft of ideas, he sat down and wrote a report for Kell, which he posted. The spymaster received it at lunchtime the following day and read it with interest. The salient points were in a few paragraphs.

I have dined with both men and extracted some details regarding their previous lives, nothing of which strikes me as being indicative of espionage. Weaver admits to growing up in Switzerland and speaks French as his mother tongue but claims to know only a few words of German. He has lived in England for many years and appears well settled here. Wragge says he speaks a little of each but not to any standard and is vague about his family upbringing. There are European connections, I think. Both express anti-German sentiments in keeping with the other staff and guests, but that may be a ruse of course.

Both their rooms have been searched. Last night, Miss Timperley told me in confidence that Wragge is a fraud with regard to the hotel's purpose and uses a clandestine partner to find out information about his clients prior to their visits. He is very good at it and has a strong following. In contrast Weaver is, I am told by Miss Timperley, the genuine article – a real clairvoyant. He also has devoted clients and may be a womaniser. I found evidence of female company in his room, although that is hardly a crime.

The German book has disappeared from its hiding place. It occurs that the advent of unrestricted submarine warfare and the consequent cancellation of the Lisbon Rose sailings may have made it redundant if the book was being used as some kind of code key for messages being smuggled on board.

You will be aware that Falmouth was bombed by a Zeppelin some weeks ago. A light in the top of the hotel's tower and a set of car headlights were switched on as the airship approached the darkened town. They pointed towards the docks and the police strongly suspect that this was a malign act intended to help the Germans. Everyone in the hotel has had to account for their whereabouts just before the raid and all appear to have done so satisfactorily. Weaver and Wragge claim to have been in their rooms and there is no way to prove otherwise. Both worked well in the aftermath of the raid, helping with the clean-up efforts.

In summary, both men appear blameless but either of them could very easily be harbouring anti-British sentiments,

*which they keep deep within themselves. I can find no
evidence that they are acting on such feelings and their time
seems generally well accounted for, with no liaisons that
might concern us.*

*I therefore am at a loss how to proceed. I remain at Miss
Timperley's disposal with regard to the hotel but intend,
unless you request otherwise, to return to London shortly.*

* * *

Kell leaned back in his chair with the report in his hand. Nascent
had done a decent job, and he made a mental note of that for the
future. But in the meantime, his point about the *Lisbon Rose* was
well made. Any reliable and regular way to smuggle messages
out of Falmouth had gone, and even if either man wished Britain
ill, it was hard to see what they could do about it.

He penned a brief note back, thanking him and agreeing to
the solicitor's return to London.

When he received it the following day James sat down with
Alma and brought her up to date.

'So there we are,' he concluded. 'There's no obvious threat
from either Wragge or Weaver so I'm going to return to town
in the morning. I like it here and have enjoyed both my stay and
getting to know you, Alma. It's been a pleasure seeing you grasp
the reins so effectively and I hope you'll have Hilda and myself
back before too long.' He grinned. 'Always assuming you can
find room for us.'

'Oh, James, you've been marvellous and you're both welcome
here at any time – you know that, I hope. And do give my love to
Hilda.' As she said this, she felt a surge of relief and excitement.

George Weaver is innocent.

* * *

In Porthcurno Alan Bricken had just finished his shift in the instrument room when Superintendent Trent caught him crossing the hall.

'Ah, Mr Bricken, just the man. Come into my office for a moment, would you?'

He followed these instructions and took a seat when invited to. This alone got him wondering what was up. Telegraph operators were normally expected to remain standing when in Mr Trent's office.

'How are you getting along?'

'Very well, thank you, sir.'

'Good. Well, I won't beat about the bush. You'll be aware that a couple of our old hands are retiring shortly, which means we've vacancies for new station heads at Cocos, which you know of course, and Ascension Island in the south Atlantic. Tyler's going to Cocos and we're giving you Ascension. It's a promotion and better terms, so congratulations. I'm not sure of the exact dates at this moment, but you'll be here for three months yet. There's a new piece of kit coming through, and I want you fully conversant with it before you leave. You'll take one with you and train the others.'

The young man was surprised and delighted. 'Thank you very much, sir. That's good news. How long will the posting be?'

'Two years, as normal. You're young for a post like this, but you're a steady man and get on with the others and that's been noticed. I'm sure you'll do well. You may tell the others; it's not confidential. And I'd have a word with Wentworth, if I were you. He came back from there just before Christmas, so he'll be able to fill you in. Carry on, then.' He gave him a nod of dismissal and Alan stood up and made for the door.

'One other thing.' The voice came from behind and he turned. 'Sir?'

'You're not married are you, Bricken?'

'No, sir.'

'I don't know your circumstances but as a station head you may take your wife with you. Something to think about perhaps.'

Head buzzing, Alan left Zodiac House and went to the Exiles Club. Two men were playing billiards, and he nodded a greeting and crossed to the bookshelves in the corner. A well-thumbed copy of the ETC relay station directory was already out on a table and he picked it up and found the entry for his new posting.

Ascension Island. Latitude 7.9467° S, Longitude 14.3559° W
Location: South Atlantic Ocean. Approximately 1,000 miles west of Africa and 1,400 miles east of South America. Nearest landfall, St Helena Island 800 miles south-east. Ascension is the main relay station for the ETC submarine cable to South Africa. The company's base is at Georgetown, the capital, and normally consists of an establishment of eight plus any family members and local staff. It is classified as a remote posting.

The young man read on down the entry, then went in search of Wentworth who he found in his room.

'I've just heard they're giving me Ascension Island. I'm to be the new head of station there,' he told him.

'I say, that's good news for you. Well done.' Wentworth jumped to his feet, and they shook hands. 'You'll be wanting the inside track on the place then, I'd imagine. How about you buy me a beer up at the pub in Treen and I'll fill you in.'

* * *

As he lay in bed that night Alan Bricken had a great deal to think about. The island was even more remote than Cocos and also had a tropical climate, although from what Wentworth had said it was much drier. And he'd told him they'd also had a brush with the war.

'In early December we were told to send the women and children to hide up Green Mountain, which is the highest point on the island. Our navy were chasing some Hun battleships around close by and the ETC was worried, but in the event they caught and sank most of them. It was in the papers back here, I think. The Battle of the Falklands they called it. I came home shortly afterwards, and I heard they'd sent some soldiers to guard the place since then.'

'And it's the main relay station for Cape Town cables?' Breckin had asked.

'Yes, and it's busy. Since the war began there's been much more military traffic of course, but commercial companies need to keep in touch with South Africa and our employer is still charging them five pounds per cable for the privilege.'

'What's it like to live there?'

'Not too bad at all. Georgetown is a little place but nice enough and there's bathing and walking in the hills. You don't half feel a long way from anywhere though. If something goes wrong, you have to sort it out yourselves.'

'All right for women, would you say?'

'The station head's wife seemed quite comfortable with the place. It depends on your attitude. Someone who is used to the bright lights and a busy social life wouldn't take to it, I don't suppose. But if you're a quieter sort and can occupy yourself with books and a bit of painting and so on . . .' He'd tailed off then grinned. 'Have you got someone in mind, my dear fellow? That young lady who came to Sunday lunch perhaps?'

And as he lay in the darkness it was this question, above all, that was keeping Alan Bricken awake. He'd been thinking about

Alma a lot and had got the impression that she was interested in him. There'd certainly been no problem with meeting her – she'd willingly agreed to that, and they'd had lunch together in Falmouth recently too.

Would she come as his wife? Would she accept his proposal?

He sensed that he'd only have one chance to pop the question and if she turned him down, he doubted she'd reconsider. Then a thought struck him. George Weaver was a pleasant fellow and knew her well. Better even than him possibly. Perhaps it would be a smart move to have a quiet word with him, man to man.

The more he thought about the idea, the better it looked. Happy that he had a plan, he turned over and went to sleep.

* * *

Two days later Weaver received a short letter from Alan Bricken proposing they meet and have lunch the following Saturday. There was no indication what the catalyst for the invitation had been but, his curiosity fired, the older man wrote back suggesting a well-run public house called the Rook at half past twelve.

They met at the appointed hour and Bricken, who was a pub man himself, surveyed the inside of the hostelry with satisfaction. It was an old building, and the comfortable interior was spilt into sections by huge oak posts blackened by hundreds of years of tobacco smoke.

'The food's good here then, George?' Bricken glanced up at a menu board as they took their pints to a vacant table under one of the windows.

'Oh yes, it's plain fare but well done and the beer's decent too. I'm a regular.'

They returned to the bar to order and when Weaver asked for a steak and kidney pie the telegraphist followed suit, thinking that local knowledge should never be ignored. Once they were settled, Bricken cleared his throat and explained his reason for the invitation.

'I've had some news from work. They're promoting me to relay station supervisor and sending me off to a place in the South Atlantic called Ascension Island.'

'Oh really? That's good news. Congratulations, Alan, I imagine you're very pleased, aren't you?' Weaver's tone was warm, his eyes ingenuous, but he was quick and suspected he knew what was coming next.

'Of course, I'm delighted and thank you for your good wishes. The thing is it's a two-year posting and as I told you in confidence the other day, I'm keen on Alma Timperley. If it wasn't for her, I'd be over the moon but, as it is, the news is bittersweet to say the least.'

'Ah.' Weaver took a long pull on his pint and set it back on the table, his mind working furiously.

How can I play this to my advantage?

Before he could respond his companion continued, 'As a supervisor I'm allowed to take my wife with me, so I've been wondering if I should ask her.' He spread his hands on the table. 'I certainly want to, but I'm terrified of her saying no.'

So there it is.

Weaver smiled sympathetically. 'At least at the moment you've got hope, you mean?'

Bricken nodded. 'The thing is, living together in the hotel you probably know her better than me. So I wanted to ask you what you thought, George. I mean, what would you do in my position?'

Fortunately the pies arrived at this juncture, giving Weaver a chance to gather his thoughts. 'You haven't had any beer yet, Alan,' he remarked with a smile. 'You've got it bad, haven't you?'

'I'm in a bit of a tizz about it, I'll not lie,' the younger man conceded, his rounded northern voice flecked with concern.

They began to eat, and Weaver asked, 'How long before you go?'

'It'll be at least three months. There's a new bit of kit coming through and I'm to be trained on it and take one out there.'

'Right, so you do have some time.' *And so do I.*

'Yes, but now it's in my mind I'd like it settled.'

'Of course. Love is the most compelling of all emotions.'

'Love?' Bricken stopped eating and stared at him. 'Love,' he repeated wonderingly. 'That's it, George, I love her. Of course I do, I hadn't thought about that.'

Weaver couldn't hide a smile. 'I'm no medical man Alan, but that's what I would diagnose as your condition.'

'You're right.' He lifted his pint and nodded in his friend's direction. 'Here's to love.' They clinked glasses. 'What do you think I should do?'

'At some point you're going to have to declare yourself, tell her about Ascension Island, and ask her to marry you.'

'Exactly.'

'You do realise that Alma owns the hotel. She has told you that, hasn't she?'

'Yes, but I thought she could employ a manager.'

Weaver gave a little shrug. 'Possibly, yes, but she's only recently weathered some major changes to her own life with moving down to Falmouth. She may not be attracted to the idea of more upheaval.'

'No, I can see that.' He leaned forward. 'So what's to be done?'

'Has she said she's interested in you?'

'We've been out a few times and I think she is. Sure she is, actually,' he said.

Weaver nodded. 'Maybe, but you don't know each other that well yet, do you? Is that a firm foundation on which to base a

191

marriage? She would not be unreasonable in wondering that. Or am I being unfair?'

'No, no, you're right. Those are good points, George. The question is how do we address them?'

Amused by the man's zeal, Weaver put on a pretence of reflecting, although his mind was already way ahead of his dining companion's. After stroking his chin for a while, he pronounced judgement.

'My instinct would be to say nothing for the moment. You do have some time after all. I appreciate you're keen to have a positive answer, but my advice is to play it very slowly for now.'

'So not even mention my promotion?'

'Exactly. Let things develop naturally.'

Bricken nodded thoughtfully. 'Yes, I can see the sense in that. At least for a while. It won't be easy holding myself in check though, George, I'll admit that to you now.'

'I'm not inexperienced in these matters and my suggestion is the best course of action for now; I'm sure of it. After all, if you do become engaged just before you leave, she could always follow you out there.'

'That's a point. Very well then, George, I'll take my instructions from you and let you know how I'm getting on.'

'You do that. The more I know the more I can help, and I'll certainly put a good word in for you with the lady in question.'

An hour later the two men parted, and Weaver spent some time walking around the town. It was a bright, cool day and not at all unpleasant to be outside. He came to a halt on the old quay and stared across the choppy grey water to St Mawes where a squall was coming in from the sea. As it steadily enveloped the distant buildings in grey mist, he reflected on his time in Falmouth.

Not for the first time, he thanked his lucky stars that when he'd first sought out Gladys Timperley, George had decided that famously neutral Switzerland was a better nationality than Germany for a fellow intending to live in England long term. So, when meeting Gladys for the first time, he had told her he was from Bern and given his surname as Weaver, courtesy of an English father long deceased. She had accepted his story without question, and they had conversed in English from the beginning.

When the British government arrested and imprisoned German and Austrian nationals at the outbreak of the war, it was well known in the town that he was Swiss. As a result, the aliens officer responsible for Falmouth left him untouched.

The British arrogance is their weak point, he mused, watching the rain drift upriver. They hadn't fought a battle in Europe for a hundred years and were used to small colonial wars with disorganised enemies in distant places. But now they were up against a first rank military power with the ability to strike directly at the British at home. The shelling of those towns in the north-east before Christmas and the Zeppelin raids since had demonstrated that.

The harsh cry of a gull broke into his reverie, and he dragged his thoughts back to Alma. The fact was, he needed peace and security to continue his patriotic work for Germany. After Gladys had found the code book in his bedroom the writing had been on the wall for her. At first, she'd merely been curious and asked him if he spoke German. Left with little choice he'd admitted he did and asked her to keep it to herself. But then, when they were alone together, she started making light-hearted comments about the amount of time he spent watching the shipping. He'd tried to discourage her, but one evening as they sat alone in the nook sharing a nightcap she'd giggled and remarked, 'Anyone would think you're spying for the Kaiser, George.'

And with that she had signed her death sentence.

It had been quite simple. The following evening he'd lured her up to the tower room, stunned her with a blow to head, and pushed her over the parapet. He regretted doing it, but knew it was necessary to protect himself. After Gladys's death there had been an uncertain period at the hotel, but Alma's arrival had steadied the ship and he needed things to stay as they were. As he watched a small boat leaving the quay, two things crystallised in his mind.

It is time to seduce the girl so that I can influence her when I need to, and I'll make sure Alan Bricken sails off to Ascension Island on his own.

Happy with this plan he turned and set off up Swanpool Street towards the hotel.

Chapter Sixteen

At nine in the evening Alma was sitting in her room at the top of the hotel when she heard a quiet knock on the door.

'Come in,' she called, and it opened to reveal George Weaver.

'Good evening,' he said with a smile.

For some reason she stood up, then asked, 'What can I do for you, George?'

'I wondered if you'd care to join me for a drink in the nook. There's something I'd like to discuss with you,' he said.

Heart beating a little faster than usual, she put her book down. 'That sounds intriguing – very well.'

They descended to the ground floor, and he poured them both a whisky from the drinks table in the lounge, which they took through. Polly was there but departed when Alma gave her a quick look, leaving the two of them alone.

Alma sat down, composed herself, and awaited developments.

The man opposite took a sip from his glass and said, 'I've enjoyed the occasions we've dined together very much, and I do hope that I can tempt you out again before too long.'

He seemed to be expecting a response to this, so Alma obliged. 'I'm pleased to hear it, George. I enjoyed myself too.' And she had. Even though Valentine's observations when they walked up to the fort had made her more cautious, the simple fact was that he was excellent company and the subtle glances she noticed him receiving from other women in the restaurant had seemed like a compliment, not a warning to her.

Valentine appeared genuine in his concern, but she'd wondered afterwards if his motivation was darker – perhaps fuelled by jealousy or bitterness about some failed romance of his own. In any event, Alma knew she was interested in George and had decided to allow him more time. And there was also likeable Alan Bricken to consider. She thought he was keen, but the likelihood of a foreign posting was an undeniable fly in the ointment and had been playing on her mind.

His voice dragged her back to the present. 'You mentioned that you were considering whether to take your place in the work as Gladys's replacement. I wondered if you'd made a decision?'

To gain time she reached for her glass. It was a fair question. Valentine had also raised it, and she guessed they had been talking, which was hardly surprising.

'As you know I turned my back on that world after my difficult experiences at school. It would not be an easy decision for me to resume work as a spiritualist.'

He nodded. 'I do recall the conversation.'

'So do I. You told me your schoolfriends called you "*Der Spuk*". The spook, I think you said it meant. It sounds German to me. Do you speak German?'

Hiding behind a lazy smile, Weaver cursed himself. *What a mistake to make.* He shrugged and said calmly, 'It was a Swiss school; some of the pupils spoke German.'

'But not you?'

'A word or two, of course. But not much. Anyway, back to the matter in hand. Are you any closer to reaching a decision? I'm asking because the workload is noticeably greater with just two of us and some help would be welcome.'

'Yes, I see that, but at the moment I am fully occupied with the hotel. It's been a huge change for me coming down to Falmouth and assuming responsibility for the place. I'm not sure I have the energy to re-engage with the spirit world. Especially on behalf of a client who is grieving and vulnerable. I imagine it is a tricky business at times.'

'That is true.' He nodded. 'May I make a suggestion?'

'I'm all ears, George.'

'Sit in with me and Lady Davenport tomorrow evening. You would not need to be involved in any way. Just observe. I think you did the same with Wragge a few weeks ago, didn't you?'

'I did, but whatever that was, it wasn't a séance.'

Weaver smiled wryly. 'No one knows how he does it but there's no doubt he's effective.' He met her eye. 'I on the other hand am the genuine article. It would give you a chance to dip your toe back in the water, nothing more.'

His gaze was on her and when he smiled, she felt like a deer being stalked. But alongside the tremor of fear there was a distinct and undeniable thrill.

Do I want to be caught?

'All right.' The words were out before she knew it and there was no taking them back.

'Excellent, I'm delighted.' He raised his glass. 'To tomorrow night then.'

She followed his lead. 'Yes, tomorrow night. Cheers, George.'

'And perhaps we can arrange another of our delightful suppers soon.'

Having given him one concession her instinct was to make him wait, but to her surprise, for the second time in less than a minute she agreed. 'That would be lovely.'

* * *

197

The following evening, she went to the medium's consulting room at nine o'clock as arranged. On entering she found George in a white linen shirt sitting at the table. His face was lit by a single candle and a standard lamp threw a low light onto a settee against the far wall. As she stood in the doorway, she heard footsteps behind her and turned to see Lady Davenport approaching. They greeted each other and Alma explained that, with her permission, she was going to join the two of them for the session that evening.

'I am only here to observe, my lady,' she concluded, and the grieving aristocrat was happy to oblige.

Two minutes later Alma was sitting on the settee at an angle that allowed her to see George's face. He in turn had reached across the table and taken his client's hands in his own. Even in profile she sensed the woman's interest as she leaned forward, her eyes on the medium's face.

'Will you call me George this evening?' he said.

'Of course,' she breathed, quietly. 'And I am June.'

He smiled his answer and said, 'And now I will concentrate and see if we can attract the attention of Edwin. Let us be hopeful.'

Present at a genuine séance for the first time for some years, Alma also closed her eyes and let her mind drift into a receptive state that was both familiar and distant – like a photograph of someone she had once known very well but from whom she had long been parted. Within a short time she was back in the Hall of the Dead, as she had been so often with Alicia Bede during her teenage years. There were people there, well dispersed as usual and she moved easily through them, as the memories and sensations flooded back.

A young man caught her eye. He was in his early twenties and wearing an army uniform. He smiled and she came closer.

'Are you Edwin?' A voice came into her head, and she realised that George was with her, even though she couldn't see him.

'I am. I heard you calling.'

'Your mother asked me to see if I could find you, Edwin,' he said. 'She is suffering greatly from your loss and needs reassurance that you are all right. Will you speak to her through me?'

He looked at Alma. 'Better than that. I can join you. She can bring me.'

Alma was suddenly back in the room. The sublime feeling of weightlessness that characterised her visits to the other side had gone and she could feel the settee underneath her again. But overriding that was an intense sensation of pins and needles that ran through her body like an electric current. It grew and grew as great waves of emotion swept over her – as if she was being rolled in the surf on a beach.

He is coming.

As she opened her eyes, she heard someone moaning and dimly recognised it was her.

George was still sitting unmoving at the table, head back, eyes closed, his hands clasped in his client's. Lady Davenport had twisted in her chair and was staring at Alma. 'Is he here?' she asked, the yearning in her voice all too apparent.

'We've found him. Edwin is here, my lady.' Alma tried to sound calmer than she felt. Communing with a spirit on the other side was one thing. Enabling its reappearance on earth was another. And yet he was here. Just like Alexander Watson had been in the hotel foyer almost two months earlier.

The overpowering sensations were easing and as she caught her breath, she could see the soldier standing next to the table and looking at his mother with a gentle smile. He seemed unsubstantial, as though a faint line drawing of a figure had been shaded in grey.

Like a ghost, in fact.

'Edwin is with you in the room,' she repeated. 'He says to ask him anything you like.'

'Can I touch him?' she whispered, her voice breaking.

'No, that isn't possible, but I swear to you he is here.'

'Eddie, my darling, I love you so much. Are you in pain?'

'No there is no pain where he is. He wants to know how Roly is.'

'Roly?' She smiled, her tears clearly visible in the candlelight. 'He misses you almost as much as I do, I think. He sleeps on your bed, Edwin. Next to your teddy. I know that he wasn't allowed to before, but he insisted when you left for France. And I take him on your favourite walk every day. Through the north field and up to Brook Cap. We talk about you, Roly and I.'

'He wishes he could still do that with you.'

'So do I, with all my heart, my darling. I stop and look at the beech tree you climbed for the first time on your eighth birthday. Do you remember? You were so proud, standing high on the branch and calling out, "Look at me, Mummy. I'm on the top of the world."' Her voice broke as she said this, and she sobbed.

'He's with some of his comrades from the regiment. They all arrived together. Jamie Lowther is there too.'

'I'll tell his mother, I promise. I'm so glad you're not alone and not in pain.'

'How's Charity managing?'

'She's coping but misses you dreadfully. Two of her friends have lost their fiancés too. It's just dreadful, what's happening.'

'Tell her I love her, but she must look to the future when she can.'

Alma saw his mother shake her head. 'It's too soon for any of us to do that, my darling. Far too soon. The house feels so empty and you're in our heads for every moment of every day.'

* * *

Half an hour later, with a tearful and overjoyed Lady Davenport having retired to her room, George sat next to Alma on the settee. His eyes gave off the same delicious threat of danger as before. She had no doubt what would happen if she gave him the slightest encouragement, and part of her wondered dispassionately if she would succumb.

He said, 'I find you very attractive, Alma, and now I discover that we are kindred spirits too. Although your abilities outreach my own. It was you who brought Edwin Davenport into this room, not I.'

She didn't reply, although she knew he spoke the truth. 'Can I ask you something?' he continued. Taking her silence as acquiescence he said, 'Have you ever tried to contact Gladys?'

Weaver kept his tone even, but inside he vibrated with hidden tension. The question was a vital one. Shocked by her spiritualist power he didn't doubt for a moment that direct communication with the woman he had murdered was a possibility.

She looked at him. 'You have a rare ability to ask me about matters that are on my mind, George. At our first dinner you wondered if I was thinking about assuming my aunt's role in the work here. And I was. And now you have again winkled out a question that I have been asking myself.'

'So not yet?'

She shook her head. 'It's true I have been reluctant to become involved with the spirit world again, but more importantly, in the letter I told you about my aunt specifically asked me not to seek her out. Even if I could.'

'I see.' He kept his face relaxed, but inside felt a surge of relief. 'And you haven't heard from her, as it were?'

'No.'

'Do you think you will try to reach out to her? Now that you are, shall we say, back in the saddle?'

'I'm not minded to at the moment, George.'

'What about taking her place in the work?'

She rose from the settee and smoothed her dress. He stood up too and she looked up at his handsome face before answering his question. Lady Davenport was clearly besotted with the man, and she could see why.

It would be so easy to sink into his arms. So easy.

But something held her back and she said, 'I think that is a distinct possibility, but I must ask you for more time.' Then she added quietly, 'As I must in all matters, George.'

* * *

The following evening Weaver went for a pint in the Rook. He was on his own and a happy man. The news from Berlin was that serious planning was taking place regarding his scheme. His brother had come through and asked him what date he proposed and, after working things out in his diary, he'd given them a two-day window during the last week of March or April.

On top of that, things were progressing very satisfactorily with Alma. He had been taken aback by the impact of her presence during the séance with Lady Davenport. The girl was in possession of a remarkable talent, and the prospect of Gladys managing to communicate with her was alarming. But that had clearly not happened, and he felt reasonably confident that Alma herself would not initiate such an enquiry.

In their conversation afterwards she had pulled back from raising her face to his for a kiss, but it was only a matter of time before intimacy occurred between them and he would make his move soon. A faint smile appeared on his face. It was a very pleasant thought indeed. From then on, the prospect of Gladys interfering from beyond the grave would be a non-starter. He'd make sure of that.

He stood at the bar and sipped his beer, then glanced round as the pub door opened and two women entered. One was a tall red-head with freckles and the other was shorter and pretty, with dark eyes. They walked past him and ordered two port and lemons. He watched them in the long mirror behind the bar. The taller one met his eyes for a moment in the reflection and he saw a brief flash of recognition before they took their glasses to a table in the corner and sat down.

Weaver took another drink. An alarm had gone off in his head and he didn't know why. The only thing that had changed had been the arrival of the two nurses. And that thought suddenly pulled him up, because the girls weren't wearing uniforms.

So why do I know they are nurses?

A shocking scene came into his mind. A chaotic madness of falling bombs, and fire and noise. Of people screaming as explosions shook the buildings along Arwenack Street, and of contorted bodies lying in the road. He'd been carrying the maid from the hotel, trying to find a place to dump her. And the tall, freckled girl had been there, in her nurse's uniform, working on a woman with a shattered leg.

They'd even exchanged a word or two. He remembered now. He'd told her the maid was dead and the nurse had said to take her to the King's Pipe. Which is what he'd done, and just left her on the ground. In the smoke and madness, no one had even noticed. But the nurse had seen his face, albeit fleetingly.

He moved slightly and found he could see the pretty nurse in the mirror. Her friend was obscured by one of the great black posts that supported the ceiling. As he watched, the girl turned to her friend and then, having listened for a moment, stared directly at his back. She looked for a long moment and then spoke to her friend again. Weaver could imagine the conversation only too well.

'That's the fellow I saw the night they bombed Arwenack Street. He was down there carrying a body. We spoke for a minute.'

'Are you sure?'

'Oh yes, it's him. I'm certain.'

Weaver tried to rationalise things. He'd been spotted. Did it matter? As far as the nurse was concerned, he was just a man helping during the bombing. But she'd seen him with the body and, if the police knew that Kate Diss had been strangled not killed in a blast, it was possible they were looking for the man who dumped her by the King's Pipe.

He was less concerned about the pretty one, but the red-haired nurse could identify him if the police called for witnesses. With his hat pulled down low, he quickly finished his pint, then left the pub without a backward glance and returned to the hotel, deep in thought.

* * *

The following evening Constable Robinson called round for Nell at the girls' flat and took her out for a fish supper. It was their third assignation. Left alone, Sally wrote a letter home and decided to take it down to the post box on the corner. She put on her coat and hat and departed, failing to notice a figure standing in the shadows opposite.

In the event she took a turn along Arwenack Street before settling down for the night and ended up meeting a doctor from the hospital who chatted to her for a few minutes, so it was three-quarters of an hour later before she walked back up her road.

George Weaver had used the time wisely. He'd worked out that although the terraced houses looked like single dwellings, the two adjacent doors in each front garden meant that they were maisonettes, each with a separate entrance. One would lead straight upstairs, the other into the hall for the downstairs flat. The nurse had come out of the left-hand entrance, and shortly beforehand the light in one of the top front windows had gone out. From that he assumed that they occupied the upper flat.

Aware the other girl had left with another man who'd seemed vaguely familiar, he had gone round to the rear of the terrace where an alley gave access to the backyards. Counting along he noted that there were no lights on in the girls' maisonette. The conclusion he reached was that there was no one else in residence and when the redhead reappeared after posting the letter she would be alone.

As Sally stood at the door with her back to the street and fumbled for her key, he glanced left and right. There was no one in sight. He moved quickly and silently over the road and through the open gate. As the unsuspecting girl opened the door he reached round, clamped his hand over her mouth and pushed her through it. The attack was so sudden and shocking that for a moment she didn't react, and he was able to kick the front door shut.

Then he moved his hands to her throat.

* * *

It was three hours later when Nell came home. Constable Robinson was keen to come in to say goodnight properly, but she put him off with a smile and a peck on the cheek.

'All good things come to those who wait,' she said and sent him on his way. She liked him – she was sure of that – but wanted some time to think about the pros and cons of being a police-man's wife in Falmouth before he was allowed any liberties.

With the front door shut she paused and sensed the still air. Her mother was fey and that sensitivity had passed to her daughter. There was a strange atmosphere at the foot of the stairs, as though there had been a disturbance. She climbed to the first floor and pushed open the sitting-room door, half expecting to see Sally there, but the room was empty and the fire out. Assuming she'd gone to bed early, Nell made herself a cup of tea and settled down to have a good think about Constable Robinson. Half an hour later she went to bed herself, leaving her flatmate undisturbed in her own room.

At half past six the next morning she woke to the alarm clock and got out of bed. She washed quickly, shivering in the unheated bathroom, and then went into the kitchen to make a pot of tea. She poured herself a cup and then, aware that there were no signs of life from Sally's room, knocked on the door.

'Come on, sleepyhead. There's tea on the table. You'll be late.'

There was no reply from inside, so she opened the door and put her head into the room. 'Come on now, Sal, wakey-wakey.' Nothing stirred beneath the eiderdown and all she could see was a flash of red hair on her pillow. Tutting to herself she crossed the bedroom and gave her a shake. Then another. Then she pulled back the covers and stared in horror.

Then she started to scream.

Chapter Seventeen

Alerted by a phone call from a neighbour, a police constable ran all the way to Sergeant Trewin's house on Norfolk Road near the bowling green, and breathlessly reported the news that a body had been found in a maisonette off Arwenack Street.

'It's a nurse that's found her, Sarge. And she doesn't think it's natural causes.'

'Hell's bells, another murder?' Trewin wrestled with his braces and jacket as they stood in the kitchen.

'Strangled, she thinks. She says she's been walking out with Constable Robinson.'

'Who has?'

'The girl that found her. She shares a flat with the deceased apparently.'

'What's her name?'

'Nell McGuigan.'

The name rang a bell with the sergeant. 'Right, give me the address then find Robinson and tell him to report to me there. It's a shame the inspector is away at his mother-in-law's for a week but we'll have to manage on our own.' This was a lie. In fact, Trewin was not sorry at all. In his view, his superior had not been as interested as he should have been in the murder of Kate Diss, and he was more than happy to be free to pursue his enquiries as he saw fit.

Half an hour later the two police officers were in the maisonette alongside a tearful Nell, Mrs Halls: the owner of the telephone from two doors down, and the dead body of Sally Regan. Once the preliminary examination had taken place a pot of tea was prepared, and the sergeant got the story out of Nell. Not that there was much to say.

'I went out with Arthur here' – she nodded at Constable Robinson – 'for a fish supper. Then we had a drink at the Farmer's Arms, and he walked me back about half past nine. I came in alone and had a cup of tea then went to bed. I didn't see Sal and thought she must have gone to bed too. This morning, when she didn't stir, I went in to wake her and, well . . .' She shrugged tearfully. 'There she was.'

Trewin looked at the girl in her nurse's uniform. She was pretty, he thought. No wonder Robinson was interested.

'So you didn't see her at all when you got back last night?'

'No.'

'Was the door locked when you arrived home?'

She shook her head. 'No, now I come to think about it. I've got a key of course but I just turned the handle and came in.'

'Was that unusual?'

'Not really. Not if one of us was in.'

'And Miss Regan wasn't expecting any visitors that you know of?'

She shook her head and he thought for a moment then addressed the neighbour. 'Did you see anyone in the street or near the house who looked suspicious?'

'No, dear.'

Sensing her hunger for more information, Trewin said, 'Well thank you for your assistance, Mrs Halls, my officer will see you out.' She departed with some disappointment, and when the constable returned he said, 'What was the name of that doctor who told us about Kate Diss?'

'Dr Grant, from Trevethan hospital.'

'That's him. Run over and see if he's there, will you. If he is, bring him here. I'd like him to have a look at Miss Regan's body before we move her.'

Constable Robinson, who had sat back down beside Nell, hesitated. The sergeant suspected they were holding hands below the table and gave him a thin smile. 'Go on, lad. She'll be fine with me until you get back.'

He departed with the same palpable reluctance as Mrs Halls, leaving Trewin and Nell alone.

'Who's Kate Diss?' she asked.

'A girl who was killed during the bombing.'

'Why do you want the same doctor who saw her to come and see Sally?'

'That's a police matter, Miss McGuigan.'

'Was she murdered too?'

Trewin hesitated. 'Look, I know you're a nurse and therefore a person of substance, but I really can't discuss that with you.'

But Nell sailed on regardless. 'Sally's been strangled. I'm pretty sure of it by the marks on her neck. Did Kate Diss have the same marks?'

'That's what I want to find out.'

'So she was!' Nell put her hand to her mouth.

The sergeant realised he'd been boxed into a corner in a few short sentences and for a moment pitied Constable Robinson, but then said, 'Look, Nell, if I may call you that, we believe that Kate Diss was murdered during the raid, but that has been kept confidential from the public for the moment. She was strangled and it was Doctor Grant who noticed, when he was checking for a cause of death. That's why I want him to come and see Miss Regan. It's possible it's the same man.'

The pretty nurse stared over the table at him, eyes wide. 'So there's a killer loose on the streets of Falmouth. Jesus, Mary and Joseph, are we all to be slaughtered in our beds?!'

Trewin stared back for a moment then said, 'Do you have any whisky in the house, Nell?'

* * *

It proved impossible to keep Sally Regan's death secret, or the manner of it. Mrs Halls had made good use of her telephone and at half past nine, just as Doctor Grant was leaving the maisonette, a man arrived from the *Falmouth Packet*. It was Mrs Wilson's son, Reggie.

'Doctor Grant, good morning,' he said cheerily. 'Here on business, I heard?'

'I really couldn't say,' he replied briskly and pushed past the reporter.

Sergeant Trewin appeared in the doorway and said, 'Mr Wilson. Always a pleasure of course but I'm afraid there's very little to tell.'

'And what would that very little be? If you don't mind me asking.'

'That the police are attending this property in regard to a deceased person being found here, but nothing more.'

'What's her name?'

'I didn't say it was a woman. Now please move along. I imagine the inspector will be making at statement in due course.'

'I thought he was away for the week.'

'Oh really? I had no idea. Good morning, Mr Wilson.' With that he retreated into the flat and shut the door.

By this time another nurse had arrived to sit with Nell and as they were ensconced in the kitchen with a pot of tea and a whisky bottle on the table, the sergeant took Robinson into the sitting room and said quietly, 'The doctor confirms death by strangulation. He's arranging for an ambulance to come and collect the body and will do a post-mortem later today to be absolutely sure, but there's not much doubt.'

'Is it the same man who killed Kate Diss?'

'The method is the same. It's certainly more than a possibility, but we can't make that assumption. It could be a sailor from one of the ships in the port, or just someone from the town.'

At this point there was a knock on the door and the nurse who was keeping Nell company poked her head round the corner. 'She's got something to tell you.'

They went into the kitchen where the girl, now on her second whisky, looked at them with soulful eyes. 'Yes, Nell?' Trewin asked.

'It may be nothing but the night before last, Sally and I were out in the Rook, and she saw the man she'd seen carrying a body the night of the bombing. The fellow you were asking about. She was sure it was him. He left later without saying anything to us, but I thought I'd better mention it.'

Robinson came to attention like a pointer spotting game. 'Why didn't you tell me before? She said she wouldn't recognise him.'

Nell shrugged. 'Well, she did. It was only a couple of days ago and I'd have told you at some point, but it didn't seem that important.'

The two policemen exchanged glances then Trewin said, 'Can you tell us what exactly happened please, Nell.'

An hour later the two policemen were back at the station, where they took stock. Constable Robinson confirmed the sergeant's feeling that he was a bright fellow who would go places by making an interesting point.

'Are we going public with the murder this time?' he asked.

'It'll be difficult to keep a lid on it. Mrs Halls is having her moment in the sun. I saw that reporter coming out of her house as we left.'

'It might be for the best anyway.'

'How so?'

Robinson cleared his throat and said, 'I see it like this, Sarge. From what Nell said it sounds like it's the same man as did for Kate Diss, and he thinks he's got away with killing her, because there's been nothing in the papers.'

'Yes, I'll give you that. Go on.'

'But say the murderer knew that Sally had recognised him. That's much more dangerous for him, because she saw him with the body. So he decides to do her in. Now then, he knows well enough that he strangled Sally Regan last night and she's bound to be found this morning. If there's nothing in the paper about her, he'll know we've hushed it up and that might get him wondering if we hushed up the first one too.'

Trewin looked at him. 'That is a very good point, lad. As things stand, he'll be expecting a fuss this morning. If there's nothing then he'll wonder why, and may well conclude that we're already after him for Kate Diss.'

'That's the one, Sarge.'

'Well let's not let him down then.'

* * *

The evening edition of the *Falmouth Packet* hit the newsstands in the town at half past five and George Weaver was one of the first people to buy one. He took it into a café on Arwenack Street and inspected Reggie Wilson's work on the front page.

Murder suspected as body is found

A young woman's body was discovered this morning in a maisonette on Bond Street. Miss Sally Regan aged twenty-three was found in bed by her flatmate, when she failed to get up for work. The victim was a Queen Alexandra nurse at Falmouth hospital and came from Sligo, in Ireland.

Sergeant Trewin of the Falmouth police told your reporter that foul play had not been ruled out. Any members of the public who were on Bond Street between the hours of half past six and half past nine on Wednesday evening are requested to come into the police station to make a statement. The sergeant emphasised that this is an isolated incident and asked that the public remain calm. The port is full of shipping at present, and it is believed the police are directing their enquiries in that direction.

Weaver read on avidly. It was clear from the tone of the report that the Falmouth constabulary suspected a seaman from one of the ships and were not connecting it with the death of the chambermaid.

He put the paper down and reflected. There had been nothing whatsoever about Kate Diss in the papers other than her funeral arrangements, and he was confident that the police had no idea she'd been murdered. Nevertheless, Sally Regan had recognised him, and he felt that he'd made a sensible decision in killing her. Any avenue that could lead to him was now blocked off. The pretty girl with her had seen his face in the Rook, but not on the night of the bombing, so she would be no use as a witness to the police.

All that remained was to find a new pub to drink in.

* * *

After dinner Weaver was sitting in his room on the top floor when there was a knock on the door. It was Valentine Wragge. 'Ah, George, did you manage to speak to Alma about the work?' he enquired.

'I did. She sat in on a séance with me and we discussed it afterwards.'

The older man eyed him. He had worked out some time ago what went on in his partner's consulting room when clients were at their most vulnerable. And elsewhere in the hotel for that matter. Weaver was extremely careful, but the fellow clearly had powerful appetites.

'What's her view?' he asked.

'She is a remarkably talented medium, better than me or you, Valentine.'

Wragge did not miss the trace of irony in the man's voice, and it irked him. 'We all serve the bereaved with the talents that we have available to us,' he said tightly.

'Indeed we do, and I imply no criticism whatsoever. You have a devoted and deserving following, my dear fellow . . .' he paused then added, 'however you do it.'

'Shall we move on. What did she say?'

'She is considering the matter and I think she will decide in our favour in due course. Her not unreasonable point at present is that she is still getting used to running the hotel.'

'Yes, she has a lot on her plate, I imagine. But your feeling is that she will assume Gladys's role?'

'In every way.'

'I noticed you've been out to dinner together a couple of times.'

Weaver looked at him then said neutrally, 'Indeed we have.'

'Are you interested in her? In that way?'

He shrugged. 'She's attractive and vivacious, but I wouldn't read too much into it, Valentine.'

'She has a young man doesn't she. Bricken, is it? Alan Bricken?'

'The telegraph fellow? Yes, I believe they've walked out. I met him once and think he's keen but I'm not sure about her. As I say, my objective is to get her involved in the work.'

'Well, we will just have to soldier on in the meantime.' Wragge sighed. The increased number of clients he was having to see was putting a strain on the partnership he had with the housebreaker who did his reconnaissance. 'How are you getting on anyway?'

Sensing the man wanted a chat, Weaver indicated a chair and rose to fetch two glasses and a bottle of whisky. 'Drink?' he asked. As Wragge nodded his agreement he continued, 'I'm all right. Lady Davenport who I am seeing at present is a pleasant woman and delighted with the work.'

'I noticed you were out on your motorbike the other day. That's unusual for the winter, isn't it?'

The German nodded. 'A little but I fancied a run and it's good for the engine to be properly warmed up once in a while.'

'Where did you go?'

'Over to Penzance and then down to Land's End,' his companion replied, knowing that the best lies are the ones rooted in truth.

'Maybe I should get one myself. I quite fancy the idea of spinning though the countryside in the summer.' Wragge sipped his drink.

'The whole coastline is quite magnificent and there a plenty of deserted coves, which are well worth a visit.'

'I'm sure.'

'How is your bridge coming along?' Weaver enquired.

'Very well as it happens. We are a lively little crowd, and the standard is quite high, though I say it myself. I'm giving a dinner for a few of them in the hotel next month. Do say hello if you're around.'

They chatted for another ten minutes then Wragge rose and left, leaving the German sitting thoughtfully in his seat.

* * *

Intent on pursuing his enquiries, Constable Robinson pushed the door of the Rook public house and went in. He walked over to the bar and asked for a word with the landlord. When the man appeared, they went through to the back.

'I'm hoping you can help me identify a fellow who was drinking in here recently,' he said.

'Oh? What's that about then?'

'I'm not at liberty to say. According to another witness he was standing at the bar about half past six on the second of March.'

The landlord thought for a minute. 'Wednesday just gone then.'

'That's right.'

'Nope, I wasn't working.' He shook his head. 'That was my wife's birthday; we went out for a meal.'

'Who was behind the bar then?'

The landlord went to the door and called out, 'Melvyn!' Moments later the large frame of a young man with rather vacant eyes filled the doorway. 'You speak to the constable now. He's got a question for you,' his commander in chief said encouragingly.

Robinson wasn't enthused. The fellow looked like the proverbial empty house. 'The landlord tells me you were working here last Wednesday evening,' he said.

'Was I?' A look of panic appeared on his face.

'So I'm told, yes. Look you're not in any trouble, I was just hoping you could remember someone who was in here.'

'Was it James Rowe?'

'Eh? No, it wasn't.'

'Was it Peter Bosanko?'

'No, not him either.'

'Carol Carlyon?'

'No. Look, Melvyn I don't know the fellow's name,' Robinson interjected before the lad ran through the entire electoral roll in Falmouth. 'But I'm told he was standing at the bar in the early evening.'

'What was his name then?'

'As I just said, I don't know his name.'

'What does he look like?' the landlord asked.

Robinson sighed and reflected that being a policeman was a thankless task on occasions. 'I don't know that either,' he admitted.

'So, you're looking for a bloke who's name you don't know. And you don't know what he looks like either,' the landlord summarised helpfully, the amused scepticism in his voice all too apparent.

'That's hard,' Melvyn observed, his face screwed up with effort.

'Bloody impossible, more like,' the landlord muttered.

'Look.' The constable attempted to take back control of the conversation. 'Do you remember anyone standing at the bar for an hour or so last Wednesday night?'

'Yes.'

'Good. Who?'

'James Rowe and Peter Bosanko.'

'I know them and they're too old. Anyone else?'

'Carol Carlyon was with them for a bit.'

'It's a man we're looking for. As I said.'

There was a long silence, so long in fact that the constable began to wonder if Melvyn was reliving his shift minute by minute. 'Anything . . . ?' he enquired tentatively.

'No. But then I only started in the bar at eight. I was in the cellar before then.'

'What? For heaven's sake, I said from half past six for an hour. Who was minding the bar then?'

'My brother.'

'Is he around?' Robinson directed this enquiry to the landlord who stared back sorrowfully.

'You won't get much out of him. Melvyn here is the brains of the family.'

'That's right,' the young man said proudly. 'I'm the one that can read. Well, a bit anyway.' He leaned forward and said, with a confidential air, 'Clem don't read at all. Mrs Lanyon at the school told my ma he's as thick as a plank. And she agreed. Can't tell a brown egg from a white, Ma reckons.'

Mystified, Robinson said, 'How do you both manage with the till?'

'They put it on the slate. The customers pay me when they see me,' the landlord said.

The constable pursed his lips and wondered how they did that if they could barely read between them. But he didn't ask. If ever he'd seen a lost cause, this was it.

'All right, we'll leave it then,' he said.

Chapter Eighteen

Felix Muller presented his plan for the raid on Cornwall at the German naval headquarters in Wilhelmshaven on the first of April. He hoped the day wasn't inauspicious. Tirpitz was there, along with three colleagues, one of whom Muller didn't know.

He spoke for ten minutes and when he finished there was a long silence.

'What do you think?' Tirpitz said eventually, well aware that the men at the table were all waiting to hear what he thought.

'It's an interesting idea,' one of them said. 'If it came off, it would be quite a coup.'

'There's no doubt about that,' the admiral agreed. 'What about you, Bauer?'

His remark was addressed to the man Muller hadn't recognised. He was about thirty-five, lean and bearded, with tired eyes. A silver badge was pinned on his lapel. It was a ring of silver metal with a submarine placed across it. With a little thrill he realised Bauer was a U-boat captain.

'Let me see the chart again.' Muller pushed it over the table and watched as the captain studied it intently for two or three minutes. Then he sat back and looked at Tirpitz. 'It's possible, providing we are not observed. Although God knows what will happen if the British realise we are there. They will have a lot of ships in the area, most of them dedicated to hunting submarines.'

He met Muller's gaze and added, 'The thing about a plan like this is that it seems feasible sitting in an office in Wilhelmshaven. But when the British spot us I'll be cursing you, Muller.'

'When or if?' Felix asked.

The man opposite him shrugged. 'You said yourself the coast is watched.'

'But it could be done?'

'Maybe.' With a thin smile Bauer added, 'Rather like a bad marriage, it's not the getting in, it's the getting out.'

A murmur of amusement passed around the table. 'And your crew, Captain. Are they capable of doing what's required?' the head of operations asked. He looked like everyone's idea of a seafaring man, Muller thought. A weather-beaten face and bearded like the U-boat man. All he needed was an eyepatch.

'I don't doubt it. But I say again, we would be placing the vessel in a very vulnerable position. If we're spotted we will have little room for manoeuvre.'

'But this is war, Captain. Surely some risk is acceptable,' Felix pointed out.

'You're confident your plan will work, Muller?' the head of operations asked.

'Yes, sir.'

'Have you ever been to sea? Or seen any action?'

You could have heard a pin drop. Tirpitz and his senior colleague were staring at him. Bauer was smiling. 'Good question,' he murmured.

'No, sir, I have not.' No other reply was possible.

He saw the U-boat commander raise his eyebrows. 'Not at all? You've never had anyone shooting at you?'

'No.'

'A paperwork man then.' The disdain was obvious.

Tirpitz stirred in his seat. 'We all have our roles to play.' He tapped his fingers on the table. 'I'm minded to approve this. The benefits are significant, and a successful operation will go down very well with the Kaiser.' He glanced at the head of operations and added, 'Is that all right with you, Willy?'

He nodded. 'Very well, we will commence preparations. Two weeks should be sufficient so we can be ready for the end of April, as suggested in the plan. I do have one condition though.'

'Yes?'

He looked at Muller with a piratical smile and said, 'The paperwork man goes too.'

* * *

In Falmouth, Alma was on Gyllyngvase beach with Alan Bricken. It was his afternoon off and they were having a stroll after a late lunch at the Rook, and chatting easily as they usually did. But in the pub Alma had sensed some kind of tension in her companion. As though his mind was occupied with thoughts he didn't want to share. She wondered whether to ask if something was troubling him but wasn't sure how to broach the subject.

What if it is something private that's none of my business?

Their relationship was at an awkward stage, she thought ruefully. They knew each other well enough to hold hands and share a kiss on the cheek, but not well enough to ask about things that might be seen as prying. She wondered how to cross the gap, because the more she saw of Alan the more she liked him. But then again, the looming prospect of his disappearance to some remote corner of the world at any moment made her wonder if there was any point.

She must have sighed because he glanced at her and asked, 'Something on your mind?'

She smiled back and squeezed his warm hand. 'No, everything's fine, thanks Alan.'

For his part he was sorely tempted to tell her about his promotion. It was a feather in his cap and he wanted her to know, and be proud of him. But George Weaver's advice had been very clear. *Don't rush things.*

And so they strolled on over the sand, happy in each other's company but with their minds full of things they should have said, but didn't.

* * *

Later that night, Alma lay in a dreamy half-asleep state in her bedroom. Not for the first time she wondered if George was awake down the corridor. It was a ridiculous thought, she told herself firmly, especially after enjoying a lovely afternoon with Alan, but when she turned over and closed her eyes, the idea lingered, strangely persistent in her mind.

He's managed to get inside my head.

But even as she wondered about that, she felt a distant summoning.

It was a feeling she recognised. By the time she left St Joseph's, Alma had withdrawn from the spiritualist world, but that didn't mean she was immune to contact from the other side. As she'd mentioned to George, there had been occasions when a spirit had come calling in a very direct way, like Alexander Watson's sudden appearance. But more often, when in a reflective state before going to sleep, she had felt a gentle sensation of pins and needles and sensed the presence of someone who wanted to connect with her. Like a faint tap on her front door or the distant tinkle of a bell. On each occasion she'd declined to answer, and the spirit had drifted away to try and find another willing to help.

And here was that same sensation again. Someone was calling, and this time Alma responded by relaxing and opening her mind. But instead of finding herself in the Hall of the Dead, where people waited to speak to loved ones they'd left behind, she felt herself tumbling backwards, head over heels, her body rigid and free of all earthly constraints – as though she was falling from a great height.

Then she was drifting in a still, quiet place. It was dark and she heard a voice. It was a child. She could see her in her mind, a girl aged about eight wearing a nightgown. Alma knew instinctively she'd died in a house fire although she was unmarked and looked positively angelic. *How appropriate*, she thought.

'Hello, are you Alma?' she said.

'Yes, I am.'

'I've a message for you.'

'What is it?'

She screwed her face up. 'I'm good at passing messages and normally they say things like "I love you", or "look in the tin in the shed". But this one isn't like that.'

'Can you tell me what it says?'

'Just two words and two letters: be careful and P. K.'

'That's it?'

'Yes. I've got to go now.'

'Wait. Who's it from? Who sent it?'

But the girl's image was already fading to black, and an awareness of being in bed in her room gently filtered back into Alma's consciousness.

The next morning she thought about what had happened and wondered if she'd dreamt the whole thing, but she'd written P and K down on a pad next to the bed and that wouldn't have happened if she'd been asleep.

The two letters were unfathomable for the moment, and she'd give them further consideration in due course, because there was a more pressing matter.

What do I need to be careful of?

If she was honest with herself, the only thing she could think of was the intense and handsome man lying in bed twenty feet from her.

Alma was no longer a Hampstead mouse. She was now a woman of means and position, and successful, charismatic, George Weaver was the sort of man she should be associating with. Always presuming he wasn't a German spy, and Alma had decided to give him the benefit of the doubt on that. Alan Bricken was a lovely man but could disappear from her life at any time. She simply couldn't ignore such a big thing. Whereas George was not just settled in Falmouth but living in the hotel. The truth was, in her heart of hearts, she knew that she would find it very difficult to walk away from whatever was to happen next.

* * *

At the police station, Constable Robinson looked up as a balding middle-aged man in office clothes presented himself at the counter.

'Can I help you?' he enquired.

'I read you're looking for anyone who noticed anything in Bond Street the night that girl was killed.'

'We certainly are.' The policeman came alert. After the gruelling visit to the Rook, he was hoping for a breakthrough. 'Did you see something?'

'There was a man behind their flat early evening. It was dark, but I saw him. I'm in the terrace on the other side of the alley, you see, and I looked out of my bedroom window at the back to see if I could spot Miss Peabody.'

'Does she live there too?'

'She lives with me, and it was her teatime. I'd got a nice bit of chopped liver from the butcher and put it in her bowl.'

The constable put two and two together. 'Miss Peabody is a cat.'

'Yes, of course.' The man's tone implied a judgement that Robinson felt was undeserved, but he grabbed his notebook and a pen and pressed on.

'What's your name, sir?'

'Mr Coren.'

'And you saw a man, you say?'

'Yes. He was definitely looking up at the back of the girls' building. They have the top flat there and he lingered for a few minutes, like he was keeping an eye on the place. Then he strolled off to the end of the alley.'

'What time was this?'

'About quarter to seven, I'd say.'

'And what did he look like?'

Mr Coren thought for a moment. 'He moved like an athlete. Sort of lithe, if you know what I mean. There is a light out there, but his hat cast a shadow over his face, so I didn't get a clear view of it.'

'What sort of hat?'

'A trilby.'

'And the coat?'

'A long overcoat. A good cut.' Coren simpered slightly, 'I'm a tailor. Not to my standards perhaps, but a nice garment.'

'What sort of height?'

'He may have been tall but it's hard to say. I was looking down, you see.'

'Did you notice anything else about him?'

'No it was just his behaviour, really. People walk through the alley, but they don't hang around there. It's not that sort of neighbourhood.' He produced a rather arch look.

'Of course not. Did he come back?'

'No, but neither did Miss Peabody and when I went to look again half an hour later someone was just finishing drawing the curtains in the back bedroom opposite.' Mr Coren shrugged. 'I'm just saying. If you live opposite someone you see them occasionally in their windows, don't you. Anyway, it didn't look like one of the girls. The outline was too big.'

'Outline?'

'The curtains are thin. You can see through them when the light's on.'

Robinson leaned forward. 'You think it was him, inside the flat?'

There was a palpable hesitation before an answer was forthcoming. 'I don't like to be indiscreet, and I don't spy on them obviously . . .'

Oh, I think you do. 'No of course not, sir, but this is a murder investigation, so I do need an answer.'

Mr Coren made an empty-handed gesture. 'I just don't think it was one of the girls, that's all.'

'And just to confirm we are talking about the redheaded girl's bedroom?'

'Yes. The brunette, the pretty one, is at the front. I believe,' he added.

Hard luck, Mr Coren. 'Is there anything else you wish to tell me?'

He shook his head. 'No, I don't think so.'

'Well, thank you for coming in. I'll just need you to come through and sign a statement for the record.'

When Mr Coren had departed, the constable found his sergeant in the kitchen filling the kettle. He told him what had happened. They repaired back to the office where Trewin stirred his tea reflectively and said, 'Sounds like it was the murderer to me. He was having a recce before he did the deed. Then Mr Coren saw him inside the flat.'

'I agree. That description strikes a chord as well, doesn't it? What did Sally Regan say about the man she saw carrying Kate Diss. "He was wearing a long coat and carried her easily," or words to that effect.'

'A long coat and a trilby are hardly unusual in Falmouth in the winter but, nevertheless, it's all starting to tie together. Sally Regan sees the man who's killed Kate Diss carrying her body during the bombing. A few weeks later they run across each other in the Rook and the murderer realises that she's recognised him. He thinks about it and decides to kill her to shut her up. And he doesn't hang about either.'

'He's got a reason for killing Sally Regan, but I wonder why he killed Kate Diss in the first place?'

'Good point. We never really uncovered a motive. It was the night of the bombing; maybe he realised it was an ideal night to get rid of a body and took the opportunity. But that doesn't explain why he wanted her dead.' He sipped his tea. 'It feels spontaneous to me, not pre-planned.'

'A lover's tiff?'

'Perhaps. Or maybe she interrupted him when he was up to something, and he had to act quickly. To shut her up.'

Robinson looked at him and the penny dropped. He sat up. 'Kate Diss worked at the hotel. What about those lights in the tower and on the car? We thought that was suspicious. If the murderer was the man who put them on, and Kate Diss stumbled over him doing it, perhaps that's why he killed her.'

'That would make him a traitor as well as a murderer. But it certainly makes sense. There are two men living in the hotel aren't there?' Trewin crossed to a cabinet and withdrew the file about the raid. He shuffled through the papers then gave a grunt of satisfaction.

'Here we are. George Weaver and Valentine Wragge. Both are residents and both gave us statements the morning after the raid. They claim they were in their beds until it all started then went down Arwenack street to help. That second bit is corroborated by others who saw them there, but there's no proof they were in their rooms before then – it's just them saying it.'

There was a silence, then Robinson said tentatively, 'Do you think we ought to tell the authorities that we think there might be a traitor in the hotel?'

'We are the authorities, Constable. It's up to us to solve this.' With a sinking feeling, Sergeant Trewin realised he'd missed a trick by not properly connecting the death of Kate Diss with the events up at the hotel. If they'd got the nurse up there to look at Wragge and Weaver, she'd probably have recognised one of them. And it was too late now.

He cleared his throat. 'Let me have a think about what's for the best, Robinson. I'll let you know.' The last thing he wanted was someone senior poking about in his mistakes with Inspector Luke's retirement less than a year away.

* * *

Having considered things carefully, a week later Sergeant Trewin called into his superior's office to report on developments in the Sally Regan murder.

'Why haven't you found this fellow yet, Trewin? It was all over the newspapers and people are asking questions,' Inspector Luke demanded.

'I quite understand, sir, and I'm sorry it's difficult for you, but we are making progress.' He told him about Mr Coren's witness statement and concluded with: 'There's a possibility there's a connection to the Kate Diss murder.'

'Kate Diss? We've closed the file on her, haven't we?'

'Indeed we have, sir. Nevertheless, there's a chance it might be the same perpetrator.'

Luke looked alarmed. 'What's your reasoning for that?'

Trewin quickly described the evidence Sally Regan had given about the man carrying the body on the night of the raid. 'The descriptions of that man and the one Mr Coren saw match . . .' he paused and added, 'such as they are. Athletic build, a long dark coat, trilby and so on.'

'You'd have to arrest half the men in Falmouth based on that.'

'I do agree with you, sir, I'm just telling you. And there's other circumstantial evidence that might suggest a link.'

'Such as?'

'The night of the bombing there were illegal lights showing at the hotel where Kate Diss worked. We think there's a faint possibility that she interrupted someone up to no good and suffered the consequences. Sally Regan might have seen the killer carrying her body that night, and was killed by him so she couldn't speak out when she recognised him in the pub.'

There was a long silence in the office, broken only by the cry of a seagull outside the window. Trewin thought it sounded as though it was laughing.

Finally, Luke said, 'It all sounds a bit thin to me, Sergeant. There's a lot of "might" and "faint possibility" in what you've told me. I wonder if you're not overcomplicating things. The Kate Diss file is closed. It was almost certainly someone from one of the ships, someone who may well be on the other side of the world now. I'd also remind you that only a handful of people know she was murdered. I'd prefer to keep it that way.'

'Yes, sir.'

'What I want you to do is find the man who killed Sally Regan. We're not interested in spurious connections to other matters. Do you take my point?'

Trewin braced himself and replied, 'There is also suggestion that the man who killed Kate Diss and Sally Regan, is a traitor. The lights in the hotel were used as a guide by the Zeppelin.'

Luke's eyes bulged. 'A traitor? What, like a spy you mean?'

'Something like that, sir.'

'Well now I've heard it all. We're not interested in bloody spies, and we're not interested in who killed Kate Diss.' The inspector rose to his feet and leaned over the desk. 'You need to do one thing, Trewin. Find the man who killed Sally Regan and find him quickly. Now get out; I've things to do.'

Having achieved his required objective, the sergeant departed. He made an official note that he had informed Inspector Luke of his suspicions regarding the connections between the murders of Kate Diss and Sally Regan, and the possibility of a spy operating from the Timperley Spiritualist Hotel and that he'd been instructed to do nothing about it by his superior. He signed and dated it, then got Constable Robinson to read it and observe him adding it to the Sally Regan file.

Chapter Nineteen

It was lunchtime on the 25th of April when Felix Muller kissed his wife goodbye, and caught the train to Wilhelmshaven. He arrived and presented himself at the office of the head of operations who kept him waiting for twenty minutes before appearing.

'Ah, Muller. Ready for your big adventure?' he asked with a smile on his face.

'Of course, sir. Anything for the Fatherland.' And to some extent that was true. The intelligence officer was a loyal servant of the Kaiser's Germany. But that morning he was also terrified, because Muller suffered from claustrophobia and the prospect of two days in a submarine as they travelled six hundred miles to Cornwall was not something he was looking forward to.

Or the rest of it for that matter.

'Leave your bag here,' the vice-admiral said.

'Pardon?' Muller had packed the absolute minimum, and the bag was small.

'There's no room for it. The men don't change their clothes on a voyage. Or wash for that matter. Don't worry, it'll be here when you get back.'

In cold wind and drizzle, they left the building and walked along a quay sandwiched between warehouses and a string of grey warships. After a quarter of a mile, they reached the U-boat. The top of the conning tower was level with the quay and as he looked down Muller thought the vessel looked alarmingly small compared to the cruisers and destroyers they had passed.

Too small, in fact. It looked like a toy for adults.

'How many in the crew, Admiral?' he asked, trying to make his enquiry seem casual.

'Thirty-six. Plus you, of course.'

The end of the quay was next to open water where the wind was much stronger, and Muller hid a shiver as a sailor on the conning tower brought himself to attention and saluted.

'Good morning,' the vice-admiral called across the gap. 'Is Captain Bauer on board?'

'Just behind you, sir,' came the reply.

Both men turned to see the sentry was correct. He came up to the two men and saluted then shook Muller's hand. 'Good morning, I'm glad you weren't foolish enough to bring a bag. We're leaving in three hours so come on board and I'll show you round U45.'

He looked at the admiral. 'Any last-minute changes, sir?'

'No, it's all on as far as I'm concerned. Good hunting, Franz.' He shook hands with them again, then turned and walked back along the quay without another word, pulling his collar up against the rain.

Bauer looked at Felix speculatively. 'Are you ready?'

'I'm not sure what to expect, but I think so.'

The captain laughed. 'Expect to be too cold and then too hot, cramped, short of air, filthy with sweat, and frightened. Anything better than that is a bonus. But it is a worthwhile mission, and the British will suffer for it.' He looked across to the conning tower where the sailor was watching them and called, 'We have a visitor, Johannes. Find somewhere for his hammock.' As the man moved, he looked at the intelligence officer and grinned. 'Come on then, Muller. Let's go to war.'

At dusk, U45 slipped her moorings and moved out of the port, staying on the surface. Half an hour later, with the island of Mellum off her starboard bow, she turned to port and rounded the point at Schillig where a fine sandy beach was popular with the locals in the summer. Muller had been allowed up onto the conning tower and it was a relief to escape the malodorous combination of sweat and diesel oil that had already soaked into his clothes and hair.

There were three other men squeezed into the limited space and Bauer said, 'We're going to stay between the coast and the Frisian Islands for as long as we can. It's shallow water but there are no British warships in here so we can remain on the surface. Once we turn into the North Sea at Borkum we really need to keep an eye open. We'll go through the Dover gap submerged, so you'll have something to tell your grandchildren about.'

If I survive. Muller nodded but didn't say anything. The prospect of being sixty feet underwater while being hunted was an appalling prospect and he hoped he wouldn't embarrass himself. Grim-faced, he stared out across the dimly lit water and tried to control his rising panic.

* * *

By contrast, in Pendennis Castle, the man looking out to sea was calm and relaxed. He'd just come on duty and had a large mug of tea at hand as he stared out of the narrow slit that ran for twenty feet across the gunnery observation bunker.

'Something out there, Sarge,' his colleague said. He was standing up and had his eyes glued to a large pair of binoculars that were bolted onto a rotating stand. 'Bearing one seventy. Two ships. One's a destroyer I think.'

There was a scramble as the other three men in the watch grabbed binoculars, and seconds later they were all combing the dark sea.

'It's *Matchless* and the *Persian Knight*,' the first man said. 'Back from the Gulf.'

'Yes, I can see them now,' the sergeant said.

As the private on the range finder called, 'Range eighteen hundred yards,' he crossed to a telephone at the back of the emplacement and rang the sighting through to the command office in the fort buildings above them.

'Back safely then. That's good news for the matelots,' the man on the binoculars said.

'Yes, at least they've got four days of peace before they're off again,' the sergeant replied. 'They're safe enough inside the estuary, moored on that berth.'

'That's true,' the private agreed.

* * *

Early the following morning Alma attempted to write a letter to James Nascent with the news from the hotel, but she struggled to concentrate and after a few lines she put the pen down and crossed to the dormer window of her sitting room. The elevation meant she had a decent view of the town. Down below she could see the backs of the houses and shops by Custom House Quay. There were some gaps after the Zeppelin raid and, through them, the water glinted in the low sun.

She stared, unblinking, at the flickering light, and for a moment she was dreamily frozen in time – connected to everything that had ever happened to her, or ever would. It was a familiar feeling and one she had experienced many times as a teenage girl at St Joseph's.

As she drifted deeper into the trance, pins and needles buzzed through her body, and an image of the angelic child who had come to her before appeared in her mind.

And when she spoke, the message resonated quite clearly. There was no mistaking it.

P. K. Now.

* * *

James Nascent had just finished his breakfast with Mrs Neal when the telephone rang. He answered and heard Alma at the other end. After the usual pleasantries had been observed she said, 'I've had a message. I'm not sure what it means, and I'm not sure what to do.'

'Err . . . a message as in . . . ?' He left the question hanging.

'Yes.'

'I see. What is it?'

'It's just two letters. P and K.'

'P and K?' The surprise in his voice was obvious.

'Yes, quite. It's all rather cryptic and apparently it's also very urgent. I've been wracking my brains to think of someone with those initials who might be in danger of some kind. Can you think of anyone?'

'Off the top of my head, no. Was there anything else?'

'It seems I need to be careful.'

'Well that is concerning. Have you any inkling of what was meant by that?'

Alma hesitated. 'In confidence, James, I have been out to dinner with George Weaver a number of times and there is an undeniable chemistry between us. I'm wondering if it's to do with that.'

'Weaver? Of all the people, Alma. I mean the possibility remains that he is a German spy.' The concern in his voice was very clear.

'I know,' she said in a small voice. 'It's inconvenient to say the least.'

'Er, in matters of the heart . . .' James paused and groped for what to say next but, attracted by a female sixth sense, Hilda appeared at his elbow. She raised her eyebrows and he willingly succumbed. 'Hold on, Hilda wants a word.'

She took the receiver and said, 'Hello, dear, can I help?' and with some relief the solicitor made himself scarce.

Alma explained the warning she'd received and the matter to which she thought it might refer, and they discussed the pros and cons of Mr George Weaver with a directness that women often display when men are out of earshot. Then Alma mentioned Alan Bricken.

'I've walked out with him a few times. He's got a good career with prospects and is a lovely down-to-earth fellow. But his job with the telegraph company means there's a strong chance that he'll be posted off to some far-flung corner of the empire at any moment, and that's putting me off for obvious reasons. I really do like him, but falling in love with Alan is a rather impractical prospect.'

'Yes, you're hardly free to follow him, are you.'

'No, my future is in Falmouth and George is very settled here, and successful of course. Famous even, in a way. I see him and talk to him every day and, well . . .' She tailed off.

'He is handsome, has a whiff of excitement about him, and seems keen on you,' Hilda observed.

Alma could feel her smiling down the phone. 'Oh dear, it's all very confusing. I don't doubt that he is much more experienced in these things than I am, but I do find him occupying my thoughts to a degree that is hard to ignore.'

'Although he may be a German spy.'

'I don't think he is. Remember James looked hard and could find no evidence of that.'

'Don't think he is, or don't want to think he is? There is a difference.'

A brief silence followed as this remark sank in, then Alma said, 'I almost kissed him in his consulting room after a séance.'

'Ah. So things are at that point, are they?' Hilda said neutrally. 'What stopped you?'

'A sixth sense, I suppose.'

They continued to talk for some time before hanging up and Hilda went to find James in the sitting room.

'And what was the outcome of that?' he asked, putting his book down.

She pursed her lips and said, 'I think she's going to ignore the warning.'

He looked at her, concern clear on his face. 'I take it that means she will continue to explore an association with Mr Weaver?'

Hilda laughed. 'What a ponderous way of putting it, James. The woman is clearly falling for him, and she owes it to herself to see where the journey will lead.'

'If it goes wrong, she may find herself in danger. I'm tempted to instruct her to stop.'

'That's hardly your decision. You have no authority over her.'

A curious expression appeared on his face. One which Hilda could not immediately decipher so she added, 'Forewarned is forearmed, James.'

'Only up to a point,' he muttered. 'Remember the Light Brigade.'

* * *

In the event, later that night in Falmouth, Alma's indecision over the two men was brought to a head because, at ten minutes past midnight, George Weaver came to her.

At first, she thought that she was experiencing the same drifting, semi-dream, that had occurred before. She heard his gentle voice and felt the touch of his hand on her shoulder and smiled to herself as she settled down to enjoy the delicious fantasy.

But the voice was gently persistent, and the soft stroking on her neck was somehow much more real than the previous occasion. With a rush she came to the surface, opened her eyes, and realised that it was no dream. He was there, in a silk dressing gown, sitting on the edge of her bed, and smiling down at her in the soft light from the window.

'George!' she whispered, eyes wide. 'What are you doing here?' Clutching the eiderdown, she struggled into a sitting position and stared at him, her heart almost beating out of her chest.

But he just smiled and leaned forward and, as the faint smell of his sandalwood cologne reached her, he let his lips caress the side of her neck sending shocking, thrilling sensations rippling through her body. With his face six inches from hers, he whispered, 'I just couldn't stay away any longer, my darling.'

Head swimming, Alma felt herself on the verge of surrender, but somewhere deep inside her a still, bright light burned, and she saw it and, with a sudden burst of clarity, came to her senses.

'No, George.' She placed her hand on his chest and firmly pushed him back. He sat on the edge of the bed four feet away and looked at her with a quizzical smile.

'You mean to deny your feelings and my own, my darling?' he said.

With him at a safer distance the fleeting madness in Alma was rapidly fading. 'You are making assumptions that you do not have permission to make. I am not your darling. Also, you seem to forget that I am walking out with Alan Bricken and would never betray his trust.'

He nodded slowly as if turning this over in his mind then said, 'I see I have misread your signals. Please accept my apologies and I hope that I have not embarrassed you.' He stood up. 'Goodnight, Alma. When we see each other tomorrow morning, this will never have happened.' And with that he walked to the door, opened it, passed through and closed it quietly behind him.

Left alone, Alma's mind was going twenty to the dozen.

Misread your signals? The cheek of the man.

But as she lay there for the next hour turning the incident over in her mind, she knew that if she was honest with herself, George had a point. She had almost kissed him in the consulting room and an experienced man like him would know that. As she had admitted to Hilda, she had been thinking about him far too much, and tonight had almost paid the price. Lovely Alan Bricken was her young man, she told herself firmly, and that was the way things would remain. Henceforth, the dangerous temptations of George Weaver would be locked away in a distant corner of her mind, there to slowly decay until there was no danger.

* * *

James Nascent also had a restless night, but for very different reasons. Because at four o'clock in the morning he opened his eyes to find the solution to the P. K. mystery clear in his head. Having woken Hilda and told her, he then had to wait, wide awake and in a fever of impatience, for five hours.

When he finally left the flat, he was carrying a suitcase. In response to Hilda's query he said, 'I'm going to Falmouth when

I've been to see Kell. There's something about Alma's phone call last night that worries me, and I'd like to be on the spot for a day or two.'

As Big Ben chimed nine, he entered the building where Vernon Kell had his office and asked for an immediate appointment. He was shown up.

'Morning, my dear fellow, what's so urgent? Have you found the Falmouth spy?' The head of MI5 was in a good mood, having won a political battle the previous evening. 'Coffee?'

'Thank you yes, I will. And no, I'm afraid I haven't. I do, however, have some news to impart to you, which is serious, I think.'

'Very well, I'm all ears.'

'You'll recall Alma Timperley of course. And the spiritualist work that takes place at her hotel?'

Kell inclined his head. 'I do.'

Nascent hesitated. *How to put this?* After a moment he said, 'I won't beat about the bush. Alma has received a message stating unequivocally that there is an imminent threat to someone or something down in Cornwall represented by the letters P and K.'

Kell's eyebrows rose a considerable distance. 'When you say, "received a message", am I to assume that this is in the context of the hotel's work?'

'You are,' James said gravely.

There was a silence as Kell considered his response. Then he said, 'And what conclusion have you reached?'

'I can only think of one thing to which those letters can be ascribed – a large tanker called the *Persian Knight* that travels regularly between the Persian Gulf and Falmouth. The round trip takes a month or so and she is often moored on her berth in the port. My concern is that the Germans may intend some kind of attack on her.'

'Knight with a K, obviously?'

'Indeed.'

'And why has Alma been singled out as the recipient of a warning?'

The solicitor raised his hands in acknowledgement of the point Kell was making. 'I completely understand if you are sceptical. As it happens, I know something of the spiritualist world. A woman with whom I was very well acquainted was a talented medium and, in a field crowded with fakes, the genuine article. She was Alma's mother. I believe her daughter has the same abilities and I'd be inclined to take the message seriously.'

Kell stared at him for a moment, then decided the risk outweighed his doubts and reached for the telephone. 'Get me the docks commander in Falmouth, will you.' He replaced the receiver, stood up, and said, 'I will act upon your information. Now you'll have to excuse me as I'm due in Downing Street in half an hour and must prepare a note. Good morning, Nascent.'

He reached out his hand and as they shook he added, 'Not a word about this, all right?'

'Of course. I'm used to keeping secrets.'

A minute after the solicitor had left, the phone rang and Kell found himself speaking to Captain Hyde in the dock office overlooking the harbour in Falmouth. He introduced himself and asked the question that was uppermost in his mind.

'Is the *Persian Knight* in Falmouth at present?'

'She is. Arrived a day ago and will be here for another three days unloading. Then she'll sail for the Gulf again.'

'I've received information that an attack might be being planned on her. Do you think that's feasible?'

'An attack? What sort of attack?'

'That's what I'm asking you, Hyde. If the Germans decided to have a pop, how would they go about it?'

241

'Well, the port is shielded from seaward shellfire by Pendennis Castle, and we have gun batteries on either side of the entrance to the estuary. The ranges are all calculated, and firing angles prepared, so it would be a brave German warship that tried to force the issue.'

'I'm pleased to hear it. What else?'

'Sabotage possibly, I suppose, although that's unlikely. There's security on the gates and someone would have to smuggle a bomb in and get it all the way down to the berth, then set it off when they were well out of range. I can't see that happening, Mr Kell.'

The man at the London end of the phone grunted, then said, 'If you were tasked with doing it, what would you do? Speaking as a navy man.'

Hyde remembered his daydream as he watched them trying to refloat the *Annie-May*. 'There is one possible way, although it's high-risk to say the least.'

'And that is?'

'This is the deepest estuary in Europe. I'd sneak a submarine in and torpedo her while she's moored on the mole.'

Chapter Twenty

Thirty-six hours after leaving Wilhelmshaven, U45 surfaced three miles off the coast of the Isle of Wight. As the conning tower hatch was opened, cold fresh air crept down into the submarine's control room and Muller thought it was the finest sensation he'd ever experienced. Like being showered with champagne.

The underwater passage through the narrowest part of the English Channel had been terrifying. Enclosed in the hot, cramped, dripping-wet tube, they had twice heard the vibrating rumble of marine engines. The first time Bauer had caught his eye, nodded upwards and said, 'Merchant ship. It's a shame we can't stop and have a look.' But the second time the noise had been faster and higher-pitched and, as the submarine vibrated and things rattled, he'd looked at Muller again, his face serious.

'British warship. Maybe a destroyer or a frigate. Going right over us.'

Something must have shown in the intelligence officer's face because the captain had nodded as if in agreement and added, 'Welcome to our world.'

Sadly, their time on the surface was brief. A sailor spotted a funnel in the moonlight, and it was quickly identified as a Royal Navy frigate. With a clang the diving alarm sounded and forty-five seconds later the conning tower slipped silently below the waves.

'At least we got a plot on the Isle of Wight,' Bauer remarked and crossed to the chart table jammed into a corner of the control room. To reach it he had to squeeze past two other sailors. Five minutes later he gave a new course to the helmsman and said to Muller, 'We'll make the attack in the early hours of the 28th, right in the middle of the range you gave us. For now, we'll make our way to the general area.'

Muller nodded. There was little to say. At least the crew all had something to do. His job was to stand there and wait, while trying not to imagine a torrent of seawater flooding into the control room.

'Excellent, Captain,' he said finally.

* * *

To say there was a flap on in the dock office in Falmouth was a considerable understatement. Captain Hyde called an urgent meeting with the senior officer from the available Royal Navy ships out in the estuary and laid bare the information he had received.

'There's an unidentified but imminent threat to the *Persian Knight*. In discussion with the powers that be in London we've reached the conclusion that it's most likely to be a U-boat attack. She's a sitting duck moored where she is, if they can get a bead on her.'

Shock showed on the face of his colleague, a rather dour Scot called MacAllister, who commanded a destroyer that was temporarily stationed at the port. 'The first we'll know of it is when she blows up,' he said.

'Yes, quite. And she'll take us and the rest of the town with her,' Hyde observed with a touch of acid in his tone. 'So we must stop it happening. The question is how.'

There was a silence then the Scotsman said, 'The U-boat will have to come in at periscope depth. They couldn't risk that passage otherwise, with no bearings and a sodding great lump of granite in the way.'

'Black Rock? That's a good point. Observers and search-lights up on Pendennis would make life very difficult for her and there's a reasonable chance we'd see the wake from the periscope. There are a couple of quick-firing twelve-pounders up there too.'

'We're up against it though, make no mistake,' said Mac-Allister. 'On a high tide there's over a hundred feet of water in the estuary. She'll have to come a ways in, I'll grant you that, but it is possible to do the whole thing underwater in my view.' He shook his head. 'It'll take some nerve though.'

'Therefore, the question remains. How do we stop a U-boat skipper making a name for himself by blowing up the *Persian Knight*.'

'Move her?' the Scotsman ventured.

'I've already considered that. I'm informed that the threat is imminent, which means the U-boat may well be outside the estuary already. I imagine the captain would be as pleased as punch to see the largest tanker Britain possesses steaming out towards him, so that's a non-starter. And there's nowhere else inside the estuary that would be any improvement on the berth.'

'So, by a process of elimination, if we can't stop the submarine sneaking in, and we can't move the target, we've got to stop the torpedo,' McAllister thought aloud. He looked at the dock commander. 'Did I see that you got that coaster refloated the other day?'

The docks commander looked at him. 'Yes, she's good for nothing though. Sold for scrap already I believe.'

'But she's floating at the moment?'

Hyde's face cleared. 'I think I see where you're going with this. If we anchored her say thirty or forty yards off the *Persian Knight*'s berth, she'd block the torpedoes. Is that what you're thinking?'

'It would be a start. She's less than half the tanker's length so there still a good chance the U-boat commander would get lucky, but it's something.' MacAllister shrugged.

'Let's have a look at the chart,' said Hyde.

By the time dusk fell the port was on high alert. The *Annie-May* had been towed out of the harbour and was anchored in position so she shielded the bow section of the *Persian Knight*, forcing any U-boat deeper into the estuary to get a clear shot. And up on Pendennis Castle a searchlight shone down onto the restless black water in the entrance channel. The tide was high and only the tip of the beacon on Black Rock showed as the bright beam combed the narrow passage. Further along the battlements two twelve-pounders and a heavy machine gun were fully crewed and waiting.

'If she tries to slip in, I'm pretty confident we'll see her,' the colonel told Captain Hyde as they sat in his office. 'I'm no sailor but I can't imagine you could run that gap underwater without the periscope up to get bearings.'

'Let's hope so. The tide will be pushing her in as well. They're brave men to have a try, but we need to kill them, Colonel. No hesitation.'

'I've told the men. They have clear instructions.'

'It's just a waiting game then.'

'As it so often is. Sherry, Captain?'

* * *

Three hours later U45 approached her target with considerable caution. Like all seamen, Captain Bauer knew that safety lay in deep water, not a few hundred yards off the coast where escape routes were limited, and reefs lurked in the shallows.

As they surfaced, he climbed out of the conning tower hatch and quickly looked around. The dark coast lay ahead, and he could see a small cluster of lights further inland, but there was no other sign of habitation. A man appeared next to him holding a pair of binoculars and he gestured over his shoulder and said, 'Face the stern, Johannes, and keep combing the horizon. I don't want anything sneaking up on us. That's your only job and you keep doing it whatever else happens.'

'Yes, Captain.' The sailor moved to the back of the tower and raised the glasses to his eyes.

Felix followed two sailors up the ladder and joined Bauer who nodded at him. 'Here we are, Muller. I'm going in very slowly. The charts mark the seabed as clear and sandy, but you never know.'

'Very wise,' the intelligence officer agreed then moved aside as best he could as a machine gun was fixed to a mounting. He heard the ratchet as it was cocked.

'Ready, sir,' a voice said quietly.

On the deck ahead of the conning tower, a group of men had appeared next to the main gun. He watched as a shell was loaded into the breech and the elevation was adjusted. One turned and gave the thumbs up to the men on the conning tower.

'Quiet, isn't it,' Felix said. And he was right. It was a still, cold, night, with a quarter moon and Porthchapel cove was calm. 'Good for the boat.'

As he spoke, three clear flashes showed in the darkness above the beach.

'Speaking of which,' Bauer murmured, then spoke into the voice tube: 'Open the main hatch and get the boat out. We're going ahead. Raiding party onto the deck and bring the charges.' He glanced at Muller. 'Once that main hatch is open, we've really got our knickers down. Let's hope no one takes advantage.'

'Excalibur is there. He wouldn't have signalled if there was any danger.'

The captain grunted in acknowledgement then said, 'Anchor,' down the tube, and an alarmingly harsh rattle echoed round the cove as the chain slipped out, then stopped abruptly. They watched as a large hole appeared on the foredeck. More men scrambled out and hauled a folding boat up through the gap. As it was assembled Bauer said, 'Come on then, Muller. We'll lead the way. Keep your eyes peeled, Johannes.'

With a quick final word to the first officer, Bauer climbed down the external ladder and Felix followed. They walked along the foredeck to where the boat lay alongside the black hull. A pile of rifles and two large rucksacks were stowed on its floor, along with some spades. 'Sit next to me at the back,' the captain said and then climbed nimbly aboard. Muller followed and took his seat next to the tiller. The sailors boarded without saying a word. Not for the first time on the mission, Felix was impressed. Bauer's command style was casual, but the crew were highly disciplined and efficient.

He looked at the deserted beach and felt a surge of excitement.

The British have no idea we're here.

The men on deck released the mooring lines and the sailors picked up their paddles and pushed off. Within seconds they were fifteen feet from the hull. Then in response to a quiet order from the captain they began to work in unison, with regular co-ordinated strokes on either side.

'They've been practising,' Bauer whispered with a quiet smile, but then added, 'It's good that it's calm, because the boat is full and there's not much freeboard.' He turned the little craft towards the beach two hundred yards away and a few minutes later they pushed through the small waves that broke in the shallows and drove the bow onto the sand. The men quickly disembarked. Muller and the captain were last out and the water leaked into the intelligence officer's shoes. It felt freezing cold. He squelched ashore and looked back at the U-boat for a moment. She looked small below the cliffs, but nevertheless, to anyone casually looking into the cove there would be no mistaking the implications.

The Germans are here!

'There you are,' Bauer said quietly. Muller turned and stared up the beach. A steep bank of rock and sand blocked any exit on the right-hand side, but to the left a narrow valley had formed where a stream ran down from the fields. In the dim light a tall figure wearing a hat and long dark coat was visible at its foot. He raised his arm and beckoned.

'Come on.' Leaving two men to guard the boat, the captain led the other four sailors across the beach. All carried rifles and spades, and two wore the rucksacks. Bauer and Muller both had pistols in holsters.

'Welcome to Cornwall,' the man said quietly in German when they got to him.

Muller stared, momentarily fascinated by the sight of the spy. 'You're Excalibur?' he asked.

The man nodded briefly. 'I am.'

'I'm Muller from military intelligence. This is Captain Bauer.' The men shook hands.

The agent gestured up the valley said in a sotto voce, 'There's a little hamlet up there called St Levan and a rough lane that leads to Porthcurno, but there's always a chance of meeting someone, even in the middle of the night, so we'll take the coastal path over the headland. It's about twenty minutes' walk to the cable beach. I'll lead the way. As quiet as possible please.'

He turned and led them up the right-hand side of the valley, as the stream rattled in the shadows below. At the top they came to a field gate. Their guide opened it and slipped through whispering, 'Last man shut it. We don't want the sheep getting out and waking the farmer.'

Moving silently, the raiding party walked up the side of a thick Cornish hedge and disappeared into the gloom.

* * *

Even though it was half past two in the morning, Kell and Bright were in the MI5 offices in London. Both men had been involved in a late-night briefing about a suspected saboteur operating in London docks and after the meeting they'd come back to prepare a new set of security instructions for distribution first thing in the morning.

'Right, that'll do it, Bright. We'll turn in now, I think. A quick snort before you head off?' Kell already had the bottle in his hand and his assistant willingly agreed.

'Very nice, sir. Thank you.'

'Did you hear about the panic in Falmouth earlier on today?' the head of MI5 asked.

'I know something was going on but not the details.'

'Intelligence came through about a possible raid. An attempt to get a tanker called the *Persian Knight*. She's a regular in the port and has just got back from the Gulf with more than twelve thousand tons of petrol on board.'

Bright blew out his cheeks. 'That would be a bad loss. Who gave us the tip-off?'

Kell cleared his throat hesitantly. 'I'll be honest with you, it's not the most regular of sources. You remember James Nascent? You met him in January when he was heading down to Falmouth to try and tease out that spy?'

'At that spiritualist hotel place, yes I do. He didn't have much luck in the end, did he?'

'No. Drew a blank in fact. Or rather "case not proven" as they say in the Scottish courts. Anyway, he's back in town now and turned up here in a terrific fuss. He'd had a message from Alma Timperley, the girl who'd inherited the hotel. She was convinced that there was a very imminent threat in the area, somehow connected to the letters P and K.'

'Really? That sounds very mysterious. Where had she got that from?'

At this point Kell's nerve failed him. 'That's confidential I'm afraid,' he said with a slight frown. 'Anyway, Nascent pointed out to me that the letters are, of course, the initials for the *Persian Knight*, spelt with a K. He also pointed out that there was widespread relief that she wasn't hit during that Zeppelin raid, because if she'd gone up while moored in Falmouth the explosion would have taken out the docks and most of the lower town.'

'Good Lord. But surely she'd be safe from attack in Falmouth Roads.'

'You'd think so, but I rang the dockmaster, who's a navy man, and he admitted that the thought of a U-boat attack had crossed his mind. The estuary is deep enough for a submarine to sneak in and if she could get lined up, the tanker would be a sitting duck. The berth is on the outside of the mole you see, not within the harbour.'

'Ye gods, what's happening down there now?'

'He said he'd think of something. I left it with him.'

There was a knock on the door and one of the duty secretaries came in with some papers. Kell gave him a nod as he put them on his desk.

'P. K. in Cornwall, who'd have thought it.' Bright shook his head. 'Well done to Nascent for getting on to it.'

'Exactly. He thought it might have been an individual but there's no one with those initials down there who'd be targeted, and the Huns aren't the type to go for assassinations anyway.' He glanced up at the secretary who was hovering. 'Something else, Carter?'

'Begging your pardon, sir, but did you say P. K.?'

'That's right. We had a tip-off about a threat in Cornwall against someone or something with those initials, but the only possible target is a tanker called the *Persian Knight*. And it's been taken care of.'

The man nodded uncertainly. 'With respect, sir, actually, it's not. I've got a pal who works for the Eastern Telegraph Company at Porthcurno, where the undersea cables come ashore. All the empire's worldwide telegraph traffic goes through there, whether it's coming in or going out.'

'Yes? And?'

'PK is the telegraphic address of the place. PK Porthcurno.'

There was a shocked silence in the room. 'Are you sure about that?' Bright asked.

'Oh, there's no doubt. He's allowed to cable me free of charge you see, so I get messages regularly. Zodiac House is the name of the building, but the sender is always PK Porthcurno. It's definitely their call sign.'

Cursing quietly, Kell reached for the phone on his desk and lifted the receiver. 'I want a call put through to the Eastern Telegraph Company . . .' he raised his eyes in a query to Carter, who nodded '. . . in Porthcurno in Cornwall. It's urgent. Call me back as soon as you have them.' He replaced the receiver and said to Bright, 'It must be a twenty-four-hour operation down there. Someone will be on duty.'

'Indeed.'

Carter left and the two men had an anxious wait until the bell rang, suddenly loud in the silence. Kell snatched it up. 'Yes? Right, put them through.' He moved round to his seat behind the desk and sat down as the operator connected the call. 'Hello, who is this please?' Bright heard a tinny voice reply, then Kell spoke again.

'Now listen to me, Kendrick. My name is Kell, and I am the head of military intelligence in London. Who is in charge down there?' There was another pause then he said, 'Very well. When we have finished speaking, you go and wake Mr Trent and tell him we suspect that a German attack on the cable station at Porthcurno is imminent. I imagine a raid from the sea is the most likely thing. Do you have any soldiers there?'

He rolled his eyes at the response. 'Normally, but not at the moment? What the devil does that mean?' The tinny voice sounded again and Kell said, 'All right, Wait a minute.'

He looked at Bright. 'You're not going to believe this. There's a unit of the Highland Light Infantry stationed there, but never in the last week of the month. Words fail me. Get onto the garrison commander in Falmouth and ask him to send some troops with all despatch. They are to go now, not in the morning.'

As the man at the other end spoke again, Bright moved towards the door. But Kell suddenly stood up and held out his arm to stop his assistant, his face slack with shock. 'Wait.'

'Is there something else?' his assistant queried.

'Kendrick says he can hear shooting,' Kell said.

Chapter Twenty-One

In the absence of the Highland Light Infantry, for the final week of every month the young men from Zodiac House performed their own sentry duty. The brunt of the work was carried out by the gallant members of the Porthcurno rifles club, which numbered twelve men, each with their own weapon.

At five minutes to midnight, as U45 felt her way towards the Cornish coast, Alan Bricken and Jerry Wentworth climbed the steep cliff path to relieve their fellow club members and man the graveyard shift in the lookout hut. Both were wrapped up against the cold and carried their rifles, sandwiches and a bottle of water. The hut was equipped with a kettle and primus stove so they could make tea.

By ten past twelve they were alone and settled in. Alan used a pair of binoculars to scan the horizon as Jerry sat alongside him. After a few minutes he sighed and said, 'Nothing.'

'What a surprise,' his friend observed in a disappointed tone. They both rather enjoyed this brush with the real war and had discussed the chance of having a pot shot at the Huns on many occasions as they sat in the darkness. On clear moonlit nights the view out to sea was stupendous and there had been the occasional thrill as a darkened ship slipped past close inshore.

'Who's that, do you reckon, one of theirs or one of ours?' Jerry would inevitably say, and Alan would invariably reply in an authoritative tone that it was the flagship of the Swiss navy, or HMS *Pinafore* with Captain Corcoran on the quarterdeck, or some similar nonsense. Young men occupy themselves thus when employed on monotonous duties.

They took turn and turn about, two hours on and two hours off, and during his watches Alan was prone to fantasising about being there with Alma, cuddled under a blanket to keep out the cold as he asked her to marry him. In his mind the dialogue was always the same.

'I love you very much you know, Alma. Will you marry me?'

'Of course I will.'

'It'll mean coming out to Ascension Island for a couple of years. Is that all right?'

'Anything to be with you, my darling.'

And at that point she would always give a deep and fulsome sigh of happiness, wrap her arms around his neck, and matters would conclude very satisfactorily. Indeed, the only fly in the ointment of these delightful imaginings was the steady snoring coming from a bobble-hatted Jerry Wentworth as he reclined in a deck chair, his overcoat pulled up to his chin and mouth open.

Sadly, tonight was no different and with a sigh he dragged his attention away from the scene in question and went outside to relieve himself. The night was still and clear and the sea looked like a rippled lead sheet, glittering gently where the moonlight caught it. He walked to the edge of the cleared area and did the necessary, idly watching the beach below him.

Is George Weaver right? Should I delay further, or should I ask her?

He adjusted his clothing and made to turn back to the hut when a movement caught his eye on the far side of the cove. He peered across the airy space, but the back of the beach was in shadow, and he couldn't be sure if there was anything there or not.

Reasoning that they were on watch, and he'd better make sure, he went back into the hut and picked up the binoculars. Returning to his previous position he raised them to his eyes and stared downwards. After a moment he muttered, 'Bloody hell,' and walked briskly back into the guard post.

'Jerry.' He shook his slumbering partner.

The man came awake quickly and said, 'Sorry, old chap, I must have nodded off.'

'Never mind that, there's something odd going on down in the cove.'

'Eh? What do you mean, odd?'

'I think I can see some fellows over on the far side. I'm not certain but it looks like one's got a peaked cap on, and others are carrying rifles. They appear to be digging.'

'Is it the Jocks?' Wentworth asked, not unreasonably.

'They're not wearing kilts.'

They went outside and walked down the path for twenty feet to where a large boulder gave cover. 'Over there,' Alan whispered.

'Yes, I see the movement. Give me the glasses.' Jerry braced his elbows on the rock and had a long and studious look. Then, eyes still glued to the lenses, he said quietly, 'Just pop back to the hut and get the rifles will you, old boy. The Germans have arrived.'

* * *

Weaver paused at the top of the cliff above Porthcurno beach and gestured for Muller and Bauer to come close.

'We can follow the path down here and get onto the sand. The cables come ashore on this side of the cove and run over-ground for the last quarter of a mile to Zodiac House, but we'll do more damage by blowing them up on the beach. When the tide comes in the seawater will get inside and run between the copper wires. It could go for hundreds of yards, which gives them a much bigger problem.'

Crouched in the heather, Muller nodded and studied the beach. 'And no sentries, you said.'

'I was definitely told they're not here during the last week of every month, but it still made sense to use Porthchapel cove to come ashore. Here there's always a chance one of the night-duty men will slip down to the beach for a cigarette. We can conceal ourselves, but you can't hide a U-boat on the surface.'

Heart pumping and every sense alert, Weaver led the way down the rocky slope, threading his way between huge granite boulders and clumps of gorse and heather. It made for good cover, although the place felt utterly deserted. The men behind were sure-footed, and they reached the back of the beach without incident.

'They're in there,' he whispered with a surge of excitement. Like great black pythons a pair of fifteen-inch-wide pipes rose out of the sand and disappeared into the darkness up the valley. 'Let's get below the high-water mark so we're sure they'll be flooded.'

Keeping in the shadow of the steep slope that loomed over them, the men crept forward, following the line the cables took off the beach. After twenty feet they passed the seaweed and marine detritus that marked the previous high tide. 'About here, I reckon,' he said.

'Yes, fine,' Bauer said, and with a few brief orders set things in motion. 'Gunther and Max, back up the beach and hide in the bushes. If anyone comes and they're alone, deal with them. If there's more than one, whistle and we'll hide in the rocks. The rest of you, start digging a trench across the line of the pipes. Once we find them, we're in business. We'll all take a turn on the shovels. Carry on.'

The sailors set to work and rapidly created a two-foot-deep trough that ran parallel to the sea. There was a false alarm when one of the shovels hit a rock but ten minutes later, as Bauer and Muller were digging, the captain said quietly, 'Here we are.'

They risked a quick flash of the torch and saw the top of one of the pipes four feet below the surface of the damp sand. 'Right, let's get them cleared and free so we can get the charges underneath.'

As he issued this order, Alan and Jerry arrived at the foot of the hill on the opposite side of the cove and crouched in the bushes. It was the last of the cover. In front of them the slope gave on to an open area of cropped sandy grass that led back up the valley.

Alan lifted the binoculars up to his eyes and stared across the beach to where the men were digging not more than a hundred yards away.

'What do you reckon?' Jerry whispered.

But his friend wasn't listening. One man was standing by the hole and to his amazement, even in the gloom the tall figure in the long coat and distinctive trilby was familiar. Remarkably so. He stared again to make sure, then uttered an astonished snort and said out loud, 'Bloody hell, it's George Weaver. With the Huns. I'm sure of it.'

Unthinking, he scrambled to his feet and bellowed. 'Oi, Weaver, George Weaver! What in damnation do you think you're doing?'

The response was immediate. The party on the sand turned and stared at the young man and the two sentries that Bauer had posted at the top of the beach opened fire. Four quick shots rang out in the silence and a bullet whined off the rock next to Alan. Realising how exposed he was, he dropped to the ground just as a kneeling Jerry Wentworth cried out and fell forward, the rifle loose in his hands.

Appalled, Alan muttered, 'Bastards,' and loosed two shots into the darkness at the foot of the hillside. These were met by a volley of return fire, and he fired again, teeth clenched, and eyes narrowed, trying to focus on the muzzle flashes. He felt the passage of a bullet past his face and then there was a sudden explosion inside his head. Disorientated he reeled back, dropping the rifle, and found himself lying on his back staring up at the night sky.

There was no pain, just a great tiredness, and he closed his eyes.

* * *

Up at Zodiac House, having sent his partner on the night shift to wake Mr Trent, Kendrick raised the men by the simple expedient of setting off the fire alarm and waiting in the entrance hall. A couple of nightbirds appeared at first, but the trickle rapidly turned into a flood as men came pouring down the main staircase in pyjamas and dressing gowns and soon the hall was full.

It was impossible to make anyone understand the real danger from the middle of the noisy rather high-spirited crowd all calling, 'Where's the fire?' Fearing they would break out into song at any minute, Kendrick hammered at the dinner gong until silence reigned and climbed up onto the reception desk.

'I've had a telephone call from London. They say a German raid on Zodiac House is imminent and I've heard shooting on the beach. Men with rifles better get dressed and we'll go down and see what's happening.'

Fortunately, the imperturbable Mr Trent arrived at that moment and briskly took command. 'Who is on watch at the hut tonight?' he asked.

'Alan Bricken and Jerry Wentworth,' a voice replied.

'All right. Rifle club members please collect your weapons, get dressed and muster back here in five minutes. Everyone else wait inside. Do not leave the building.' He turned to the young telegraph operator and added, 'Now then, tell me exactly what they said in London, and what you heard outside.'

His calm authority settled the rather febrile mood. Less than ten minutes later the supervisor led his troops out of the building and down the lane in single file, moving cautiously in the shadows beneath the skeletal winter trees.

A hundred yards from the beach Mr Trent held up his hand. Kendrick was at his shoulder, and he turned to him and asked quietly, 'See anything?'

'Nothing.'

They crept forward following Trent's lead and crossed the last ten yards to the top of the slope overlooking the beach on their stomachs. Cautiously the supervisor raised his head and peered between two clumps of marram grass. The great pipes that climbed the slope were intact and the sand appeared to be deserted, but a large trench had been dug parallel to the sea about twenty yards away.

'So that's their game,' he muttered. 'They are trying to blow the cables, Kendrick.'

'There's no sign of anyone. Do you think we disturbed them?'

'I imagine so. Bricken and Wentworth must have spotted them and opened up. That would be the shooting you heard. I wonder where they are.' He looked at the men lined up along the crest to either side of him. 'Anyone see or hear anything at all?' he asked in a louder voice.

No one replied. Suddenly confident that the Germans had gone, he stood up. 'Gentlemen, I think we're on our own but stay alert. Spread out and try and find Bricken and Wentworth, will you.'

And at that moment the charges exploded.

* * *

Once the firing started, Bauer and Muller knew they were on borrowed time. The captain sent another man up to the back of the beach and then jumped down into the hole to lay the charges. It took a while. The explosives officer in Wilhelmshaven had emphasised the importance of packing them tightly.

'We've come this far, we might as well do it right,' he observed to the second engineer as they laboured, crouched in the hole. The shooting had stopped, and a sailor arrived to report.

'No casualties on our side, Captain, and they've stopped firing, so I think we hit them. We had a quick look, but in the dark it's not easy in the scrub over there.'

'All right. Here, take the fuse cable roll. There's a hundred metres of it. I want you to climb back up the path we came down. Go to that overhang and lower one end so we can attach it to the charges. It's going to be a very big bang, so we'll blow them from up there.'

'Yes, sir.'

As the captain and the second officer completed the packing of the explosives, the sailor scrambled back up the slope and made his way to the edge. He tied a stone to the end of the cable and lowered it to another crew member who crossed to the hole. They connected it to the charges. At that moment the other sentry appeared.

'There are men coming down the lane, sir. We can hold them if you like.'

'No, we've finished here. Tell the crew to head back up the path. We'll follow directly.' He looked at Weaver. 'Do you want to stay for the bang?'

'Yes, I'll come back to Porthchapel with you. My motorbike is hidden at St Levan.'

'Very well.' The German sailors slipped one by one into the chaotic jumble of rock and gorse that covered the steep hill and disappeared into the shadows. When they reached the overhang, the captain inched forward until he could see over the vertical drop to the sand a hundred feet below.

He watched as the party from Zodiac House crept into view and then wormed their way to the lip of the slope at the back of the beach. He noted the rifles. Some kind of yeomanry perhaps, but not soldiers, he guessed. It was remarkable that the British had not thought to defend this Achilles heel, tucked away on such a remote stretch of coast.

Their arrogance will lose them the war.

As the men below climbed to their feet, Weaver murmured in his ear, 'About now, I'd say, Captain.'

'Indeed.' He twisted the handle on the box and an electric signal pulsed down the cable and into the charges. Even though he was expecting it, the explosion shocked him, as every seabird within a quarter of a mile soared into the air, the night suddenly alive with their alarm calls. The men from Zodiac House disappeared in a haze of sand.

Muller grinned at him. 'Mission accomplished, Captain.'

'Nearly. We just need to get home safely now.'

'This way, then.' Weaver stood up and the little troop followed him into the night.

* * *

Down on the beach chaos reigned for a minute. A man called Bailey was unconscious, knocked out by a flying rock, but it slowly became clear that the lip of the slope had shielded them from the worst and although they were covered in sand there were no other injuries.

Suddenly a single shot rang out. Trent span round to see Kendrick kneeling with his rifle trained at the top of the slope. He fired again, before saying, 'There are men up there, sir. I clearly saw an outline and movement against the sky.'

Everyone stared at the summit of the cliff and for a moment the silhouette of a stooping figure showed then disappeared.

'They're on the coast path,' Trent called excitedly. 'Royce, you stay with Bailey; the rest of you, let's get after them.' With a cheer the men from the rifles club surged towards the hillside.

Spurred on by the shots, Weaver led the men at a fast pace along the twisting path high above the sea, his mind racing. Alan Bricken had recognised him and, if he was unhurt or only wounded, would inform the authorities at the first opportunity. His position at the hotel would become untenable. Arrest and a firing squad in the Tower of London would follow as surely as night follows day.

What to do? Could I kill him before he spills the beans?

The thought flashed through his mind, but he dismissed it just as quickly. Bricken might well be back at Zodiac House already, telling everyone who he'd seen on the beach. He hurried on, mind churning, as Porthchapel cove appeared below them. Then he saw the submarine lying like a toy on the grey and black sea, and the solution struck him with startling clarity. It was the only way out. If he stayed in Britain, the police would find him sooner or later.

They arrived at the gate that led into the field, and he took Muller's arm and stopped him. 'What is it?' the intelligence officer said.

'You've got to take me with you. That man recognised me. I'm George Weaver and you heard him call out my name. He's probably telling them now. If I stay, I'll be arrested and shot.'

Bauer ran past, bringing up the rear of the file. 'Come on. No waiting.'

They set off again. Muller's mind was also working hard and by the time they reached the boat he said to the captain, 'We'll have to take Excalibur. He's been identified. The British will get him if he stays.'

Bauer stared at George for a long moment then shook his head. 'Sorry, the water is choppy now, and the boat will be overloaded. We can't make two trips. The British are right behind us.'

Muller looked at him, wide-eyed. 'What? Excalibur is behind this whole operation. Without him it wouldn't have happened. You must take him.'

But Bauer's reply was steely. 'You don't give me orders, and I won't endanger the boat. There's only room for one of you. You'd better choose who.'

There was a tense silence then shots rang out and sand kicked up close to where they were standing. The captain spun round and stared at the top of the cliff. He could see movement and figures running down the path towards the back of the beach.

'Open fire!' he bellowed to the crew on the submarine, pointing upwards. It was two hundred yards, but his voice carried clearly to the machine gunner on the conning tower who sent a long raking burst towards the muzzle flashes.

'Decide now! One or the other!' The sailors were in the boat and paddling out in knee-deep water.

Muller looked at Weaver and said, 'Sorry. Good luck. You'd better take this.' He handed over his revolver, then he waded out.

The night was suddenly rent with a colossal roar and flash of light, and a split second later the footpath at the base of the cliff disappeared in a shocking explosion of smoke and fire.

Bauer grinned and said to the crew, 'Main gun, that'll keep them busy.' Then, as Muller was hauled over the stern, he looked at Weaver standing twenty feet away, shrugged and called, 'Sorry, my friend, the fortunes of war.' He pointed to the far side of the beach. 'Run. You can make it to the valley before they cut you off. Go now!'

The agent didn't hesitate, sprinting towards the valley, his long legs eating up the ground. But as he reached the dry sand his pace slowed and a lucky shot from one of the rifles hit his shoulder. He felt the impact rather than the pain and staggered briefly before pounding into the shadowy gap and safety. Feet splashing through the stream he ran on, crouching and half expecting another shot, but nothing came and after a hundred yards he was on the narrow path between two chest-high Cornish hedges that led to St Levan. His arm was aching, but it was manageable, and he guessed the bullet had grazed him but not lodged in his shoulder. He slowed his pace to a brisk walk, eyes alert for any movement.

Ten minutes later he reached the hamlet. Lights were on in all the cottages and in the rectory, which was hardly surprising. It sounded as though a full-scale battle was taking place in the cove. The shattering roar of the submarine's main armament firing and shells bursting, supplanted by machine gun fire and the pop-popping of the sports rifles borne by the men of the Eastern Telegraph Company carried clearly to St Levan.

He slipped round the back of the church and crossed to where he'd left his motorbike in a little copse. A gate led into a field and from there a rough track ran for a quarter of a mile to Tresillion farm above the Porthcurno valley. He started the bike and gingerly tested his wounded arm. It was painful but he could cope. Face set he steered across the open field and when he reached the farm, joined the lane that ran up towards the main road.

Five minutes later he reached the T-junction with the bus-stop, where Alan Bricken had given Alma a quick peck on the check eleven weeks earlier. He stopped and turned the bike's lights on, then swung the machine onto the main road and accelerated away into the night, face set and mind busy.

At the cove, the folding boat was well away from the shoreline. The crew paddled quickly but steadily. There was no panic, just a steely concentration on the job in hand. Within a minute they were thirty yards from the sand, and then a hundred, as the machine gunner and the crew of the big gun maintained a steady fire over their heads.

In amongst the cacophony of noise, a sailor suddenly cried out and fell backwards, the paddle loose in his hands.

Bauer cursed. 'Damn. Keep going. Paddle hard, boys.' When they neared the black hull he bellowed across the narrowing gap, 'Close the hatch now! We'll leave the boat! Main engine start!'

There was a flurry of action behind the deck gun as the crew loosed another shell, which screamed over the men in the boat, barely seven or eight feet above them, then they were alongside, and willing hands were reaching out to take the wounded crewman.

Bauer ran to the conning tower and climbed the ladder. A bullet whined off the steel panel below him as he reached the top where the machine gun crew were focused on the beach and still firing. The noise seemed incredibly loud, and the floor was covered in empty cartridge cases.

'Raise anchor!' the captain called down the speaking tube, then shouted, 'Keep firing,' to the deck gun crew. The square hole in the deck had disappeared and the empty boat was drifting twenty feet from the hull.

Minutes later U45 was moving astern, as the deck gun kept up a steady rate of fire. When they passed the headland the seabed fell away sharply and Bauer ordered them to cease firing and go below, before tapping the machine gunner on the shoulder.

'That's enough, Hans. Well done. Down you both go. You too, Johannes.' As they unclamped the gun, he conned the submarine to starboard until it was lying parallel to the coast then spoke into the voice tube again. 'Slow ahead. Submerge. Fifty feet. Course one seven five.'

Then with a last quick look around at the deserted sea, he descended the ladder and slammed the hatch shut. Five minutes later all that was left of the submarine was a gentle disturbance on the surface a quarter of a mile south-west of Porthchapel cove.

Chapter Twenty-Two

As the submarine sank beneath the surface, and the withering incoming fire they had endured finally ended, Trent called out 'Cease fire!' and summoned the men. The shelling had been appalling and he'd twice been covered with sand and shattered granite. At some point among the chaos and explosions he'd heard screams and feared the worst.

He waited for the men to assemble and did a mental head-count. Out of the twelve members of the rifles club, Bricken and Wentworth were unaccounted for, and Royce was looking after the unconscious Bailey who was presumably still at Porthcurno beach, although help might have arrived over there by now.

So he should have eight men. Six appeared. 'Henning's brought it,' one of them said in a flat voice, blood flowing from a gash on his forehead. 'That bloody machine gun got our range. I ducked down but he was unlucky.'

'Same with Mills,' another man said. 'I think the first shell got him.'

'That's a hellish bad show,' Trent said, then looked at them. 'I'm proud of you all though. We showed the Huns they can't just come marching ashore and expect to have it all their own way. Well done to all of you.' He stared out to sea for a moment, as if to confirm the U-boat had indeed gone, then said, 'You'd better show me the two casualties and we'll work out a way to get them back to Zodiac House. The lane from St Levan is probably the best bet. The farmer up there will have a horse and cart.'

'Did anyone else see that tall man running across the beach?' a man enquired. 'When we were coming down the path. I think I winged him.'

There was a murmur of agreement. 'He disappeared into the valley that leads up to St Levan,' someone said.

'They left him behind,' another confirmed. 'I wonder who it was.'

'He wasn't in uniform,' the first voice observed.

The pensive silence that followed this remark was broken by a tremulous voice that sounded from the field behind them. 'Hello? Is anyone there?'

'Over here,' Trent called back, making himself visible. 'Who is it?'

'The Reverend Alston, from St Levan. The whole hamlet is awake, and I thought I'd better come down and see what's happened.'

'We've had a visit from the Germans, Vicar. And we fought back, I'm proud to say.'

'Good Lord!' The churchman appeared to allow himself this modest blasphemy under the circumstances and walked forward. He stopped at the little group.

Trent said, 'We've got two casualties. I fear both men are dead, but we will double-check. Either way we'll need to get them back to Zodiac House.'

'How awful. There's a handcart up at the church. That might be the best way. It's small enough to get down the track. I'll go and get it.'

'Yes please. Do you have a telephone at the rectory?'

'I'm afraid not.'

'I'll come back with you anyway. You fellows hang on here for now and please have another look at Henning and Mills – you never know. Bring them back to Zodiac House when the cart arrives, and we'll reconvene there. I'm going on ahead.'

He paused and looked at the silent group clustered together in the grey light. 'I'll say it again. I'm proud of you. It takes some guts to keep firing when you're being shelled over open sights from less than a quarter of a mile away.'

He turned to the vicar. 'Right, on we go then.'

* * *

When he got back to Porthcurno the supervisor telephoned Pendennis Castle.

Even though it was half past three in the morning, the colonel was awake and impatiently waiting for news following the order to send troops to Porthcurno. 'Yes, Trent, what the devil's been going on over there?' he demanded. 'I rang earlier but the only thing some fellow could tell me was that the Germans had arrived, and he could hear heavy artillery.'

In a few short sentences the supervisor summarised events, concluding with: 'I mobilised the rifles and we chased them over the cliff path to Porthchapel, where they'd come ashore from a submarine. A pitched battle developed, and we were shelled, and machine-gunned at short range.'

'That was plucky. Did you take casualties?'

'Two dead, one wounded. Two others missing at the moment. The submarine got away.'

'It sounds as though you did well under the circumstances. What on earth happened to your regular soldiers?'

Trent briefly explained and there was a silence at the other end of the phone as the colonel wondered if the blame for leaving the empire's most important communications hub unguarded was heading his way. Mentally bracing himself, he asked, 'Were they successful? Are the cables blown?'

'When I arrived last autumn, I was worried about how exposed we were even with the troops here and repeated a little wrinkle I tried out in the Cocos Islands. We put a working party together and sunk a couple of empty pipes into the beach for thirty yards and made them rather obvious as they emerged and disappeared into the undergrowth heading towards Zodiac House. If asked, the men were instructed to give it out that the cables were secured inside them, but the real cables come up on the far side of the cove and are laid up a sand-filled gulley.'

Relief flooded through the colonel. 'Are you telling me the Huns blew up the wrong thing?'

'I am. Just like they did on Cocos. You'd think they'd have learned their lesson, although perhaps they never knew.'

'I tell you what, Trent, that is a feather in your cap and no mistake, and I'll make sure the powers that be know all about it.'

The two men talked for some minutes more, then the colonel rang off and asked for the number for MI5 in London. Vernon Kell, resigned to an overnight shift, was also in his office and listened in silence as the colonel described the events at Porthcurno. They disconnected, and he summoned Bright and filled him in.

'Do you think that this is the work of our spy down there?' his assistant asked.

'That's what I'm wondering. Porthcurno isn't exactly a secret but it's hard not to think that someone put the German High Command onto it, especially as the raid took place when the regular troops weren't present. That's surely a sign someone local was involved.'

'Someone actually working there?'

Kell frowned, thinking hard. 'Not necessarily, but the timing is no accident.'

'So he's still active.'

The head of MI5 looked at his assistant. 'Oh yes, I don't think there's much doubt about that. The colonel says the raiding party came ashore along the coast, which means they knew there weren't any other troops nearby. Someone would have needed to go and do a reconnaissance beforehand. It all points to a man on the ground.'

Kell scratched his chin and added thoughtfully, 'One other big question remains, and it's worrying me more than anything else at this precise moment.'

'What's that?'

'Whoever he is, he's obviously in regular contact with Germany. How the devil is he doing it?'

* * *

As dawn showed in the eastern sky things were still busy in Porthcurno. The troops from Pendennis Castle had arrived and were conducting a sweep of the valley and cliffs, and the local doctor had been summoned and was waiting at Zodiac House when the handcart arrived with its dismal load. He pronounced both Henning and Mills dead but just as he was arranging to have the bodies moved to Penzance a man arrived at a run to say a search party had found Bricken and Wentworth at the foot of the path up to the lookout hut.

'You'd better come now, Doctor, neither of them looks too good,' the man said.

They hurried down to the cove and found the casualties behind a large granite boulder. Two men were standing nearby. A quick examination of Wentworth revealed more bad news.

'Dead, I'm afraid,' the medical man said briefly. He moved on to Bricken who was lying on his back on the grass, his hands thrown above his head in a graphic illustration of the impact of the bullet that had caused the bloody wound above his ear.

'There's a pulse here. It's faint but he's alive. Get the handcart, will you, and ask Mr Trent if we can borrow his car. If we can get this young man to hospital there's a chance.' He glanced up at the remaining members of the search party. 'Now please, gentlemen. He needs urgent care.'

* * *

Four miles away, George Weaver's motorbike was tucked round the back of an isolated cottage off the road from Porthcurno to Penzance. Inside, he was sitting at the kitchen table watching as an elderly woman cooked bacon and eggs on the range. His shoulder was bandaged, and he was wearing his bloodstained shirt.

The woman's husband was sitting in a battered armchair by the sink. His eyes were fixed on the large black revolver that lay at the German's elbow.

Since knocking them up in the middle of the night, he'd insisted the woman tend to his wound herself, rather than sending for the doctor, by the simple expedient of pointing his gun at her husband and threatening to shoot him. He was tired but not exhausted and, in the hours since then, had formed a plan.

He had to assume Alan Bricken had given him away. It was therefore inevitable that the police would be alerted and looking for him. His German passport was in a deposit box in the bank and there it would remain, but he needed the cash he'd hidden under the floorboard in his room. His time in England was over, certainly for the moment, but the money would pay a fisherman to smuggle him across the Channel to Brittany. He knew a couple of them in the Rook that would perform such a service, but the money had to be good. Especially in wartime.

And then there was the notebook tucked away with the money. The book in which he'd written down every piece of gossip and indiscretion he had extracted from the aristocrats he'd hypnotised in his consulting room. It was all in there – the hushed-up scandals, astonishing secrets, murky deals, and self-serving compromises that characterised high society across the empire. And many of the people involved were household names. In the hands of Muller and his people in Berlin it would be gold dust. A license for blackmail at a minimum, and all kinds of coercion beyond that.

He just needed to get back to the hotel and sneak into his room. He would do that tonight, and then he would be gone, with no goodbyes.

* * *

At eleven o'clock in the morning a police inspector from Penzance telephoned Sergeant Trewin in Falmouth.

After explaining about the raid, he said, 'You can expect a call from a Mr Bright of MI5 in London. I spoke to him earlier and gave him your name rather than Inspector Luke's,' he remarked, without offering any further explanation. 'I've been over to Porthcurno and spoken to Mr Trent. The Germans came ashore at Porthchapel and took the coastal path. The detonator was found above the cove. There are three dead from the Eastern Telegraph Company and one still unconscious in hospital, but they put up a good fight by all accounts.'

Sergeant Trewin listened carefully and took some notes. Just before they rang off the inspector said casually, 'One other thing.

I'm told by the men in Zodiac House that Bricken, the fellow in the coma, is walking out with a girl called . . .' there was a pause as he consulted his notes '. . . yes, Alma Timperley. She works at the Timperley Spiritualist Hotel in Falmouth, I believe. You might send someone over there to inform her.'

'I will, sir, thank you for that.'

When the call had ended Trewin sat back and had a think. The hotel kept cropping up. First there was the suspicious death of Gladys Timperley before Christmas. Then the unsolved murder of Kate Diss who had worked there, and that business with the lights during the Zeppelin raid. And now a connection to the events at Porthcurno. Was it all a coincidence? Either way the girl deserved to know about Alan Bricken before she heard it from someone else.

He summoned Robinson, told him what had happened and despatched him to pass on the bad news.

At the hotel, the constable asked for Alma and waited. When she appeared, she recognised him.

'Hello, Constable. What can I do for you?'

'Good morning, Miss Timperley, can we go somewhere private?'

Something in his tone alerted her and she gave him a direct look, then led him into the office, where he continued, 'You might not have heard yet, but there was a German raid down the coast at Porthcurno last night. We have been advised that a man was badly wounded and I'm sorry to say we believe he is an acquaintance of yours. His name is Alan Bricken.'

He spoke slowly and stopped there, frowning in sympathy. He'd passed on bad news on many occasions and knew she wouldn't hear anything else he said until the initial shock had passed.

'Alan? Injured?' Her hand was to her throat, eyes wide.

'That's right. We believe he was shot by the Germans. I am very sorry to say he is gravely ill. He's being brought to the main hospital in Falmouth today, so perhaps you can visit him, if he improves.'

If he improves. Stunned, Alma just stared at him. At that moment Gracie Banks put her head round the door. Robinson looked at her and said quietly, 'Miss Timperley has had bad news. The Germans raided Porthcurno last night and Alan Bricken was badly wounded.'

'Oh, dear Lord.' Eyes swimming, the older woman pushed behind the desk and hugged Alma as she sat there. 'I am most terribly sorry.'

The constable stayed for another five minutes but there was nothing else he could do, and he left shortly afterwards, leaving Alma wracked with guilt. As she had ruefully acknowledged after her surprise nocturnal visitor, she had become far too distracted by George Weaver and had not spent enough time thinking about Alan Bricken. The idea of him lying unconscious in a hospital bed was terrible. She resolved to go and see him as soon as he was fit enough to receive visitors.

If he survives.

The appalling thought swept over her as tears ran down her cheeks.

* * *

At the police station the call from London came through.

'My name is Bright from MI5 in London, Sergeant. I believe you are expecting to hear from me.'

'Yes sir, good afternoon.' Trewin sat to attention.

'And to you. Now I'll be circumspect because this is an open line at your end, but we suspect that the person who provided local assistance regarding the events you are aware of may well have a base in the Falmouth area. Do you understand what I'm saying?'

'Yes.'

'In that context, is there anything we should be aware of? Any local perspective you can give us?'

The police officer thought fast. 'Possibly. There's a hotel that's been connected to a couple of serious incidents in the town. It may be a coincidence, or it may not. My gut feeling is not.'

'A hotel?' There was a pause, and the sergeant sensed some serious thought going on at the other end of the line. Then Bright said carefully, 'Are the initials of the place you're talking about the T-S-H. Run by a surprisingly young woman?'

Relief flooded through Trewin. 'That's the one, sir.'

A grunt of satisfaction came down the line, then the man from MI5 said, 'We need to talk on a secure line. Go to Pendennis Castle and give my name on the gate. They'll take you to a telephone you can use. Write my number down now. It's Whitehall four-four-five. Have you got that?'

'Yes.'

'I'll tell them to expect you. Quick as you can please.'

'Very good, sir. I'll be with you in half an hour.'

* * *

George Weaver stood unmoving under the cedar trees in the back garden of the hotel. It was half past ten in the evening, and he'd left the elderly couple tied up securely and driven carefully back to Falmouth an hour and a half earlier. His arm and hand were becoming increasingly numb, making the journey difficult, but he'd managed.

For the last twenty minutes had been studying the rear windows for any signs of movement. It was cold, but when his life depended on it, George Weaver was good at waiting. His back door key was ready in his pocket but he reckoned he'd give it a while yet.

* * *

At the railway station Trewin and Robinson were waiting on the platform when the last train from London rolled in. A few people got off, including a stocky, pugnacious-looking man in an Ulster and a bowler hat, who glanced around, spotted the police officers, and walked purposefully towards them.

'Good evening. Sergeant Trewin?'

'Yes, sir. Mr Bright, I presume? There's been a development since we spoke,' Trewin said without further preamble. 'Alan Bricken recovered consciousness while you were on the train. He's sitting up in bed telling everyone who'll listen that George Weaver is the man we want. He clearly saw him with the Germans on the beach at Porthcurno apparently.'

The man from MI5 cocked his head. 'Really? He actually named him?'

'Yes. I've concealed a man outside the front of the hotel to keep an eye on the place and we're ready to go there now.'

'Are you armed?'

'Rifles in the car, sir. Yourself?'

'I carry a revolver. Very well, Trewin, to horse. Let's go and catch this blasted spy.'

* * *

Alma was in her room, in bed, but sleep eluded her. She had a strong premonition that significant events were occurring, without being able to pin down what. Since the constable's visit, news of the raid had filtered around the town and there had been widespread shock at the idea of Germans landing on Cornish soil. After telling James Nascent what had happened, she'd gone to the main hospital and asked to see Alan but been refused by a doctor who said he'd only just arrived and was still unresponsive. She'd left the hotel phone number in case of developments and come away in tears.

Then there was George's unaccountable absence from the hotel. He'd been due to do a séance that afternoon but hadn't shown up and, asking around, she realised that no one had seen him since dinner the previous evening. With James at her side, she had unlocked his room but found it deserted, with the bed neatly made.

Where are you?

Restless, she sat up and decided to make a cup of tea. She put on her dressing gown and descended by the main stairs. To her surprise, as she crossed the entrance hall, a figure appeared beyond the glass front door. For a moment she thought it was George, but then a helmet showed in the front door light. It was Sergeant Trewin and three other men.

She opened the door. To her astonishment the policemen were carrying rifles.

'Yes?' she asked. 'What on earth is the matter?'

'We're looking for George Weaver, Miss Timperley. Is he here?'

'So am I, and no, he isn't.'

'You don't mind if we check, do you?' The urbane voice came from a man wearing a bowler hat who eased past the others. 'My name's Bright, from MI5 in London. We have reason to believe George Weaver is a German agent and it's very urgent that we locate him. Have you seen him today at all?'

Shocked, Alma said, 'No. His room is empty, and his bed is made.'

'Hello, Bright.' James Nascent's voice sounded from behind them. He was standing in the doorway of the lounge holding a glass.

'Nascent.'

'It's Weaver, then.'

'Yes. I'm informed he's been named by a man called Alan Bricken. A positive identification during the raid at Porthcurno.'

'Alan says it's George? Is he awake?' Alma stared at the sergeant.

Trewin nodded. 'Mr Bricken regained consciousness earlier this evening.'

'We'll have a look upstairs, I think, Miss Timperley,' Bright said. 'Would you lead the way.'

Trying desperately to control the turmoil of emotions that were searing through her, she nodded. 'Very well. Follow me.'

'It'll be all right, Alma,' James said, but his expression was grim as he joined them.

They climbed to the guest floor using the main stairs and then started on the flight that led to the staff bedrooms. Alma went first with James behind her.

Halfway up, Bright put his hand on the solicitor's arm and stopped him, then turned to the policemen and said quietly, 'If he's here he may be armed, so be ready. Safety catches off and shoot if necessary. He's better dead than running free.'

The men eyed him, as if suddenly recognising the reality of the situation, then they set off again, with Alma now half a dozen steps in front. As she arrived on the landing she came face to face with George Weaver.

'George!' she cried in surprise. He stared at her, alarm showing in his face as the armed men appeared round the corner of the stairs. But his reactions were lightning fast. Even as Trewin shouted, 'There he is!' he grasped Alma's arm and hauled her through the door that led up the stairs to the tower room, then slammed it shut behind them. She heard the lock turn.

'Up to the top, if you wouldn't mind,' he said calmly as a crescendo of hammering and shouts sounded from the other side.

'Open the door, Weaver! You won't get away.' Bright's voice came clearly through panelling, but the German ignored him and pushed Alma upwards. When they reached the tower room, he paused indecisively and she turned to him, her face drawn with tension.

'George, what's happening? Please tell me.'

But he shook his head and pointed to the door that gave access to the balcony. 'Out there, please.' As he steered her into the moonlight, she noticed he was favouring his right arm and saw the dark stain of blood on the other shoulder of his coat.

'You've been injured,' she said.

A shot sounded from the foot of the stairs as Bright fired his revolver into the lock, then put his shoulder to the door. It burst open and the empty flight loomed in front of them. 'What's up there?' he said to Nascent.

'The tower room and access to the outside balcony. That's where Gladys Timperley fell from.' The solicitor pushed past him and led the way. Bright followed, his revolver in his hand. At the top, Nascent peered cautiously into the room and found it empty and silent. The door to the balcony was open.

'Is there any other way off?' Bright whispered from behind.

'Not unless he jumps down onto the roof,' Nascent replied.

The men entered the tower room and crept over to the door. Bright risked a glance outside. In the moonlight, the iron railing ran along to the corner where it turned to the front of the building. Even in extremis the incredible view across the estuary struck him. 'Come on, Trewin, the rest of you guard the door,' he said, but the solicitor put his hand in his shoulder.

'I'll go first,' he said, and led the way out onto the balcony.

'Wait, man! You're not even armed,' Bright hissed, but the man in front ignored him.

When he got to the corner Nascent stopped and craned his head round the brickwork. At the end of the next section Weaver and the girl were standing together facing the sea. He had his arm round her waist, and they looked for all the world like a courting couple enjoying a romantic moment.

'Weaver,' he said quietly.

The man turned and Alma turned with him. He had a revolver in his hand, and the end of the barrel was pressed against her ribs.

'Can I help you?' he said.

The solicitor walked towards him but stopped six feet away as Weaver said, 'That's close enough.' He nodded slowly, as if turning things over in his mind, then added, 'So you're part of the opposition, are you? That was clever, I must admit.' He glanced over Nascent's shoulder and gestured briefly with the gun as Bright and Trewin appeared behind him. 'Stay there,' he ordered, then said, 'Let us down and I'll release the girl when I'm clear of the hotel.'

But the solicitor's eyes were locked on his and he ignored this proposal. 'You know this ends here, don't you? The game's up, I'm afraid, and for what it's worth I think you've shown some guts. But let her go. She's an innocent party in all this.'

Alma turned and looked at him, her face pale in the moonlight. 'You're the spy,' she said flatly. It wasn't a question.

He nodded. 'Yes, I'm the spy. Jürgen Weber, at your service, and German through and through. Sorry and all that.' He offered nothing more, but Alma's mind was working quickly.

'This is the place that Gladys fell from. This corner above the front door. But I think you know that, George. Did you kill her?'

As she said this, she unconsciously moved out of his grasp, as though being close was unthinkable. He didn't resist and turned to face her, his back to the railing.

They stood looking at each other four feet apart. Finally, he said, 'I'm afraid I did. She'd worked it out you see, and I couldn't allow that.' He looked at her and his face creased in a sardonic smile. 'What was she to you anyway? A woman you never knew or cared about, until she left you this damned place.'

His taunt hit home, and Nascent saw Alma's face change as tears of grief welled up in her eyes.

'She was my mother!' she screamed and taking a step forward, pushed him hard in the chest. He was tall and his buttocks hit the top of the railing. Panic showed in his eyes as his feet rose. He tried to grasp her arm but the shooting agony in his injured shoulder forced him to let go and he rocked back, dropping the pistol, and scrabbled for the rail with his other hand.

'No!' Alma shouted and reached for him. But she was too late. The momentum was too strong and suddenly, shockingly, George Weaver was gone.

He fell silently and there was a thump as he hit the ground in exactly the same place as the woman he had killed five months earlier. Horrified, Alma gripped the rail and stared down at him, her cheeks wet with tears. Nascent leaped forward and grabbed her, thinking for a second that she would follow him over.

He hugged her tightly, trying to ease her violent shudders, but she pushed him back. 'Why are you here, James? Why do you care so much?' she cried, her voice raw with emotion.

Their eyes met, and to her astonishment she saw he was smiling through his own tears.

Then he said, 'Because I am your father, Alma.'

Epilogue

In Falmouth, James and Hilda had just finished viewing a Georgian townhouse on Wood Lane not far from the hotel. As the agent loitered discreetly out of earshot he asked, 'Will this do, do you think?'

'I like it, James.' She nodded firmly.

'It won't be full-time immediately, but even so . . .' He pursed his lips and smiled.

'But even so, we'll be near your daughter and when we do move down permanently you can play a full role in each other's lives.'

'And you, of course. You don't mind throwing your reputation to the four winds and living in sin with me then?' His kind brown eyes crinkled at her.

She took his hand. 'The war is changing everything, James. I really don't think people will care too much about that, and neither do I.'

'I think you're right. Families have got much more important things to worry about now.' There was a short silence then he said, 'You knew about Alma, didn't you. You'd worked it out.'

She nodded, eyes smiling. 'Oh yes. Once Alma told me Gladys was her mother it wasn't a great leap to understand your interest in her. But I thought I'd wait for you to tell me in your own time.'

'Yes well, once she came into my life I knew I needed to tell both of you, but then the whole spy thing started, and the right moment never seemed to come up.'

'Until the balcony . . .' She squeezed his hand.

'Until the balcony,' he agreed.

They were standing at the entrance to the drive and as he glanced back along Wood Lane, James noticed he could see the top of the hotel's tower and his mind drifted back to the tumultuous events in April.

After Weaver's plunge and his declaration that he was Alma's father, the two of them had clung to each other as a strange madness rippled the air, then he heard Bright say, 'What did you see, Trewin?'

The sergeant replied without hesitation, 'I saw Mr Weaver stumble and fall over the edge, sir. A tragic accident.'

Bright nodded, but as he opened his mouth to reply, a piercing scream sounded from below. He looked over the railing. Weaver was lying flat on his back, arms and legs extended like a starfish, clearly visible in the light cast by the front door. A girl in a maid's uniform was standing on the step, hands to her mouth. Behind her a well-dressed mature woman appeared. Their voices carried clearly in the night air.

'Be quiet, Rankin, for heaven's sake. Now, what is all this?'

'A dead man, my lady, fallen from up there. I heard the thump. I think it's Mr Weaver.'

'So it is. How extraordinary.' She peered upwards and Bright gave her a wave.

'Hold on down there, please. The police are coming.' He looked at Trewin. 'Would you mind . . .'

'Right you are, sir.' He turned and walked briskly round the corner.

Still holding tightly to her father, Alma looked at the MI5 officer. 'I've killed a man,' she said, flatly.

'No, you didn't. It was an accident,' he said firmly. 'I'm certain of that.' He met her eyes and after a moment said, 'You say Gladys Timperley was your mother? I thought she was your aunt.'

'So did I, but she left a letter explaining things. There's no doubt.'

He looked out at the moonlit estuary and gathered his thoughts, then said, 'Look, Alma, if I may call you that, George Weaver was a self-confessed spy and murderer. If we'd taken him alive a date with a firing squad was inevitable under the Defence of the Realm Act. I am satisfied that you didn't mean to kill him and there will be no repercussions as far as you are concerned.'

As voices below heralded the arrival of the police outside the front door, he addressed the father and daughter. 'Come on, the pair of you. I think a stiff scotch is in order. We've just rid Britain of a dangerous enemy and George Weaver won't bother us again.'

Alma's curious reply would stick in his mind for a long time.

'I hope not,' she said.

The remaining loose ends were tidied up over the next few days. Gleaning what thin pickings he could discover, Reggie Wilson wrote an article for the *Falmouth Packet*, and Weaver's deposit box at the bank was opened where a German passport in the name of Jürgen Weber, a direct translation of George Weaver, was found. His room was emptied, and his possessions disposed of. No one noticed the floorboard with the two scratched screws under the rug.

With Constable Robinson firmly holding her hand, Nell McGuigan viewed the body and confirmed it was the same man she'd seen in the Rook, and Trewin concluded that George Weaver was the man who killed Kate Diss and Sally Regan. Their parents were informed.

And faced with of a full set of bookings for the next three months, Alma threw herself into the work, which she found a valuable and fulfilling distraction. The reality was that many people were suffering far more than she had done, and it was cathartic to be able to assuage their grief. And there was no sign of George in the Hall of the Dead, to which she was now a regular visitor.

* * *

On the first of July, as Valentine Wragge happily closed his copy of *Who's Who* and drafted a brief note that would send his partner in crime to Ashbourne in Derbyshire a week later, Alma got off the Happy Wanderer at the top of the lane that led down to Zodiac House. She exchanged a smile with a farmer's wife who was waiting to board.

'He's just coming up the road,' she said. They were becoming acquaintants as Alma was a regular Sunday visitor to the telegraph station and the woman was often at the stop.

'Right. Enjoy your day out,' she replied.

As the bus drove off, Alan Bricken appeared beneath the trees. 'Morning,' he called and gave her a kiss on the cheek.

'Hello,' she replied, warmly. 'What's for lunch today then?'

They set off towards Zodiac House, holding hands as he pondered her question. 'The third Sunday in the month, so it'll be roast pork. Did you bring your costume?'

She raised her arm and gestured with the bag she was holding. 'And a towel. I've remembered this time.'

'Shall we swim before lunch then, we've an hour yet.'

'Lovely.' Then she added, 'Any news?'

A lot had happened since the dramatic raid on the telegraph station. Alan had suffered a relapse, and Alma had been a devoted daily visitor to the hospital as he slowly recovered. In the many quiet conversations they'd had as she sat at his bedside, their relationship had developed and deepened in a way that had surprised her.

Then one day, as she was leaving, she'd spontaneously leaned over the bed, given him a lingering kiss on the lips, and said, 'I like you very much, Alan Bricken.'

After his discharge he'd been up to Burnley to see his family and then returned to Zodiac House and started work. In his absence the Ascension Island job had been allocated to someone else, and he was waiting to hear where the Eastern Telegraph Company was sending him. And the decision was imminent, hence Alma's question.

He gave her a sideways look. 'Oh aye, there's news.'

She stopped. They were under a gap in the thickly leafed trees and a pool of warm sunshine lit the couple, as though they were actors on a stage. 'What is the news?' She tried to sound calm, but the aching tension in her voice shone through. She knew she loved Alan Bricken and he was about to disappear from her life for two years. She didn't know how she'd stand it.

Eyes watering, she braced herself. 'Where are they sending you?'

'Nowhere.' He was smiling at her.

'Nowhere?' Heart beating, she leaned forward, and he took her other hand as they faced each other.

He shook his head. 'Nowhere. They've said with my injury it's unsafe to pack me off to somewhere without access to a decent hospital. Just in case. And they've reorganised a bit and created a new post called Head of Training, here at Porthcurno. That'll be me. It's a promotion and more money and it means I'll be staying here for the foreseeable future.'

'Oh Alan.' Tears were welling up in her eyes. 'I'm so pleased.'

Then suddenly he was kneeling on the gravel lane before her. 'This seems as good a place as any,' he said, grinning from ear to ear. He held up a ring box that had appeared in his hand. 'I love you, Alma Timperley, and I'd like to marry you. Will you marry me?'

With her heart doing somersaults she replied unhesitatingly, 'Yes I will, Alan Bricken.'

He stood up and slipped the ring onto her finger. It was a solitaire diamond and the sunlight caught it as she held up her hand. Then, with joy surging through her, she raised her face to his.

Author's note

Like my earlier *Great Tew* series, much of the background to this fictional tale is true. Spiritualism reached its peak in the latter part of the nineteenth century when a widespread belief emerged in Europe and the United States that the dead could be contacted and connections to 'the other side' were available to those capable of using them. Public interest had faded by the turn of the century, but when World War One broke out in 1914, spiritualism in Britain experienced a huge revival. As casualties mounted, desperate mothers were prepared to try anything to keep their dead sons in their lives, especially among the upper classes where many of the junior officers who suffered the highest casualty rates of all the combatants originated.

Early in the war, the German cruiser *Emden* did attack the Cocos Islands and was caught and destroyed by *HMAS Sydney*, while the Eastern Telegraph Company employees and the German raiding party sat together on the beach and watched the action. And the ETC men had constructed a dummy cable, which the raiders duly destroyed, leaving the real one untouched.

For this and much of the other information regarding the cable station I am indebted to the terrific museum at Porthcurno, which is well worth a visit. Young telegraph operators spent nine months training there and were then despatched to some of the most remote places in the world. Given the insular nature of life in the Edwardian era, it must have been quite an adventure to be sent to Cocos, or Ascension Island, for two years.

Records are sketchy for World War One, but a squad of the 4th Highland Light Infantry was despatched to Porthcurno to defend the cable station. The troops were inexperienced and in training, but both the flawed monthly rotation and the German raid are my own invention. However, the story about the drunk soldier being shot dead by his own corporal appears to be true. His name is in the burial register for the church at St Levan, above Porthchapel.

The Zeppelin raid on Falmouth is also fiction, but the town was a busy place during World War One and was fortified early on according to a well-established plan. The sea-facing batteries were augmented, and trenches were dug on the landward side to defend against a major assault. Pendennis Castle became the HQ for the garrison, which numbered seven thousand troops. Nowadays the castle is run by English Heritage and is a fascinating place to visit.

Modern Falmouth is much bigger and the area between the top of Swanpool Street and Pendennis is now urbanised. In 1915 it was mainly open fields and orchards, and I am grateful to the excellent people in the archives at the National Maritime Museum for access to the maps and photographs of the town during that period. The large house at the top of Swanpool Street is the imagined location for the hotel.

As before, the spiritual side of the book is informed by my own experiences. The existence of life after death, and the nature of 'the other side' and reincarnation are curious concepts for some, but I hope you have been able to enjoy the ideas that are explored. For people like me they are real.

Thank you for your support and, as ever, a review on Amazon and Goodreads would be greatly appreciated if you've enjoyed the book. We will be back with Alma at the Timperley Spiritualist Hotel before too long.

F. H. Petford

Somerset, England, 2025

RAISING READERS
Books Build Bright Futures

Dear Reader,

We'd love your attention for one more page to tell you about the crisis in children's reading, and what we can all do.

Studies have shown that reading for fun is the **single biggest predictor of a child's future life chances** – more than family circumstance, parents' educational background or income. It improves academic results, mental health, wealth, communication skills, ambition and happiness.[1]

The number of children reading for fun is in rapid decline. Young people have a lot of competition for their time. In 2024, 1 in 10 children and young people in the UK aged 5 to 18 did not own a single book at home.[2]

Hachette works extensively with schools, libraries and literacy charities, but here are some ways we can all raise more readers:

- Reading to children for just 10 minutes a day makes a difference
- Don't give up if children aren't regular readers – there will be books for them!
- Visit bookshops and libraries to get recommendations
- Encourage them to listen to audiobooks
- Support school libraries
- Give books as gifts

There's a lot more information about how to encourage children to read on our website: **www.RaisingReaders.co.uk**

Thank you for reading.

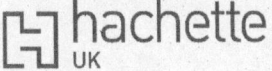

[1] National Literacy Trust, Book Ownership in 2024, November 2024
https://nlt.cdn.ngo/media/documents/Book_ownership_in_2024

[2] OECD. 2021. 21st-century readers: developing literacy skills in a digital world. Paris, France: OECD Publishing.
https://www.oecd.org/en/publications/21st-century-readers_a83d84cb-en.html